DEAD PRETTY

A police doctor gets embroiled in a murder investigation

CANDY DENMAN

THE BOOK FOLKS

Paperback edition published by

The Book Folks

London, 2020

© Candy Denman

ISBN 978-1-913516-32-1

www.thebookfolks.com

DEAD PRETTY is the first in a series of medical crime fiction titles featuring medical examiner Dr Callie Hughes. More information about the other five books can be found at the end of this one.

Prologue

She lies there, on the dishevelled bed, mocking him. Her scrawny, naked body covered in old scars and bruises, courtesy of her job, her profession. And there she is, this hag, this whore, laughing at him and his limp dick. Soft as ice-cream, unresponsive to her sucking and wanking. No use to man nor beast, let alone a woman. She laughs. Cackles. Her mouth gaping wide. Stained, uneven teeth. Furred tongue. Lipstick all gone. Left on the glasses of vodka and coke he's been buying her all night. He's paid out for this pathetic body, this diseased bit of stubble covered cunt, but it's her that's laughing at him.

He has to shut her up, shut up the stream of humiliation from her mouth. Going on and on. Ringing, echoing, in his ears. He reaches for her discarded tights, her grubby, laddered tights, wraps them between his hands and winds them around her neck, tightening, straining, until the abuse stops, replaced by a hoarse, terrified, rasping noise. A croak. A silent scream. She scrabbles at his hands, scarlet nails ripping in vain at his skin and her own neck, desperately trying to free herself. The tights are buried too deep in the flesh of her throat. Eyes bulging, she lashes out with her bare feet, landing bruising blows to his legs, but only making him pull tighter. Slowly, her frantic but pathetic attempts to stop him become weaker and then cease.

Her body twitches and lies limp. Limp as his dick. Still he keeps the pressure on, until he can be sure. Sure she is dead. Sure she is silenced forever.

He loosens his hold, slowly unwinding his hands from the tights. A line of drool hangs from her mouth. He looks at the body. The stillness of the flesh. The cool slackness. At last he feels a stirring, and looking down, sees his cock getting hard.

Chapter 1

The sun was shining through the grimy windows, making the dust motes dance and giving enough light for Dr Calliope Hughes, Callie to her friends and pretty much everyone else, to take a good look around the bedroom before entering. Tall, slim and elegant in an understated way, Callie divided her time between being a local GP and working on-call for the Sussex police as a forensic practitioner. It was in this second role that she had been called out to reports of a body found in a council flat.

From the doorway, Callie took in the pink and grey colour scheme in the room; very fashionable, very feminine. The mirror was hung with fake jewellery, there were make-up bottles and brushes strewn across the dressing table and a variety of plaques and pictures on the wall urged her to *Live, Love, Laugh; Never Regret Anything;* and *Make Today Great.* The king-size bed had a slightly grimy padded headboard, the bedding was messed up and in the middle of it, naked and with legs splayed, lay the body of a youngish woman. Today certainly wasn't going to be great for her.

Callie took a couple of photos using her phone, and slowly approached the bed. There was a smell of body fluids and death, but no drug paraphernalia or bottles visible by the bed. Callie thought there could be a mark around the throat, so she didn't check for a pulse there, but instead, with gloved hand, reached carefully for the woman's wrist.

Unsurprisingly, there was no pulse and the woman's arm was limp and cold. She had been dead for some time. Callie carefully leaned in and took a closer look at the neck. Yes, she could definitely see a line that might be from a ligature, and there were some possible petechiae on the face. She very carefully backed away from the bed, touching nothing and trying, as best she could, to follow the same path as she had taken in.

As she reached the door into the living room, she turned and walked towards the front door of the flat, where she had left the policemen who had called her out to pronounce death. She was surprised when the front door opened, as she had quite clearly told them to wait outside and stop anyone else from coming in.

"Don't come in!"

Startled by this sudden order, the two men in the doorway froze. The one in front was in his late thirties, she guessed, and dressed in a dark blue suit, pristine white shirt and subdued silk tie – he looked more like a businessman than a policeman – but the older man, peering round from behind him, was definitely, unmistakeably, CID. His crumpled suit and the loosely knotted tie that failed to cover the tea stains on yesterday's shirt, were a dead giveaway.

"What?" Mr Clean queried as he backed out into the hallway.

At least he was wearing gloves, Callie thought.

"I don't want any further contamination of the scene," she explained as she walked towards them. At least one of the constables as well as herself had already been in the room, and she wanted to keep it to that until the forensic team had been over the place.

"Are you the duty doc?" he asked.

"Dr Hughes. Callie Hughes, Forensic Physician," she said, pushing past him as she left the flat, suddenly realising that he was surprisingly tall, at least six inches taller than her, unlike his sidekick who must have struggled to make the minimum height restriction back in the days when he would have joined.

"And you are?" she asked.

"Detective Inspector Steve Miller. And this is DS Jeffries." He gestured at the older man with him.

Callie nodded, and noted that, rather than the scent of beer and stale smoke she had come to expect from policemen, DI Miller exuded a fresh and pleasantly soapy smell, as if he had just this minute stepped out of the shower.

"As a forensic physician, you should know better than to touch evidence then, Dr Hughes."

The shower image disappeared like a cloud of steam and the look Callie gave him was blatantly hostile.

"This was reported as a possible overdose, I had to check firstly that life was extinct, you'd be surprised how many apparently dead bodies come back to life once the drugs have worn off, or they've been revived with the antidote," she told him in a voice that was flat and clipped with barely restrained anger, and if Miller had known her longer than a minute he would have apologised and backed off.

"But not this one." It was a statement, not a question.

"No." Callie was equally brusque. "Why are you here, Inspector? I can't imagine you attend the scene of every sudden death."

"Part of a new initiative. I am collating information on every drug-related event."

Callie suspected this was a response to a recent report on the unexpectedly high mortality from heroin and fentanyl overdoses in the area.

"You'll be pleased to know that there's no overt evidence of an overdose. No syringe, no bottles, no tourniquet, no spoon, no silver foil, no baggies."

"But you don't think it's a natural death?"

"No."

"Are you sure?" he asked. "I mean, not having any drug paraphernalia visible doesn't mean it isn't a simple overdose, does it?"

A further slight hardening of Callie's features, and a cold glint to her eye, should have warned him that she did not take kindly to having her professional judgement questioned. A slight twitch of Jeffries' lips showed he had seen her irritation and that he was enjoying it.

"No, Inspector, until there is a PM I can never be quite sure," she told him. "But there is enough evidence for me to insist that you treat this as a suspicious death."

"Suspicious?" he queried.

"Like what?" said Jeffries.

"Like the presence of a ligature mark around the neck but no ligature still in situ, visible petechiae and no other cause of death evident." She couldn't help a little triumphant smile as they both looked surprised. They really had thought it was just another drug overdose. "So, you will need to roll out all the crime scene procedures required and yes, I'm sorry if that blows your budget for the next six months." She snapped off her gloves and walked away from them, back ramrod straight and head held high, rigid with anger, and knew that they were watching her every step of the way. She just prayed she didn't trip or stumble before she was out of their sight.

Chapter 2

The mortuary at Hastings General Hospital had been built slightly apart from the hospital, and an attempt, of sorts, had been made to hide it from view by planting a row of leylandii between the main hospital block and the entrance, presumably to screen the sick and dying from the physical reminder of where they themselves would end up. The trees had not prospered; perhaps their proximity to the incinerator chimney had choked the life out of them. Whatever the cause, the result was that these specimens, whose family is renowned for their hardiness and hyper-virile growth, were so thin and spindly that the closed metal trolleys which they were supposed to shield from public view, could clearly be seen as they came and went with their lifeless cargoes.

Callie ignored the main door marked "Chapel of Rest" and instead entered by a small, anonymous side door. Behind it stretched a windowless corridor with naked, expressionless walls interrupted only by an unmarked door on the left – the back entrance to the chapel of rest – and terminating in a set of plain steel, double lift doors. Once inside the lift, there was only one direction to go: down.

Having descended, Callie stepped out into the subterranean mortuary where she could hear the clank and chink of metal instruments being laid out on metal trolleys as she headed for the autopsy suite. Looking through the porthole window in the door to the first room she could see the chief technician, a huge, bear of a man, whose name she struggled to remember. Callie watched him prepare for a post-mortem, XXL scrubs straining across his chest, with the shroud-covered body already laid out on the table. He looked up as Callie pushed open the doors, having to press hard against the positive air pressure, the cooler atmosphere and smell of disinfectant hitting her simultaneously.

"Is Dr Dunbar about?"

"In the office with the coroner's officer, Dr Hughes." He waved latex-covered hands at her, gesturing in the general direction of the corridor, and smiled. "Sorting out the PM for the murder you were at this morning." He seemed excited by the prospect; Callie supposed that he didn't get to see too many murder victims. Of course, this one might not be, she could have been mistaken, in which case, she would probably never live it down.

"Thanks." She ducked back out of the autopsy suite, leaving the technician who had gone back to opening sterile packets of instruments out onto the already loaded surface. In the corridor, Callie opened the office door to see Dr Ian Dunbar, seated at the well-ordered desk. In his early sixties and fighting any suggestions of retirement, Dr Dunbar was also dressed in theatre greens, but he was a small, thin and spare man in direct contrast to his much larger assistant. Mike Parton, the coroner's officer, a man of great physical dignity with the bearing of a funeral director, was waiting patiently as Dr Dunbar struggled with his computer. Technology was not his strong suit.

"Hello, Calliope, how nice of you to drop in on us." Dr Dunbar always liked to use Callie's proper name, and was always telling her it was lovely and that she shouldn't let it be shortened. Callie wondered if he had helped choose it, having been a family friend from before she was born, and being her godfather to boot. Someone had to take the blame for saddling her with such a ridiculous name. "We're just organising the PM on your body from today."

"I've spoken to Professor Wadsworth and he would like to start tomorrow morning, nine o'clock," Parton told them.

Dr Dunbar snorted.

"Does Wally Wadsworth think we can just drop everything else?" Dr Dunbar had never liked the local forensic pathologist who covered the south east coastal region, feeling, probably quite rightly, that Wadsworth believed himself to be superior because he handled the criminal cases instead of just the 'unimportant' sudden deaths due to natural causes. Both Parton and Callie had already had the Dunbar lecture on every life being valuable and every death a personal tragedy for someone. Several times. Parton checked his notes for the pathologist's details.

"He has a very tight schedule and…"

Dr Dunbar held his hand up to stop Parton's stream of excuses and leant slightly towards the door, calling: "Did you hear that, Dave? The Very Important Home Office Pathologist is coming to do the PM on the probable ligature strangulation tomorrow morning, so we'll have to do the old dear found in her chair at the residential home this afternoon, as well as the two-day post-op and the OD."

Dave Ball, of course! That was his name. Callie mentally stored the information: she really mustn't forget it again and she was relieved that Dr Dunbar apparently concurred with her initial thoughts on the cause of death. It would have been embarrassing if it was a natural death, although not as embarrassing as the other way round, calling in forensics after the body has been removed and the scene trampled by all and sundry because she missed a suspicious death. She would always err on the side of caution and insist on a full forensic workup for everyone who might need it, even if that did mean that sometimes it turned out to be a waste of time and money. Dave appeared at the door, looking disgruntled.

"Haven't you got a pathology dinner to get to this evening, Dr Dunbar?"

Dr Dunbar stood.

"Hmm. I'd forgotten that. Looks like the OD will have to wait until tomorrow afternoon." He turned back to Callie. "Do you want me to ask Dr Wadsworth if you could come and watch? Hmm?"

"Actually, yes, that would be interesting, if you're sure I won't be in the way."

Dr Dunbar waved away her concerns.

"You don't take up as much space as the rest of us, don't you agree, Dave?"

"No, Dr Dunbar." Dave smiled. "Nowhere near as much."

"Right then, young Dave. Chop, chop. Let's clear the decks as much as possible and get ready for tomorrow. Can't upset the man from the Home Office and anyway, it will be the flu season soon and we'll need all the room we can get."

* * *

Still thinking about the poor woman who had died that morning, wondering if the police had been able to find her relatives or the person who had anonymously called the emergency services to report it, Callie went to go into the lift as soon as the doors opened, and bumped into a man as he was coming out, dropping her bag in the process.

"I'm so sorry," the man said and bent to pick up her bag just as she did so, causing them to bump against each other again, almost knocking her over. The man grabbed her elbow and steadied her, picked up her bag and returned it to her, all in one graceful movement. Callie, grateful that her bag had stayed closed and hadn't strewn its contents across the floor, automatically gave him the once-over. He must have been in his early forties, but was well-preserved and dressed in what Callie suspected was a bespoke shirt and suit. An expensive silk tie, held in place with a gold tiepin, completed the ensemble. No lowly white doctor's coat for this consultant, because Callie instinctively knew that's what he was.

"That was so clumsy of me. Are you okay?" he asked as she pulled herself together.

"Absolutely fine," she assured him. "I should look where I'm going."

"No, no, it was my fault, in too much of a rush as usual," he explained, but he didn't seem to be in a rush and, having taken a good look at Callie, asked, "Have we met? Kane, Jonathon Kane."

Callie recognised the name. Even if she had never met him, she knew that he was a senior surgical consultant at the hospital. As a GP, she had referred many patients to him over the years.

"Er, no, I don't think so, I'm a local GP, Dr Hughes, Callie Hughes." Callie was unusually hesitant. Mr Kane definitely fancied himself as a bit of a charmer and the look he was giving her was an open evaluation, but then, she'd given him the once-over herself.

"Callie? What a delightful name. Almost as delightful as its owner."

Callie tried to extract her hand and he seemed to suddenly realise that he was still holding it in his own.

"I'm so sorry. Do have your hand back. I was getting a bit carried away there, and who could blame me?"

Callie smiled; that little trace of humour, of self-awareness that almost amounted to self-mockery, even though she suspected that it was a well-practised line, redeemed him in her eyes. He wasn't just another hopeless smoothie.

"That's all right, Mr Kane."

"Jonathon." He corrected her, looking directly into her eyes.

"Um, Jonathon." Callie felt flustered by the intensity of his stare.

"Would it be frightfully presumptuous of me to ask if you'd like to go for a drink with me? Tomorrow?" Jonathon asked and Callie hesitated, surprised by the request. "I'm sorry. Of course, it would, ignore me, I'm being a bore."

"Not at all. I have other plans tomorrow night but maybe some other time…" Callie startled even herself.

"Terrific. What about the next night, Wednesday? About eight? Or do you have something more interesting to do?"

Callie was caught on the spot. It had been a while since anyone had asked her out quite so directly and she hadn't prepared her excuses. She thought for a moment and realised that it might actually be nice to go out for a drink with a charming, intelligent, good-looking man who was unlikely to be short of money. He saw her waver.

"A country pub? Or a wine bar? You choose."

If she was seriously going to meet him for a drink, she had best make it home territory, she thought, and walking distance from home.

"Porters," she told him. "The wine bar in the Old Town High Street." At least then she might persuade him to stay there for dinner as well, if the evening was proving a success.

Jonathon Kane smiled and Callie, feeling uncomfortably self-conscious, slipped past him into the lift.

"Until Wednesday, then," he said as the lift door closed.

Chapter 3

As she entered the large modern building that was the East Sussex Police Headquarters, Callie was not exactly sure what she was about to face. On the telephone, all the duty sergeant would say was that a prisoner had been slightly injured during arrest and that he wanted her to check and document said injuries. Whilst most of her work for the police was mundane, there was always the possibility of something more interesting, something other than the seemingly endless parade of drunks and the aftermath of petty violence.

She knew most of the uniformed sergeants and many of the constables by sight if not by name, but was much less familiar with the detectives, as had become all too evident at that morning's scene. Her world and theirs rarely coincided and, as a relative outsider, she was not privy to their gossip; all she heard were the moans and groans about them from the uniformed officers, who she suspected, were biased. She nodded at the civilian at the desk as she entered and was buzzed through the door into the body of the police station, where she walked briskly along the corridor and down the stairs to stop at another locked door, smiling up at the CCTV camera as she waited to be allowed in. The lock clicked and she was able to enter the reception area of the custody suite, stepping up to the desk and only just managing to stop her face from showing her dismay as she saw which custody sergeant was on duty that evening. He greeted her with a nod and grunted, "Evening, Dr Hughes."

Sergeant Barlow was a well-known jobsworth with only three years to go until early retirement. He would be polite, do things rigidly by the book and not let her forget to dot an 'i' or cross a 't'. Absolutely nothing was going to come between him and his pension.

"The prisoner is this way," he gestured, leading her down a narrow, brightly lit corridor to the cell area, where he unlocked the gate and ushered her through before turning and locking it again behind them. Even though she knew they were being constantly watched on the camera screens at the desk, Callie always felt a slight frisson of excitement and fear when she was locked in with the mixture of thugs, sad cases and hardened criminals held in the cells.

"I'll bring him down to you," Sergeant Barlow told her as he began to unlock a cell, and Callie headed towards the treatment room at the end of the corridor.

* * *

The custody suite treatment room was slightly smaller than her consulting room, but felt much more spacious as it had less clutter and a somewhat different array of equipment. No box of toys by the door or cartoon posters on the wall. Nothing to soothe the troubled soul. Here the emphasis was on the job in hand: syringes and tubes for taking blood samples from drunk drivers in one cupboard, first aid equipment such as dressing packs, plasters and steristrips, to patch up both prisoners and policemen, in another. A sink to wash your hands, complete with the obligatory notice reminding her to do so frequently. As if she needed reminding. Most of the patients she saw here hadn't bathed in recent memory and were sweating off an excess of alcohol anyway. It always took a good soak in scented bathwater before she could get rid of the custody smell.

As well as two chairs and a desk, the room also had an examination couch so that patients could lie down, if it was absolutely necessary, but this was currently covered with several boxes of swabs for taking DNA samples. It was more like a nurse's room than a doctor's, and that was what the work was most of the time. In some areas the police employed nurses to do the routine blood tests and dressings, cutting down on how often the forensic practitioner, as police surgeons had been renamed, had to be called out. Nurses come cheap and it was a case of anything to save money.

Callie had been thinking about giving up her two days a week at the surgery for some time, but, although those days and her occasional stints doing out-of-hours cover meant she often worked long hours, she was loath to stop when the police authority might decide to reduce her main job to the sort of walk-on part that had happened just up the road in Maidstone. What with paramedics and nurses even being allowed to pronounce death as well, it was getting to the point where being a forensic practitioner could end up being very part-time work indeed.

Callie looked up as her patient – Jimmy Allen according to the custody record sheet Sergeant Barlow handed her – came in, and tried not to wonder what he might have done. She preferred to think of him as just another patient at this stage. Knowing whether a prisoner was a suspected rapist, or a wife beater, would colour her attitude towards them, no matter how hard she tried not to let it. She might even be tempted to feel they deserved to suffer a little unnecessary pain, which would be human but distinctly unprofessional. So, staying ignorant of his possible crimes, she tried to examine Jimmy just as she would have done if he'd presented to her in her consulting room at the surgery rather than in the custody suite of the local nick.

She gestured to him to sit down and, pulling on surgical gloves, looked closely at his battered face. It clearly wasn't the first time his features had been re-arranged. There was a scar across one eyebrow, and the suggestion of another on his chin, though it was hard to make that one out clearly because of the two-day stubble that covered the lower half of his weaselly face. An unpleasant-looking person if ever she saw one, Callie thought to herself as she pulled down his swollen and split lower lip with her vinyl-covered finger. The frenum was intact. His lip would be sore for a few days but nothing more. She moved her hand up to his bloody and swollen nose and tweaked it.

"Fuck!"

Jimmy flinched away, but there had been no give or crunch when she tried to move the nasal bone.

"Not broken, Mr Allen. No need for you to go to hospital."

She dipped a cotton wool ball from the dressing pack in sterile saline and firmly wiped all the blood away.

"You a fucking sadist or what?"

"Or what, Mr Allen. Definitely an 'or what'." She bundled up the used pack and threw it in the contaminated waste bin, stripped off her gloves and chucked them in after it.

The door to the examination room was open and she leant out, catching the custody sergeant's eye.

"No major damage. Fit to be detained." She came back in and sat at the desk, writing up her examination on Jimmy's custody sheet as Sergeant Barlow approached.

"I want to make a complaint," Jimmy said.

"Oh yes?" She barely looked up, still busy documenting her findings.

"It was that bastard DI. He did this. Hit me when my hands were cuffed. He can't do that, can he? I mean, I know my fucking rights."

"No need to swear, Mr Allen."

But he had Callie's attention now. She looked at the doorway, where Sergeant Barlow stood, looking as if he wanted to use a few choice words himself. His shift had just got complicated. So close to knocking-off time, and yet so far.

Like Sergeant Barlow, Callie was not happy about this turn of events and her dismay showed. She ushered Jimmy out of the treatment room and thought longingly of her bed. And a bath. But both seemed a very long way off now. Whilst she waited for Sergeant Barlow to return with the officer involved, she tried not to think about how difficult this could turn out to be. A bit of a disaster all round. Whatever else, she had to work with the police and was employed by them: she didn't want to suddenly find herself ostracised, considered an enemy rather than a friend. That was exactly what would happen if she found Jimmy's accusation to be true. She was under no illusions about her job. Many officers considered that she was only there to support their side of the story, not the scumbags they arrested. That said, she never had been and never would be on the same side as the sort of policeman that went around thumping people already subdued or restrained, unable to hit back. There was nothing she hated more than a bully.

As she rubbed at a place on the bridge of her nose that seemed to be the focus of her fast-developing tension headache, there was a sharp rap on the door.

"Come in," she called, hastily sitting straight and putting on her serious professional face.

Miller opened the door and came quickly into the room, almost doing a double-take when he saw Callie sitting at the desk.

"Oh, great, Dr Hughes, I didn't realise it would be you."

"Only one forensic practitioner on duty at any given time in Hastings, Detective Inspector Miller. Have a seat."

17

He sat and appeared to rapidly try to regroup his thoughts.

"If I had a pound for every prisoner who said I'd used unnecessary force…"

"And if I had a pound for every policeman who said he never touched the bloke…"

They looked at each other, both knowing exactly where the other stood. Callie took the opportunity to size up the man in front of her.

He still looked good. Clean, neat, nothing flashy and as if he was, in general, a solid and reliable sort of bloke. A man's man. Closer inspection showed him to be on the downward slope towards forty, but his once taut, rugby player physique was only sagging a little. He obviously kept up some sort of physical exercise other than propping up the rugby club bar. Squash, Callie thought, he probably plays squash. His hair, a rich brown – still thick and with a tendency to curl where he had let it grow a little longer than he should, had developed a sprinkling of grey above his ears – not that it was likely he would have noticed, she thought. He didn't seem the type to be overly troubled by either vanity or introspection. Like many men, he might worry a little that his hair may start receding one day, but Callie was willing to bet that that was as close as he got to navel-gazing. As he sat in front of Callie, giving her an unashamedly appraising look, he appeared unworried by what she might think of him, but she suddenly found herself feeling less secure about the impression he was getting of her. She looked away, tucked her hair behind her ear, and mentally kicked herself for letting him get to her.

"Hold out your hands, please, Inspector."

Miller held out his hands, well aware that the grazed and swollen knuckle at the base of his right little finger looked exactly like a punch injury.

"Caught it on the car door," he explained, "as we were putting the prisoner in the back. He tried it on; my finger got whacked against the edge."

Callie pulled on gloves and took his hand, gently feeling along the fifth metacarpal towards the knuckle. Miller winced.

"You ought to have it X-rayed."

"It's fine, honest."

She looked him in the eye.

"I would expect there to be a line, or ridge across the injury, if you hit it against the edge of the car door. This" – she indicated his hand – "is more indicative of hitting a flattish surface." Like a face, she left the words unspoken, but still hanging in the air.

"The edge of the door, the side, whatever, makes no difference; it was the car I hit, not Jimmy Allen."

"And how did he get the bloody nose?"

"Struggling. Resisting arrest. My hand went into the car door; his nose met the car roof." Miller looked her straight in the eye, challenging her to rebut his version of events. "He should have been a good boy and got in the car when he was told. Have you finished?"

She had, but she certainly wasn't going to admit it now.

"I should clean the graze."

"It's fine. I washed it as soon as I got back."

"As you wish."

"Is that it?"

"Yes. You can go now, Detective Inspector."

He stood.

"And what are you going to put in your report, Dr Hughes?"

She gave him her most impenetrable smile. Small, cold and getting nowhere near her eyes.

"You'll have to wait and see, won't you?"

He looked at her, weighing up his next move.

"Jimmy Allen is a rapist. A torturing, perverted, violent rapist who finally went too far and killed his victim. If I don't prove it before we have to release him, he'll do it again. Think about that and the amount of time we've already wasted with this when you make your report,

Doctor, not to mention the added pressure for an early release if you support his ridiculous claim." And he left.

Callie felt her colour rise. This was exactly what she didn't need to hear. If he was so worried about giving Jimmy a get-out-of-jail card, why had he hit him in the first place? Because she was pretty sure that that was what he had done. And why blame her? The moment a complaint was made, there was a set procedure that had to be followed and he knew that. The doctor had to check the alleged assailant, Miller, for wounds that might be consistent with the injuries inflicted on the alleged victim, Jimmy Allen. End of story. It wasn't her fault all this had happened, it was his. She slammed the pen down on the desk and took a deep breath, considering what to put in her report, when there was another knock at the door.

"Yes?" she almost shouted before getting herself under control. "Come in."

The door opened and Detective Sergeant Bob Jeffries came in. He'd managed to put on a clean, roughly ironed shirt but that was as far as he had been prepared to go to smarten up for work.

"Dr Hughes? I just thought I'd let you know that I was a witness. To the alleged assault on Jimmy Allen."

"How convenient. Don't tell me, you support DI Miller's story?"

"Exactly."

Callie looked at the sergeant and weighed up the options. Should she try and get the real story out of him? He was one of the few CID men she had heard about, even if she hadn't met him before. Older than his boss, more experienced perhaps, his once-ginger hair now faded and laced with white. Everyone, except possibly Jeffries himself, knew he would never make it beyond detective sergeant because of an inability to play the political game or keep his mouth shut when a smart remark came to mind. Tact and diplomacy were foreign territory to

Detective Sergeant Bob Jeffries. But he was loyal to the force, and to his boss, in his own way.

Callie sighed. If it was the case of two officers' word against Jimmy Allen's, her report would make very little difference. Besides, it could have happened the way they were telling it, even if her gut reaction was that it hadn't.

* * *

When Callie returned to custody reception with her report, she saw Miller and Jeffries at the desk along with a man she recognised as Harry Worthing, a legal executive rather than a qualified solicitor and almost certainly there to represent Jimmy Allen.

He was smiling as he turned to Callie.

"Ah, the good doctor. I trust your report makes it clear that my man was punched whilst already under restraint?"

Callie was irritated, her dislike of Harry Worthing was almost as strong as her negative feelings towards Miller and Jeffries.

"My report makes no such judgements, Mr Worthing. I am a doctor, not a clairvoyant. The only people who can tell you how exactly your client got his injuries are Jimmy himself and the two arresting officers."

Miller looked relieved and Jeffries grinned.

"Bad luck, Harry."

Worthing scowled. "You won't be smiling half an hour into a no-comment interview. You've nothing on Jimmy and you won't get it whilst I'm around, of that you can be sure. He'll be out of here first thing in the morning, you'll see." He turned to Barlow. "I'll speak to my client now, Sergeant."

He nodded at Sergeant Barlow to let him through into the custody area so that he could make sure that Jimmy was well-schooled in repeating the words "No comment". Probably a lesson Jimmy had no need to learn as he was hardly a virgin to police interviews.

Callie slammed the report down on the desk in front of Sergeant Barlow and turned towards the exit.

"If you could let me out first, Sergeant." And she walked towards the door with Sergeant Barlow scurrying after her. She didn't see Miller's appraising stare as she went out but she could feel it, hot on the back of her neck, and she was uncomfortably aware of a flush coming to her cheeks. Thank goodness she had her back to him.

Chapter 4

Darkness was falling fast and a light drizzle had started as Callie hurried out of the police station to the carpark and her midnight blue convertible Audi TT. A frivolous car, her father had told her disapprovingly. Not a suitable car for a serious person, a career woman, a doctor. Callie loved it. Her little piece of rebellion. God knows what he would have said if she had bought the scarlet version, and she had been sorely tempted.

She slipped into the driver's seat, glad she had put the roof up before leaving the car earlier. There were few things worse than driving home with a wet seat, and it happened to her regularly. She slammed the door shut, still seething about her second encounter with DI Miller.

"What an arrogant–" She struggled to find a word that was acceptable, but finally chose: "prick!" The nearest to a swear word that she could bring herself to use but, she told herself, entirely justified in the circumstances.

She switched on the wipers and punched buttons on the radio, in no mood now for anything soothingly light and airy. She wanted something angry and discordant but that didn't seem to be available. She hit the off button and drove away with nothing to distract her thoughts from

Jimmy Allen's bloody nose and DI Miller's classic punch injury. A bully in uniform – even though he wore plain clothes. She realised now that he must suspect Jimmy Allen of killing the woman she had attended earlier that day.

She drove fast down the hill and along the seafront, past the strip of amusement arcades and fish and chip shops that linked Hastings Old Town to the town centre. Past the mini-golf and the kiddies' funfair, and further on to the fishermen's beach where the largest beach-launched fishing fleet in Britain stood, the boats looking strange and awkward on the stones, like fish out of water; with the net shops towering, black and menacing, close by. There was no doubt in Callie's mind that the heart, and particularly the soul, of Hastings were housed in the Old Town, where she lived. She slowed to make the left turn up the valley, feeling the tension slowly slip away from her shoulders on the familiar road up the East Hill.

* * *

Callie left the car parked at the back of the square, brick-built, Georgian manor house that she called home. With its tall windows and graceful lines it stood out as different from the Victorian villas more common in this part of town. The house was situated in a commanding position high up on the East Hill and at some time in the past twenty years it had been converted into flats, or apartments, as the estate agent had insisted on calling them when Callie bought the one that was up for sale on the top floor.

It was just three rooms: a bedroom, a bathroom and a living room with a kitchen area along one wall, divided from the living area by a breakfast bar. The rooms were large and well-proportioned, the conversion having been sympathetic, not like the amateurish efforts she had seen elsewhere: plasterboard walls sectioning off bathrooms in the corner of the bedroom, chopping through ornate ceilings, making a mockery of the original features. But it wasn't the ceilings, the sympathetic conversion or the size of the rooms that had sold the flat to Callie the moment she walked into it: it was the views.

From the main living room, you could see the coast, the funfair and promenade she had just driven along, almost as far as St Leonards. Down and to the right was the Old Town nestling in the valley, crowded and compact, and further, across to the West Hill, the castle ruins, and the swathe of green parkland crested by a terrace of white houses. It was a view that never ceased to impress her, whether it was early morning with the rooftops floating in a sea mist, the castle backlit by a setting sun or, like now, with the streetlights in the valley twinkling invitingly below.

Callie switched on the lights as she came into the living room, throwing her bag onto the cream sofa, and purposely ignored the flashing light of the answer phone as she headed straight for the modern beech wood and stainless-steel kitchen area. She took an open bottle of white wine from the fridge and poured herself a glass. Sipping as she stood at the breakfast bar and looked out at the lights shimmering in the rain on the window, she wondered if she should risk the wet and walk down to the town for something to eat. Or perhaps she should get back in the car and head for the supermarket? A brief glance at what was on offer in the fridge hadn't inspired. A carton of milk that was several days past its best, half a lemon, slightly shrivelled, some unsalted butter and an open packet of mixed salad leaves that, on closer inspection, had begun to get slimy. Maybe someday soon they would genetically modify salad leaves to last long enough to be eaten. And perhaps the rain would stop, too.

Callie enjoyed cooking; it was the shopping she hated. Wandering around soulless supermarkets, which always seemed to be filled with screaming children, and God knows she had enough of screaming children at work; then there was the muzak and tinny announcements, all combining to give her a headache within minutes of her arrival. Not to mention the risk of running into a patient. On more than one occasion she had been quizzed about test results in the middle of the frozen food section, desperately trying to remember the person's name, let alone their results.

She checked out the cupboard. Passata, garlic paste, extra virgin olive oil, freeze-dried basil, not as good as fresh, but a reasonable compromise. All the ingredients for chicken parmigiana. Except the chicken. And the buffalo mozzarella. And the shaved parmesan. Not to mention fresh salad and crusty bread. She opened the freezer door and looked at the stack of frozen ready meals that were her only choice. As usual, they didn't appeal. They seemed so appetising, not to mention quick and easy, when she was doing the shopping, but when it came down to it, she never fancied them. Some of them must have been in the freezer for months. She was too tired to play salmonella and listeriosis roulette. She closed the freezer without taking anything out and refilled her glass, wandering reluctantly over to the answering machine.

Callie had a mobile phone, but only work, family and Kate Ward, her best friend, were allowed to have the number, and they all knew better than to use it when all they wanted was to chat. She preferred her home phone for that. She pressed play and a synthesised voice announced that she had three new messages. The first, as usual, was her mother, asking how she was, fishing for news on the boyfriend front. The second message was from her friend Kate, reminding her that they were due to meet for their regular Tuesday night calorie-laden meal and giving her usual excuse about being too tired to meet at the gym beforehand. It was the same every week. The third message was silent apart from some audible breathing. Callie replayed the last message. Was the breathing threatening? Or sexual? It seemed too quiet for that. Just gentle, silent, somehow reproachful breathing.

Callie erased the messages and looked around the room. The stillness, the emptiness, seemed less peaceful and more accusatory to her now. No cat or dog, not even a goldfish to welcome her home. Maybe her mother was right, maybe it was time she got a husband, or changed her life in some way, or at least changed her phone number.

She went into the kitchen and poured herself another glass of wine whilst she gave it some thought.

Chapter 5

One last sip of coffee and a quick check to see that there were no biscuit crumbs on her lap or desk and Callie was ready for the next onslaught of patients. Her consulting room was small and utilitarian, but had a few soft touches to put patients at their ease: a Disney poster on the wall, an easy-clean children's toy on the floor and thank-you cards from grateful patients pinned on the board above her desk alongside a variety of public health notices. Callie looked at her computerised appointment list. Next in line was the ten-forty patient. She was only running five minutes late – that was a turn up for the books. The name, Timothy Lockwood, meant nothing to her. Callie pressed the buzzer and double-clicked on Timothy's name to reveal his records, flicking through what little information there was in them.

There was a light tap on the door as she read that Timothy Lockwood was aged nine and had only recently registered with the practice so there was no past history to go on, yet.

"Come in," Callie called, and Timothy and his mother appeared in the doorway. She smiled reassuringly, as both mother and child seemed apprehensive.

"Have a seat, Mrs Lockwood. Hello, Timothy. What can I do for you?"

She listened as Mrs Lockwood, in her thirties and good-looking, in a high-maintenance style, explained that Timothy had been feeling increasingly unwell over the last few days.

"It's not like it's anything specific, Doctor. He just isn't feeling well. Of course" – she glanced at Timothy but he sat quietly, apparently not listening to what she was saying – "he's not helped by all the stress. My situation. My husband and I, well, we're in the process of getting divorced. We are legally separated for now, and I have an interim settlement. I'm in the middle of changing lawyers because my last one was useless. That's why I'm here. Hastings was all I could afford thanks to him."

Callie swallowed the remark that sprang to her lips and kept it professional.

"What about Timothy? You have sole custody?"

"Joint, supposedly. Not that Philip's ever around to do his fair share."

Callie turned to Timothy, deciding that he was probably going to be more use.

"So, Timothy, let's take a look at you, shall we?"

Whilst he was taking off his shirt, Callie warmed her stethoscope in her hand. She listened to his chest, front and back, felt for glands in his neck, peered in his throat and ears, took his temperature, and all the while he was quietly cooperative and polite but listless. Listless was definitely the word, Callie thought.

"Have you been drinking more than usual? Been thirsty?"

Timothy shook his head.

"Can't seem to get him to eat or drink anything much."

"Up on the couch, young man, so that I can feel your tummy."

He did as he was asked and lay back, letting Callie palpate his abdomen.

"Does it hurt anywhere?" she asked, but he shook his head.

"Right, off you pop and get your shirt back on."

"It's nothing, isn't it? Just the stress?"

"It might be that, Mrs Lockwood, but I always think it's best to be sure." Callie was already pulling out blood test request forms.

"There's nothing in his past history I should know about? Anything that could be relevant? His old notes haven't arrived yet," she explained.

"No, he's been quite healthy. But sensitive. That's all." Mrs Lockwood seemed more surprised Callie was taking it seriously than she was worried that her son might really be ill. "What could it be? If he has got something wrong, that is."

"It could be any number of things, Mrs Lockwood, but he isn't showing signs of anything acute. We'll wait and see if the picture gets clearer, or if Timothy gets better, and, in the meantime, these blood tests will narrow it down if he doesn't."

She held out the form to explain it.

"I've asked for liver function tests, full blood count in case of anaemia, although I saw no signs of that when I checked his eyes, and ESR, to see if he shows signs of fighting an infection, blood sugar for diabetes, and one to tell me how his kidneys are doing. And I'd like a specimen of urine, too, in case he has a kidney or bladder infection brewing." She opened a cupboard and took out a specimen bottle.

Mrs Lockwood turned and checked Timothy had finished getting dressed.

"Just wait outside for a minute, will you, Timothy?" She smiled at her son and he left obediently. Mrs Lockwood turned back to Callie.

"You don't think it's all in his mind then? Just a bit of attention seeking?"

It was clearly what she wanted to hear, wanting some reassurance that there was nothing seriously wrong. Callie took a deep breath.

"It might be, Mrs Lockwood, but that doesn't mean we should ignore it. Whatever is causing Timothy to feel so unwell will need to be treated, one way or another."

* * *

Later, Callie sat in Dr Dunbar's office, drinking Earl Grey tea from the delicate china cup and saucer provided by the pathologist.

Dr Dunbar bustled back into the room.

"Right, that's all done and dusted, the great man has left, having imparted his great knowledge to us all."

Callie smiled. She had been very disappointed that she had arrived too late to watch the autopsy itself, Dave was busy tidying up by the time she had made it to the mortuary after a prolonged morning surgery. She had patiently waited in the office with Dr Dunbar, whilst the home office pathologist organised the samples that needed to go to forensics with Mike.

"Did he say what the COD was?" she asked him anxiously.

"Ligature strangulation. Probably with some sort of thin stretchy fabric, he got some fibre samples to send off but his preliminary view was that she was strangled with a pair of tights."

Callie was relieved that her original opinion of ligature strangulation was right, although the thought of being strangled with your own tights sent a shiver down her spine.

"Have they found out who she was yet?"

"Yes, a Christine Trent. Mike said she was known locally. Went by the name Jade."

"A working girl then?"

Dr Dunbar nodded acknowledgement that she had been a local prostitute. Callie had quite a few on her list as a GP, but she was pretty sure Christine, or Jade, wasn't one of them. Prostitutes often used a different name when they were at work, not, as some people thought, to make them sound more glamorous, but because they needed to distance themselves from what they were doing. It wasn't Christine who was having oral sex with a stranger, or giving him a hand job, it was Jade. A different person altogether.

Dave popped his head around the door.

"Are we keeping the body for a while Dr D., or can she be released to the relatives?" he asked.

"Need to keep her I'm afraid, Dave. I know space is tight, but they haven't even located her relatives yet, according to Mike." He sighed.

"No problem, I can just about manage to squeeze her in." Dave was relentlessly upbeat in contrast.

"I hope you two youngsters are both going out to enjoy yourselves tonight. If ever you needed reminding that life can be all too short, working down here should do it."

He went out and Dave and Callie exchanged looks. Dave shrugged.

"Guess it's been a bad day. You going out at all tonight, Dr Hughes?"

Callie picked up her bag.

"Having dinner with a friend. How about you?"

"Oh, I have plans, I certainly do. I will be tripping the light fantastic, don't you worry. So, if the earth moves, it's not an earthquake, just me boogieing on down." And he gave Callie a private display of his skills as he went down the corridor, a wobbly, disco-dancing green giant, light on his feet despite his great weight. Callie laughed, and he turned at the end of the corridor to give her a grin and a wave before disappearing into the post-mortem room, his natural habitat.

Chapter 6

Callie had arranged to meet her best friend Kate for a quick drink in The Stag, so that they could discuss where to have dinner over a drink. The Stag was a convenient place to meet, close to both their homes in the Old Town and to the restaurants that they were likely to visit. It had everything you could want from a pub: a warm welcome and an open fire, beer that met Kate's rigorous standards and a display case containing an ancient mummified cat for some obscure reason.

The evening had turned out warm but damp and they sat in the window seat, far enough away from the fire not to roast but sheltered from the door and the people coming in and out shaking wet umbrellas.

"So, what do you feel like?" Callie asked Kate. "They've got a jazz pianist at the wine bar, a Spanish guitarist at the tapas bar and muzak at the bistro."

"Can't say that I'm fussed what the music is like, so long as it soothes the fevered brow; much more important is the food. I'm thinking braised lamb shank at Porters or an Italian. I could quite fancy an Italian."

"Nothing new there, then." Callie looked affectionately at her friend as Kate took a swig of her pint of Spitfire. If

Callie was a tall, thin glass of Pinot Grigio, Kate was a large, round bowl of a glass, filled to overflowing with Merlot – warm, dark and full bodied. Kate swirled the inch of beer that was left and looked at Callie's almost untouched white wine spritzer. "You want another drink to play with while we decide, or do you want to talk about what's bothering you?"

"There's nothing really bothering me."

Kate clearly wasn't convinced, so Callie continued.

"I'm just feeling dissatisfied with life at the moment. You know, being a GP can be..." she struggled to find the right word.

"Trying?" Kate suggested.

"Yes, that and, well, boring sometimes too."

"You could always go full time as a police doctor."

"Not enough work and anyway, that can be trying and boring at times too. Maybe I need a complete change. Or at least a new challenge."

Kate finished her pint and put it down decisively.

"I vote for the Italian." She stood and picked up her coat. "What you really need, my girl, is a man."

And depressing as that was, Callie thought, she was probably right.

"Just as well. I've got a date in Porters tomorrow night, as it happens, and I don't want to go there two nights in a row. They might think that I can't cook for myself," Callie said as she shrugged on her coat.

"Fantastic. Tell me all about him. Come on, come on. Is he rich? Good-looking? And has he got a brother?"

Callie was laughing as they headed for the door. It was an undeniable fact: an evening spent with Kate always made her feel better.

* * *

"Bye, Callie. Good luck tomorrow, and you'd better call me and give me all the gory details about this consultant bloke after your date. And don't forget to ask if he has a brother, right?"

"I promise." Callie waved and hurried up the narrow flight of steps that led up from All Saints' Street to the lanes on the hill above. In the nineteenth century, as Hastings town grew, house owners had sold their gardens for building plots and sometimes several homes would be built on the land between two houses whose gardens had previously backed onto each other. The only way of reaching these infill houses was by a complicated network of steps and alleys called "twittens" and "cat creeps". Callie knew her way round these sometimes dark and unlit paths like the back of her hand; she often had to visit patients who lived down them and had never found them scary but, as she walked up the steps towards her home she thought, for a moment, that she heard footsteps further down the hill.

She stopped, thinking that if someone was hurrying up the steps behind her they might want to get by and, after the enormous meal she had just eaten, she didn't want to race up ahead. She'd probably throw up if she tried. As she waited to see if the person wanted to get by, the footsteps stopped. Maybe they had turned off, gone down one of the side passages or into a house, Callie thought as she started up the steps again, listening carefully as she climbed. She could be imagining it, but she was sure she could hear the footsteps start up again after a pause. For the first time, Callie felt frightened by the darkness of the alley and had to remind herself that the houses on either side were very close. If she screamed someone would hear, she was sure, but she wasn't about to hang around and put it to the test.

She leapt up the last steps two at a time, despite her full stomach. It was amazing what an adrenalin surge could do for your energy levels. She reached the well-lit street above with relief and hurried on towards her flat, and safety.

Chapter 7

Callie took a long hard look at the woman sitting next to her desk at the surgery. In her late thirties, Marcy had not had an easy life, and it showed.

"I know I'd done well, cut right down, but these last few weeks, it's been bad, Doc."

"It's bound to happen, some weeks you feel the withdrawal worse than others."

"Don't I know it. But it's not just the withdrawal, I really have had a bad few weeks."

Callie had heard this one before. Many times.

"There are always reasons, excuses, to fall off the wagon, Marcy. A bad day, an argument, a court appearance."

"Don't worry about them anymore." She was dismissive.

"Addicts often deliberately provoke confrontations to give them a reason to slide."

"I know all that, but I mean it. Look, I knew that woman that was murdered. You know? The one in the news. I did. I haven't made that up, and it's upset me."

Callie was interested.

"You knew Jade Trent?"

Marcy fiddled with her cigarette packet, looked as if she was thinking of lighting up before remembering where she was and putting the packet away again.

"Me and Jade went way back." Marcy's lower lip trembled despite her well-cultivated, hard-as-nails image. "We were going to get out of the game. Buy a house and run it as a bed and breakfast. With extras, if you know what I mean. We'd put some money aside where no one could touch it. Okay, so it's not enough yet, but we would have got there. Honest truth, but I can't do it now, not on my own, can I?"

"Why not?"

"It was Jade who had the business sense, worked out the money side. I'm hopeless at that sort of stuff. What am I going to do, Doc?" Callie tried to look reassuring, but there was little she could say that would help and she knew it.

"She can't even be buried 'cos they have to keep the body till they get the killer, so I can't even get – what's it called? – closure. That's it. Closure. I mean, what if they never catch who did it? They can't keep her forever, can they?"

Marcy looked as though she was about to cry.

"Of course not. They usually organise a second PM for the defence, if they do find someone to charge, and then release the body to the family."

"And how long is it, until the second what's it?"

"Post-mortem. It's usually in three to four weeks, and you aren't allowed to have them cremated, in case, you know, they need to check things later."

Marcy's lip wobbled slightly and Callie hurried on, "But they usually allow a burial. I can talk to them, see if they are happy to get it done sooner rather than later."

"Could ya? I'd really appreciate it, Doc." Marcy really did seem pleased.

"Do you know if she had any family? They may need to give permission, and also may want to arrange the funeral."

"Just a worthless shit of a brother. He won't want to pay for no funeral."

"Well, I'll speak to the coroner's officer and get him to contact you when she is ready to be released."

Callie knew that Mike Parton would have to contact the brother first, but if Marcy was right and he didn't want to know, then he would be very relieved that there was someone else willing to arrange the burial, and pay for it. She turned to her computer keyboard and keyed in M for medication. "I can't give you any more temazepam, Marcy, but I will let you have some diazepam to tide you over the next few days." She typed in the drug name, dosage and frequency and pressed P for print, ripping the prescription off the printer as soon as it was done, and signing her name along the bottom.

Marcy sniffed and took the prescription.

"It'll have to do, I suppose. Better than nothing."

"Try not to mix it with anything else, Marcy, okay?" They both knew that was a forlorn hope, so Marcy didn't bother to reply, she just sniffed again and then wiped her nose on the back of her hand.

"I'll use our savings to give her a proper send-off. I don't want her being given a council ceremony, without any, you know, class. I want her to have the works. We can afford it." She folded the prescription and put it in her bag.

"Maybe you'd be better off using the money to get yourself off the street, like you planned. It's a dangerous game."

"That's what gets me. I mean, I know it is, but that night? Jade wasn't even working."

"Maybe she changed her mind, decided to earn a bit extra?"

"No. She couldn't have been working."

"How do you mean?"

"She was strangled at home, wasn't she? Her flat up on The Priory. Jade wasn't stupid. She never took punters there. Always took them to the place we used on Wigmore Street. Other people around, see. Other toms. We look out for each other there. If she was in danger, she woulda screamed and someone would have come to help there."

Callie had been to the dilapidated four-storey Victorian terrace on Wigmore Street where the working girls rented rooms by the hour. She had been called out when a man had died "on the job" and, remembering the place, she realised that what Marcy was saying was true. The rooms, just big enough to accommodate a bed and a basin, had been divided off using sheets of plasterboard nailed into place, and everything that was happening in one room could be heard in several others. A turn-on for the clients and a built-in safety feature for the girls.

"No, if she was at home, she was killed by a bloke she picked up on the side, like. A leisure fuck." Marcy stood up and pulled at her micromini in an attempt to make herself half-decent, missing Callie's wince at her choice of language.

"Have you told the police that, Marcy?"

Marcy seemed indignant at the suggestion.

"No."

"Don't you think you ought to? I mean, anything that would help catch the man who did this has got to make you and the rest of the girls safer, hasn't it?"

Marcy hesitated.

"They're not going to listen to me. I'm a junkie whore with a record."

"You have relevant information. They'll listen."

Marcy didn't seem convinced.

"Probably bang me up on some soliciting charge."

Callie realised where the problem lay.

"Is there an outstanding warrant on you, Marcy?"

Marcy was defensive.

"There might be, I'm not sure I made it to a court appearance. Hard to keep up with things, you know?"

Callie did know, only too well. The working girls seemed to be in and out of the police station with monotonous regularity, and Callie was often called in to certify them as fit to be detained if they were high or in withdrawal, or to patch them up if they were injured.

"What if I went to see them for you, to explain the situation to the detective in charge, and arrange for him to meet you somewhere neutral." She held up her palm to stop Marcy's anticipated interjection. "He's really not going to be interested in you missing a court appearance for soliciting, Marcy. Believe me, I've met the man."

Marcy still didn't seem too sure.

"Look, if you get done, I'll pay the fine, okay?"

Marcy smiled.

"You're on, then, Doc. If you got a monkey to throw away, don't let me stop you."

Callie's smile was a little taut as she wondered just what she had got herself into: meeting Miller again, voluntarily, and risking losing five hundred pounds into the bargain. She wasn't sure which was worse. Why on earth did she get herself into these situations? She reached out for the phone. Mike Parton was the person to talk to about getting the second PM sorted, and getting the coroner to release the body. Thank goodness she had a good relationship with him, unlike Miller. Telling him what Marcy had told her was not going to be a pleasant experience.

Chapter 8

As Callie was shown into the incident room, Miller was in his shirt sleeves, watching the cheap office desks and chairs being stacked up ready to be moved out. He looked towards the door and managed a tight smile.

"Dr Hughes, to what do we owe this unexpected pleasure?" he said, but his expression made it clear that it was no pleasure. "Don't tell me, you suspect me of beating up another prisoner."

"And how is Mr Allen?" she replied coldly.

"Free. And quite possibly out looking for his next victim. I wouldn't know as he seems to have disappeared."

Callie frowned. His look suggested that she was at fault for Jimmy Allen's disappearance. Like every other bully she had ever met, he blamed everyone but himself.

"Maybe you should have concentrated on collecting evidence against him rather than attempting to 'persuade' him to confess."

"Look, is there a reason for you being here, or have you just come to gloat?"

"I don't think losing a murder suspect is any reason for me to gloat. I came because I have some information for you, actually."

"On Jimmy Allen?" Sergeant Jeffries cut in, startling Callie because she hadn't seen him under the table where he had been unplugging a computer.

"No," she replied, rather shortly. God, the man irritated her.

He stood and coiled the wire as he pulled it up.

"No, I have some information on Jade Trent." She had their undivided attention now. "It comes from a patient. So, it's a slightly sensitive area."

"This is a murder case and murder isn't sensitive. What's the information and who is it from?"

Whilst Miller had no time for niceties, Callie wasn't about to let herself be pushed into giving them Marcy's name, not without her say so.

"I will need certain assurances before I give you a name."

"I don't have time to argue the semantics of patient-doctor confidentiality. I don't have the time, and certainly not the energy. Just tell me what she has got to say, Doctor. I'm assuming it's a she? That you got the information from a tom?"

Callie felt herself redden, but kept her voice steady and calm.

"Jade had a room in the house on Wigmore Street that she used for work."

"Most of them do."

"She never took her work home to her flat. It was an absolute rule with her. That was her sanctuary away from all that. Ergo, the man who killed her was not a client."

"Bet she didn't use the word *ergo*." Jeffries muttered under his breath, but both Miller and Callie ignored him.

"This patient of yours? Did she know Jade well?"

"Yes. They were good friends." Callie hoped Marcy hadn't been exaggerating their friendship, or her reputation would be worth even less if Miller found out.

"Is there any chance we could meet her?"

There was a cough behind them, and they turned to see Mike Parton, the coroner's officer, standing in the doorway. Like most coroner's officers, Parton was an ex-copper who hadn't managed to get fully away from the job when he retired. It was his responsibility to take possession of the body in all sudden deaths, report directly to the coroner, and deal with the relatives, keeping them informed about what was happening if their relative's death didn't warrant a family support officer on the police team. Only major investigations had big enough teams to allocate a person to help support the family. In this case, a WPC had been named family liaison officer on top of her other duties, but one meeting with Jade's brother had brought her to the decision that this was one family that didn't need liaising with or supporting, so it had fallen once more to Parton to talk to him.

Sombre, concerned and reassuring as Parton doubtless was with the bereaved, he was like a spectre at the feast when he had to deal with his colleagues. He irritated the hell out of them. Silently disapproving of how they spoke and acted towards the dead, his presence had the effect of restricting conversations. Of course, the dead should be treated with respect and dignity, they all had to concede, but a certain level of sick humour was to be expected from police officers, particularly Bob Jeffries, and Parton should have understood that. His possession of absolutely zero sense of humour did not help him, and his pride in the fact that he was teetotal was unlikely to improve his standing amongst his colleagues.

"The second post-mortem on Christine Trent, the strangulation victim, has been arranged for next week and I have informed the family that the body will be ready to be released for burial after that, although I understand they are not interested."

Callie was relieved to hear that Parton had managed to organise it and gave him a quick smile of gratitude.

"Typical," Jeffries muttered.

Parton hadn't moved, he seemed to be deciding whether to say more.

"And?" Miller prompted.

"Miss Trent's brother was asking about the crime scene. When will you be finished there?"

Jeffries wasn't taken in for a moment.

"You mean he was asking when he can get his hands on her possessions. I've met the man. You remember, guv? He wanted to have her purse to make sure none of us nicked the cash out of it. First thing he said to me wasn't: how terrible, my sister's been strangled; but: can I have her purse, because I know what you lot are like."

"He's still her next of kin, and in the absence of a will…"

"He's sole heir to her condom stash, I know, I know."

Parton's upper lip curled in distaste at Jeffries' remark, and even Miller looked embarrassed and sneaked a look at Callie to see how she was reacting. Her face was impossible to read. He rubbed the back of his neck and looked like he was wondering why he'd bothered to come into work today. Maybe it would have been a good day to develop flu, or food poisoning, let his colleagues handle things and come back when it was all over. He sighed and looked at Parton.

"We'll meet him over there this afternoon, after we've taken a last look round, okay? Say threeish?"

Parton nodded to Miller, but couldn't bring himself to even look at Jeffries as he went out.

Miller turned to Callie. "Would your client, or patient or whatever, be willing to meet us at the flat too? Earlier than the brother? She might notice if there's anything missing or out of place."

"I can try." Callie wasn't overly optimistic. "She said she might speak to you, so long as I was present, and so long as I got an assurance from you that you wouldn't arrest her for any warrants that might possibly be outstanding. Or not."

"Typical!" Jeffries snorted, but was silenced by a look from Miller.

"No problem. Tell her I won't have time to check outstanding warrants. I don't even know her name, right?" His voice was softer now, less antagonistic. "It would be really helpful if you could persuade her."

"I'll do my best. We'll see you there if I succeed."

Miller smiled and Callie turned to leave.

"Tasty bint, I'll grant you," Jeffries said, not quite quietly enough, as he watched her leave the room. "But got too much of a mind of her own for my taste."

Miller just rolled his eyes heavenward and said nothing.

Chapter 9

The Priory Estate was in the process of being renovated. Two of the four blocks had been finished, and now boasted little balconies in blue plastic and brushed steel, stuck incongruously onto the front of the buildings, partly to make the flat concrete slabs of the original design look less dismal but also to give the residents somewhere to hang their washing or stick their rubbish. What was more important was that the blocks that had been refurbished all had new windows to keep out the cold, wet, seaside air and security doors to keep out the muggers and burglars that operated on the estate. At least, the security doors would stop them provided they weren't also residents, which they were more often than not.

The Priory Estate wasn't popular, having been run-down and crime-ridden for years, but in recent months the council had started an extensive refurbishment programme, adding balconies and security doors. Callie could see that work had not yet started on the block they were headed towards.

"Just Jade's luck," Marcy said, as she and Callie looked up at Whitefriars House. "She lived on this poxy estate for years but managed to get herself killed just days before the council were due to move her to a new flat and start doing up her block. She would've liked a balcony. She coulda sat out there with a glass of wine and pretended she were somewhere flash like Ibiza. When it wasn't raining, that is."

Marcy and Callie climbed the open stairs, littered with fag ends, empty beer cans and polystyrene takeaway cartons, and turned the corner at the top. As soon as they started to walk along the dimly lit corridor that led to Jade's front door, they could see her brother Darren waiting for them, jiggling about from one foot to the other. Dressed in a grubby sweatshirt and jeans that seemed too big, Darren sniffed loudly and wiped his nose on his sleeve, unaware that he was being watched.

* * *

"He's not supposed to be here yet," Callie explained. "Do you want to wait until he's gone?"

"And he's nicked all Marcy's stuff? No way."

"He is the next of kin."

"Yeah, I know. We get to choose our friends, but family… we're stuck with what we're given." Marcy shook her head. "I was always telling Jade to stop giving him money. But he was her little brother, the baby of the family…"

Darren turned and spotted them and started towards them aggressively.

"What are you doing here? You can't have anything, it's mine."

"And you're welcome to it, you ungrateful little tosser." Marcy was not intimidated.

"So, piss off then and take your social worker with you."

He was closing in on them and Callie was just wondering whether or not to grab Marcy, who seemed to be spoiling for a fight with the man, and run for it, when Miller and Jeffries appeared behind her.

"Oi, Darren, learn some manners, will you? We asked the ladies to meet us here. Hello, Marcy, nice to see you again," Jeffries said in passing as he grabbed Darren, none too gently, by the arm. "You are not supposed to be here for another hour."

"Yeah, well, I thought you might be trying to pull a flanker. And I was right, wasn't I? You were going to let the whore have first pick of Jade's stuff. Weren't you?"

Jeffries shook his head as he started pulling the police tape off the front door of the flat.

"You know what? You are a sad and suspicious individual."

Miller got out the key and unlocked the door.

"If we could just have one last look round before you take anything, Mr Trent, okay?"

Darren followed them into the flat, with Marcy and Callie bringing up the rear.

"Just don't take too long about it, all right? I ain't got all day."

"Yeah, right." Marcy was unsympathetic. "Meaning you ain't got no money as usual and you've got to flog some of this stuff to get your next hit."

"Takes one to know one."

"At least I work for mine."

"Yeah, right. On your back."

"Kneeling, more often."

"That's enough."

Callie was thankful that Miller had had enough of their bickering, because she had too. In fact, she could feel another headache coming on and rubbed at the spot between her eyebrows where it always seemed to be centred.

"Darren, sit down and shut up, or I'll make you wait outside. Marcy? It is Marcy, isn't it?" Miller asked.

She nodded, sullenly.

"Can you take a look round, tell us anything that might have been moved, out of place, or whatever."

Marcy nodded again, and Callie followed her as she went slowly through the flat, taking her time, looking at everything. It was just as she remembered from her visit to pronounce death, despite the fact that many people must have been through the flat before them, checking and logging the contents. Every inch had been dusted and photographed by the crime scene investigators; their grey fingerprint powder covered almost every surface. Although she had never met Jade Trent, Callie tried to picture the person who had lived here as she went from room to room. Somehow it made her feel less of an intruder.

The living room was quite comfortably furnished. Nothing flash, but homely. Not a bordello, or a brothel, just an ordinary living room, the sort that she had seen many times when visiting patients. Large telly – not new but a good make – a green patterned sofa with a cream throw over it, and assorted cushions artfully arranged. Prints of African elephants, lions and giraffes on the wall. Maybe she had dreamed of going to Africa one day, on a safari holiday, to see the animals in the flesh.

The kitchen was clean and tidy, the bathroom spotless. Nice fluffy pink towels hung on the rail. Callie hadn't expected Jade to be quite so house-proud, showing that she was as prejudiced about Jade's profession as anyone else would be. Callie could feel Marcy steel herself before stepping into the bedroom, almost as if she expected the body to still be there. Miller stood by and watched them, and Callie was relieved to see that the bed was stripped of its sheets and that even the mattress, which would most probably have been stained with the body fluids involuntarily released at death, had been removed. It had gone to the forensic laboratory to be sampled and scraped, she supposed, just in case any particle or cell from the killer remained.

"Jade's clothes, what she had been wearing that night, we think, were on the floor by the bed, where they must have fallen as she undressed," Miller explained.

Looking at the bed now, Callie could still see Jade's body as she had that first visit – her naked body, legs akimbo, head lolling – and she suppressed a shudder. She looked up and realised that Miller was watching her and was surprised to see him moved. She turned away quickly, taking a last look at the rest of the room.

He had been hoping intensely that Marcy would spot some vital clue, but she shook her head.

"No. It looks like it always did. Apart from the mattress being gone, of course."

Miller couldn't hide his disappointment as they left the bedroom and Jeffries jerked his head to Darren.

"You can start on the bedroom." Darren didn't wait for a second invitation and they could hear him opening and closing drawers as they stood in the lounge.

"Did she suffer?" Marcy asked.

Miller wished that he could say no. "She put up a bit of a fight, but not for long."

Callie's interest was piqued.

"What about under her nails? Strangulation victims often claw at their assailants." Callie looked up at Miller and read his expression that spoke volumes about teaching grandmothers and egg-sucking, but Marcy hadn't noticed.

"She used those stick-on ones; they kept pinging off. It was so she could still take them off and bite her nails when she wanted. Disgusting habit, but not as bad as some, I suppose." Marcy looked at Callie, acknowledging that drug dependence was probably worse. "Me? I prefer the acrylic nails, much harder to shift, although they are expensive." She looked down at her talons.

"There were some traces of glue on her nails, which were bitten down, but there was no sign of the false nails we assumed she was wearing."

Callie was perplexed.

"Her killer took them with him? He must have realised that he'd been scratched and known the significance."

"Doesn't mean much these days, every bugger watches CSI." Jeffries was unimpressed.

"But it does mean that the killer was cool-headed," Callie persisted. "Cool enough to collect any damning evidence even though he'd just killed her."

"Cold-hearted bastard," Marcy said under her breath.

"Organised and calculating, yes," Miller said. "Which is what makes me believe that this isn't an isolated incident. This killer will strike again, if we don't catch him."

Callie shuddered. She hoped he was wrong, but something about this crime told her that he wasn't. It wasn't a rage killing. It wasn't a one-off. This was just the start.

"You found her, didn't you?" Miller said, looking intently at Marcy. "It was you who called it in."

"What if I did?" she said, covering her fear in belligerence. "I didn't kill her, if that's what you think. I was working all night, you can check. I just came up for a coffee. Like I always did. Let myself in and, and..." Marcy broke down.

"There's nothing worth having in the bedroom." Darren's return to the lounge made Marcy turn away and look out of the window to hide her tears. "Can I start in here now?"

"You can take it all, Mr Trent. If that's what you want."

Darren looked round the room and shook his head.

"What would I want with most of this stuff? Worthless crap. Nah, I'll leave it for the council to clear, that's their job, innit? Unless you want any of it, Marce, a memento of your best friend."

Marcy looked like all she wanted was to punch him on the nose.

"I just want the telly, video, stuff like that."

"Stuff that's easy to sell, you mean. You never did give a monkey's about her."

Darren ignored Marcy and picked up the telly.

"Don't lock up or nothing, will ya? I'll be back up for the rest in a mo."

They watched him stagger out of the flat under the weight of the television.

"Hope he drops it." Marcy had said what they were all secretly wishing.

Miller took the opportunity of Darren's absence to ask her a few more questions.

"We'll need to check your movements, Marcy, but we think the killer was man. For a number of reasons. So, help us out here. Where would she have gone on a night off, so to speak?"

"There are a few places she used to go. The vodka bar on George Street. The sports bar, and that new place near it, in the town centre, Bateman's, or Yates's. Those are the most likely."

Callie had gone to the window and watched as Darren carefully placed his haul onto the back seat of a decrepit H-reg Ford Orion. She saw that Jeffries was watching too.

"Could run a vehicle check on it," he said, but Miller shook his head.

"No point. So, what if we bring him in for possession of a stolen vehicle, or we slap a producer on him" – he turned to Callie to explain – "get him to bring his car documents into the station within two weeks. We know he's unlikely to have anything as expensive as insurance or an in-date MOT, but even if he can't produce his documents, all he'll get is a fine."

"And a ban if he's got enough points." Jeffries still seemed keen to give it a go.

"He won't pay the fine, or stop driving if he's banned. His sort just laugh at bans. And he'll get away with it. That's the way it is. Always has been." Marcy sighed.

"Only the law-abiding middle classes ever pay their fines, not the likes of you or Darren, eh, Marcy?" Jeffries was disappointed not to be allowed to do anything.

"So, why do you bother running us working girls in all the time?"

"Fun."

Callie could believe that someone like Jeffries would do it for fun, too.

Darren came back into the flat and started collecting together the video, mini hi-fi, and the few CDs on the rack.

"What about the body? I understand the coroner's officer told you, you can have Jade's body next week," Miller said to Darren.

"What would I want with her body?"

"To bury it, Mr Trent. It is the normal procedure after death, I've found." Miller was unable to keep the sarcasm from his voice.

"Can't afford a funeral, right? So, if I just leave it, like, the council have to do it an' all, don't they?"

Neither Miller nor Jeffries felt the need to answer. The man was right, of course he was, someone always pays up in the end.

He backed out of the flat laden with the last bits he wanted.

"That's it, you're welcome to the rest," he told Marcy as he paused in the doorway. "You're wrong, I will miss her, you know, she was always good for a bunce," he said as he left.

Marcy waited until he had gone before turning to Miller.

"It's okay, isn't it? If I see to the funeral? I went to the funeral directors and they thought it was okay."

"Fine. No problem at all," he replied.

"Won't tell him when it is, though." She jerked her head towards the door. "Don't want him to spoil it."

Marcy turned to leave, with Callie following her.

"And if there's anything else, anything at all that you remember, you will tell us, won't you?" Miller asked her.

"Depends. If I think it will help catch the killer, of course I will, but I might not feel too helpful if I'm under arrest or anything."

Marcy looked at Jeffries pointedly and left.

Chapter 10

It was nearly ten past eight when Callie pushed her way into Porters wine bar. It was packed, as it always was on a Friday night.

No chance of a table, she thought to herself, but then spotted Jonathon ensconced at a small table for four in the corner, with his coat, a newspaper and his briefcase spread proprietarily over the other chairs to fend off anyone else who might get ideas about sitting there. Callie smiled. He definitely got brownie points for getting a table, and extra points for having a bottle of red and two glasses ready and waiting.

She wound her way through the heaving masses, towards the table.

"Sorry I'm a bit late. Visit that went on a bit," she explained as he stood and cleared a chair for her to sit.

"Don't mention it. I know how difficult a GP's life can be."

Callie tried to suppress a smile; he was going to have to stop being quite so smooth.

Jonathon noticed.

"Too much? Sorry," he said. "Let's start again, shall we? Sit down, have a glass of wine and relax. I got red, but I could get white as well, if you'd prefer?"

"Red is perfect."

Callie sat as Jonathon poured her a glass and passed it to her. He then raised his own.

"The weekend starts here." They both took a sip of wine and Callie could immediately feel it easing the tension of her stressful day.

"Or are you on call?" he asked.

"Only for the police, and even then, not until tomorrow."

He looked surprised and Callie explained about her work as a forensic physician.

"I had no idea. Now that must be really interesting. Come on, don't stop there, I want to hear some gory stories or, at the very least, some salacious gossip."

Callie was surprised by his interest and she entertained him for quite some time with stories of unusual injuries and their unconvincing explanations, tiddly old ladies who insisted they'd had nothing but sherry trifle, and the weird and wonderful things that drunks get up to.

"You clearly like your work very much," he commented when she ran out of stories, and Callie realised that yes, she did. She also realised that the wine bottle was almost empty and she didn't think that Jonathon had drunk much of it.

"I'm sorry," she apologised, "I've monopolised the conversation and drunk all the wine. Let me order another bottle." She stood up, but Jonathon placed a hand on hers and stood up himself.

"I'm really sorry, but I have to go."

Callie couldn't hide her disappointment. She had been enjoying herself.

"Can I give you a lift home? My car's just up the road."

"No, that's fine. I could do with a walk. Clear my head."

Callie was embarrassed, wondering if perhaps all her talk about working with the police had put him off, and not sure what she should do as he hastily put on his coat.

"I've bored you. I'm sorry. You should have stopped me going on and on like that."

"No, not at all. I've found it absolutely fascinating; I think your enthusiasm is wonderful, it's just that I have something that I need to do, and I'm going away for the weekend, so I have to do it tonight."

"I'm not sure I believe you," she admitted.

"It's true, I'm afraid. Sad and boring, but I have some work I need to finish. An article I'm writing. But look, I've really enjoyed this evening, Callie. What's that short for, anyway?"

"Calliope."

"That's beautiful. The Greek muse of poetry. Your parents must have known..." He noticed her expression. "Sorry. Too much again?"

She smiled and Jonathon took her hand.

"I mean it, though, I really have enjoyed this evening, and I'd love to do it again, only maybe next time we can make it dinner as well? Next week, perhaps? Damn, my firm's on call all week, let's make it the following week. I don't want to be called out to an ectopic halfway through the first course." He smiled and Callie found herself believing him. "How about Wednesday? Here? I had a look at the menu and it made me feel quite hungry. How does that sound?"

Callie smiled back. If he had been bored rigid, he wouldn't have suggested a specific date, would he? Callie was useless at reading the signals given by men; contrary to common belief, she thought women were much easier to understand.

"That sounds terrific, Jonathon. I can certainly vouch for the food here. I'll look forward to it."

And, as he gave her a smile and a quick peck on the cheek, she realised that she was looking forward to it already. And also that she hoped that it would go a bit further than a peck on the cheek next time.

Outside Porters, Callie was relieved to see that at least it wasn't raining. She hesitated. She could turn right, to the sea front and the more direct route up the steep steps and twittens, or she could turn left and use the well-lit main road. Silently telling herself she was being a wimp, Callie took the longer, safer route. She still felt as if she was being watched all the way home, but she saw and heard no one. As she locked her front door behind her she felt a wave of relief, then gave herself a mental slap. It was stupid to live your life in fear, particularly as she had no proof or even genuine reason to believe that she had ever been followed or at risk at all. It wouldn't do, she told herself, it really wouldn't do. She'd end up with agoraphobia like one of her patients, a little old lady she visited every week – a spinster who never left her home for fear of what might be out there. Too frightened of death to ever live.

* * *

He saw her at the karaoke night at The Jolly Sailor, a large, soulless pub out on the London Road. She was on her own, although she obviously knew a few people in the bar to nod to, to say hello to, to pretend to herself she was friends with. Plain and fat and scarred by acne. The fat was all too obvious under her tight synthetic top, bulging either side of the crease of her bra strap, and over the waistband of her low-cut jeans. Her dull, straggly, mousy hair was at least clean, but when she laughed, imitating happiness, being one of the gang, he could see that her teeth were yellowed and stained from the cigarettes she smoked endlessly, thinking they made her look cool, perhaps.

Probably never had a boyfriend in her life, he thought. Not a proper one. Not a bloke who wasn't blind or drunk, anyway. The look on her face, when he caught up with her on her way home, suggested they go back to hers for a coffee. She'd been pathetically grateful. Tried to hide it, tried to make out she wasn't normally that easy, but there was no doubting it, she was astonished and flattered to have a bloke come home and fuck her. Someone to tell her mates about without having to lie. If only she'd known, Fat Denise, shelf stacker and checkout girl at the supermarket; if only she had known just what she was going to get once they got back to her pathetic rented basement flat. She wouldn't have been grateful then, she would have been terrified.

She'd thought it was a joke at first, a dressing up game, and happily went along with it, giggled at the outfit he put on, and sniggered dirtily at the latex gloves. Doctors and nurses, now this really would be something to tell the girls. It was a shame she hadn't got any tights on; she chuckled coyly when he'd asked about that, said she always wore trousers and socks, so he'd had to use his key chain. Next time he'd be more prepared, bring some tights with him, or something better perhaps.

It wasn't until he'd got the chain wrapped round her neck that she began to realise it wasn't a game, and by then it was too late. Her eyes bulged and her tongue stuck out as she gasped; it almost got cut off when she bit down on it. Didn't bleed much though, because she was dead soon after. Cooling fast, almost as fast as his prick rose. Strong and hard. He unwrapped the chain from her neck and tried to put the tongue back in, but it kept flopping out. That put him off her a bit. It stopped her looking so nice. Not that she was ever going to be pretty, and there was no denying it, she was fat. He looked closer at her fat thighs, dimpled with cellulite, her pubic hair — wild and untrimmed, leading up to the stretch marks crossing her sagging belly. He'd felt disappointment then, as he looked down at her, and quickly lost his erection. She just wasn't good enough. Even in death, Denise was disappointing. If only she knew.

Chapter 11

The rain had started in earnest by the time Callie got to the small chapel in the corner of the cemetery. Callie was running late as usual, but she was relieved to see that they hadn't yet taken the coffin inside, and also that Marcy had resisted the temptation to go for a horse-drawn hearse, a lone bagpiper or anything over the top like that.

She hurried inside the chapel, shaking the worst of the rain off her umbrella as she sidled into a pew at the back and was surprised to see several people in the chapel. Marcy was at the front in a dramatic black hat and full-length leather coat, regularly dabbing at her eyes with a lacy handkerchief. Behind her were two men in suits who turned as they heard Callie come in. Miller and Jeffries.

Probably here in case the killer turns up, Callie thought scornfully. As if life was ever that simple.

There were three or four other working girls, a couple that Callie recognised, but all of them easily identifiable by their clothes. Battered stilettos, mini-skirts and an awful lot of cleavage for a funeral. They can't have been planning on taking the whole afternoon off, then. And Edna. Callie wasn't surprised to see Edna there. Edna went to pretty much every funeral service going, said she liked to be sure nobody went without at least one mourner, but Callie suspected that her real reason was the after-funeral drinks. Most people felt it only polite to ask her along, even if she had never met their Aunt or Dad or whoever the deceased actually was, and they quickly discovered that Edna was very partial to a glass of sherry.

There was also a slim, elderly man – sleek, silver hair cut stylishly – wearing a slinky black polo neck jersey, tucked into neat black trousers. An aging trendsetter, stuck in the Sixties. At first Callie thought he must be a relative of Jade's but, as the coffin was carried into the chapel by the pallbearers provided by the funeral director, she realised that he was actually taking the service. Callie was relieved that this wasn't going to be religious; somehow she couldn't believe that Jade would have wanted hymns and prayers. The humanist service arranged by Marcy turned out to be short, simple and very moving. A couple of inspirational readings, the Auden poem made famous by *Four Weddings and a Funeral*, and the silver-headed man then read out a sanitised version of Jade's life, that somehow left out pretty much everything that Callie knew about her.

As they all followed the coffin out, to the inevitable Robbie Williams' song *Angels*, Callie thought she would try and slip away, but Marcy took her hand and gripped it firmly before she could escape.

"Thank you so much for being here, Doc. You've no idea how much your support means to me. Just got the actual burial bit to get through now, then we can all go back to The Hastings Arms and raise a toast to Jade. Eddie's laid on some food. You will stay, won't you?"

Callie didn't have the heart to refuse, even though the rain showed no sign of easing off. She put up her umbrella and followed the dismal procession to the graveside, where the freshly dug soil was already fast turning to mud.

* * *

The Hastings Arms was a traditional English seaside resort pub. It had fishing nets dotted with shells and plastic crabs hanging from the ceiling, a cheery feel and during the summer it was always packed. On a wet autumn afternoon in midweek, Eddie, the landlord was probably delighted to have the funeral group in there, otherwise he would have been on his own apart from Old Jim on his favourite stool in the corner. By the time Callie re-emerged from the ladies, having removed the worst of the mud from her shoes, most of the working girls had gone back to work, or to get ready for the evening rush at least, but Marcy, Callie, Miller, Jeffries, a neighbour of Jade's whose name Callie had forgotten if she had ever known it, and Edna had stayed. Edna, of course, was already clutching a nearly empty glass of sweet sherry. Half a dozen people at that time of day were a good crowd as far as Eddie was concerned, even if some of them were only drinking mineral water.

As she sipped her fizzy water and exchanged pleasantries with Edna, Callie saw Miller looking over in her direction more than once.

"I always think rain is good for a funeral. There's something wrong about laying someone to rest when the sun's out, don't you think?"

"Mmm, yes, I suppose you're right." She looked at her watch. "Going to have to go in a minute, Edna. Evening surgery."

Edna didn't seem to have heard.

"Shame about the turn out, though. I do like to see a packed chapel. Makes for a livelier do afterwards." Edna tossed back the last of her drink and looked meaningfully at her empty glass.

"Can I get you another, Edna? Sweet sherry, is it?"

"That's very good of you, Doctor. I don't mind if I do."

At the bar, Callie was joined by Miller as Jeffries headed off to check out the facilities.

"Always attend the funerals of your patients, do you, Dr Hughes?"

"She wasn't my patient." Callie glanced round at Marcy, who seemed more relaxed now that she was on her second large glass of Chardonnay. "I came to support Marcy, that's all, and I have to go in a minute. Evening surgery awaits. How about you? Do you always attend the funerals of your victims? I mean, do you honestly think her killer is here? Or is it just standard procedure?"

"Standard procedure. And more in the hope that a friend or relative we don't know about attends rather than the killer. Speaking of which" – he indicated Edna – "is she...?"

Callie shook her head.

"Never met Jade. Just here for the free drinks."

"Oh." Miller was disappointed. He looked around, wanting to find something or someone of interest, and failing.

Callie paid for Edna's sherry and was about to head back with it when Miller put his half-empty glass on the bar.

"No point in hanging round," he said and headed towards the door. Jeffries quickly downed his pint and followed with a cheerful wave to Callie, who was left wondering whether the pair of them practised irritating the hell out of her or if it just came naturally. Once she had handed over the sherry to Edna, she made her excuses to an already tipsy Marcy and left the wake. As she hurried up the High Street back to the surgery, her mobile rang and she hesitated when she saw that the caller was Jonathon. A little part of her braced herself for an excuse, a sorry-but-I've-changed-my-mind-about-a-second-date call, but then was pleasantly surprised when she finally answered and he seemed as keen as he had been when they last met.

"Is Wednesday night still all right with you?" he asked her. "I thought I might book a table at The Dining Room.

It's in the Old Town so, your neck of the woods, so to speak, and it's a bit quieter there."

More intimate, Callie thought but was relieved he wasn't cancelling so she agreed.

"That would be lovely." She wondered if he could tell over the phone that she was smiling.

"Eight o'clock?"

"Lovely," she said again and almost groaned at how stupid she sounded.

"I'll see you there then." He hadn't seemed to notice, fortunately, and once they had finished the call, Callie walked the rest of the way back to work giving herself a good talking to about keeping her cool and not acting like an infatuated schoolgirl.

Chapter 12

The relentless drizzle that seemed to have settled on the town in the days since Jade's funeral showed no signs of lifting as Callie hurried up the steps towards the address she had been given, high up on the West Hill. As she reached the top and looked along the road, she assessed the run-down Victorian terrace, each four-storey house divided into as many flats as could be crammed into the available space. The upper floors would have a nice view over the town centre to the sea and would bring in good money, but the lower floors, even the so-called "garden flat", with its bit of concrete patio out back, where the residents stored their wheelie bins and chained their bikes to the railings, looked dark, damp and dingy. A flight of cracked concrete steps led down to the basement flats in each house.

There was no mistaking the address that she was supposed to be visiting. Apart from having a police car parked outside, a cluster of interested neighbours and onlookers had gathered on the pavement, and a middle-aged man was sitting on the steps, head in hands, with a young police constable, looking unsure and awkward, next to him. Callie was surprised that the witness-comforting was being left to a rookie, until she spotted the more experienced policewoman in the panda and could tell from the look of her that she had been the one who went in and discovered the body and that it had been a very unpleasant experience.

The constable stood up to let Callie pass and she patted the other man on the shoulder as she went by. She was not sure that he noticed, he was so engrossed in his misery and shock. As she went down the steps to the tiny concrete area that allowed a modicum of light into the basement rooms as well as giving access to the front door, she could understand why. The smell of decomposed human tissue was unmistakeable. There was a small splattering of vomit over the steps and Callie trod carefully round it, glad that she was in jeans and easy-to-clean, dark leather shoes; she wouldn't want the mess from this death scene on her cream suede Ballys or her dry-clean-only silk-mix suit. She would want everything she was wearing today to be thrown straight into a hot wash to get rid of the smell as soon as she got home.

She paused on the bottom step by the open front door, the broken glass on the doorstep and missing window-pane revealing how the policewoman had gained access, and fished a pot of vapour rub out of her medical bag. Taking a large dab, Callie smeared it under her nose knowing that, even if she stuck a whole pot full of menthol and eucalyptus up there, there was no way it was going to disguise the smell from this body. With one last deep breath of not-so-fresh air, she entered the flat.

The hallway had no natural light except for what was coming through the open front door and a second door at the end. It took Callie a few moments to adjust to the dim light, before she could make out the hallway. The floor, covered by a well-worn, stained carpet, led to the back of the house and she could make out three doors off the hallway, all closed, except the one at the end which was slightly ajar, and through which a muted light and a terrible smell emanated.

"Hello?" she called out and was relieved to see Mike Parton appear from the doorway.

"She's in here, Doctor."

She hurried along the hallway and followed Parton through the open door at the end, pulling on a pair of gloves as she went.

Standing in the doorway, Callie looked round the cheaply furnished bedroom. Parton, aware that she liked to do this, stood silently to one side, waiting for her to take it all in.

The curtains were drawn across, but a weak light was seeping through the gap where they did not quite meet in the middle. Behind them she could glimpse dingy, grey nets that looked as if they had hung there, unwashed, since the flat was first built. The central ceiling light was on, but the bulb was dim and insufficient to light the room properly. The furniture was a mix of second-hand junk and cheap flat-pack pieces, inexpertly put together. It was an unloved and utilitarian room, typical of cheap, rented accommodation of this type, a type that Callie had often seen when visiting the sick and poor of the town. The council put homeless people on the housing waiting list in this sort of place, when they could find it. Students, the unemployed, the old, the vulnerable; this was where they often ended their days, overdosing on drugs or alcohol, or just giving up the struggle.

The room was warm, despite the cool temperature outside. There was a night storage heater under the window. It would be on a timer and would have continued to come on regardless, speeding up the body's decomposition. There were several flies buzzing at the window. Callie was thankful it wasn't summer or there would have been several hundred.

She finally turned her attention to the bed. This was clearly the source of the smell. The naked, bloated and partially decomposed body of a woman was lying on top of the covers. It was hard to tell if she had always been overweight or if it was just the effects of the putrefaction gases building up inside her bowels and abdominal cavity that gave her such an obese appearance. Probably both, Callie decided as she moved closer to the body, checking the surrounding area for anything that might give her a clue as to why this lady was deceased.

"Do we know anything about her?" Callie asked Parton.

He looked down at his notebook.

"Her name is Denise Gardner. Twenty-two years old. Lived alone. Worked in Morrisons, on the checkout. Hadn't turned up for work for the last two weeks. That's her manager outside, came round as he hadn't been able to reach her on the phone and it was out of character for her to no-show for more than a couple of days. I think he was just covering his bases before forwarding a P45."

"Next of kin?"

"Her manager doesn't know of anyone but I went through her bag and found her driving licence, still with an address in Croydon, and there's a telephone number for Mum in her address book."

Callie nodded. Parton had been as thorough as always.

Close up, Callie could make out more of the girl's features but light was still a problem. She flicked the switch on the bedside light but the bulb had gone so Parton opened the curtains and pulled back the nets. It was a grey day and the already weak sunlight was no match for the many years' build-up of dirt on the windows. It wasn't going to be easy to see what she was doing.

Callie stooped over the body and checked for any obvious signs of trauma. There were no apparent wounds or limbs at odd angles. Her mouth was open and her tongue was lolling out slightly. The girl looked as if she had died in her sleep but healthy twenty-two-year olds don't usually die in their sleep, not even obese ones, not without some kind of help. So, Callie looked round for any signs of drugs or alcohol. There was nothing on the bedside table. The top drawer was sticky and difficult to open and contained nothing more than a pack of contraceptive pills, some condoms, a vibrator and several used tissues.

Callie pulled down the girl's lower jaw. There was a pool of blood in her mouth from where she had bitten her tongue but no sign of vomit, and if there had been froth on the lips it was hard to tell now that decomposition was so advanced. Callie tried to keep the revulsion from her face as a single maggot crawled out from under the tongue.

"Any history of epilepsy? Fits?"

Parton shrugged.

"There's no anti-epileptic drugs in the drawer, were there any in her bag? Or the bathroom cupboard?"

"None in her bag. I'll check the bathroom." He went out.

Callie gently moved the head to one side and stopped.

"Just some paracetamol," Parton reported as he came back in.

Callie held up her hand to stop him and indicated the girl's neck.

"Have you got a torch, Mike?"

He moved back towards the door.

"There will be one in the panda."

He went off to fetch it, leaving Callie with the body. There was no point trying to examine it any further without light and she didn't want to disturb or touch anything if what she suspected was right, so she stood still and patiently waited for Parton to return. It was less than two minutes but seemed like an hour before he hurried back in and handed her a black police-issue Maglite. She shone it on the girl's neck and tilted the head slightly to one side, aware of Mike leaning close, trying to see what had obviously caught her attention.

"There." She pointed at a slightly darkened line around the neck. It was hard to see as the skin tone was already unnaturally dark due to the putrefaction process. "Looks like it could be a ligature mark to me."

Parton leant back.

"Right. Best call for back-up then."

And he went out, Callie following, making sure that she took all her things with her and left everything just as she had found it.

* * *

As she waited for the back-up to arrive, she spoke to Denise's manager, who was still feeling very sorry for himself.

"I didn't notice the smell at first. It wasn't until there wasn't any answer at the door and I opened the letter box to shout that I smelled it. Now I can't get rid of it. I don't think I ever will."

Callie handed the manager her pot of vapour rub.

"Here, a touch of this helps, just pop it under your nose."

He took the pot gratefully and stuck a large glob of the stuff right up his left nostril before digging his finger in again and getting more to stick in the right. He went to hand the pot back, but Callie shook her head. Did he really think that she would want it back after he had contaminated it like that?

"It's okay. You keep it."

They were sitting on the kerb a little along from the flat, where she and Parton had moved the manager and, realising how distressed he was, she felt obliged to attempt to comfort him. A thin, almost scrawny man in his early forties with thinning hair and a care-worn expression, Callie rather doubted that he would ever go looking for any missing employees again.

"So, how come you were visiting Denise?" Callie asked, searching for something to break the silence, and get the man's mind off the lingering smell.

"I was coming to see what the problem was. Why she hadn't come into work for the last ten days." He looked down at the pavement, absentmindedly scraping at a lump of discarded chewing gum with his cheap plastic shoes. "Thought it might have been something I'd said."

He was shifting his position nervously, guiltily.

"Did she kill herself?" He looked directly at Callie.

"What makes you think that?"

"The last time I saw her, at the end of her shift on the Saturday before last, she asked me to go to a karaoke night with her, up at The Jolly Sailor."

"And you turned her down?"

"No. I said I'd go, meet her there, like, but…"

Callie let the silence linger on, knowing that he'd fill it sooner or later. He only left it a few seconds.

"I know she had a bit of a crush on me, but well, I mean, fraternising with the staff is looked down on. You know. From head office."

"So, why did you say you'd be there?"

"Because it was getting embarrassing. She kept asking me to things and I'd run out of excuses. It just sort of came out and she looked so happy. It just seemed kinder."

"To let her go to the karaoke and then let her down publicly?"

He went back to digging at the gum with his foot.

"I'll never forgive myself if she killed herself because I stood her up."

A silver Toyota pulled up, and Callie stood as she saw Miller and Jeffries get out.

"We'll have to wait for the post-mortem but I don't think she did."

He looked at her with a mixture of relief and disappointment. God save her from the egos of men, Callie thought.

"I've got to go," she told the manager. "Just remember to tell the police everything you told me." He nodded and she hurried towards the steps down to the basement, already several paces behind the two detectives.

* * *

Miller and Jeffries were standing just inside the bedroom door as Callie came in. Both men exuded pent-up excitement and anticipation, convinced that this second death would be the break they were looking for, had been waiting for.

"You say you think you saw a ligature mark on the neck, Dr Hughes?" Miller asked.

"That's right. It's hard to tell with the decomposition, but I thought it better to be safe."

"Have you touched anything?"

Callie glanced at Mike Parton, who was looking slightly uncomfortable.

"We opened the curtains to let in more light, that's all," Parton answered for her.

Miller nodded.

"And I opened the bedside drawer, looking for signs of drug use," Callie added.

"Did you find anything?"

"No. Just contraceptives."

"Okay. Show me the mark." He almost ordered Callie.

She moved forward, pulling on a fresh pair of gloves, tilting the girl's head slightly to one side, and pointed.

"Here. It's faint, but I'm sure." Callie tried to sound more convinced than she was. The line seemed even less obvious now than it had when she first saw it.

But it was enough to convince Miller. He turned to Jeffries.

"I want the full team out here, everything, and get on to Professor Wadsworth, see if you can persuade him to come out to the scene. Now let's get everybody out of here until the crime scene boys have done their bit."

They all traipsed back to the front door and Callie wondered if they all felt like naughty schoolchildren, or if Miller only had that effect on her.

* * *

Callie was not sure if she should hang around, see if she could do anything else to help, or if she had been dismissed. Jeffries and Miller were questioning the manager and she didn't want to interrupt and ask but, on the other hand, she had things to do, places to go. It was her day off from the surgery so she couldn't claim an urgent need to leave but she really needed to do some food shopping, take several weeks' worth of clothes to the cleaners, and go to the bank. All the little jobs that, one way or another, she never quite found time to do. She knew the investigation took priority, the dead girl deserved that, but this sitting around waiting was beginning to irritate.

She saw Parton returning from having made a telephone call from the privacy of his car, presumably to brief the coroner about this case, and went over to him.

"Hi Mike, do you think they are likely to need me anymore?" She nodded towards the two detectives.

Parton frowned.

"Hard to say. Professor Wadsworth will be here soon but–" He shrugged.

Callie sighed. Best to wait until class was dismissed. She glowered over towards Miller and was embarrassed when he turned and looked straight at her, as if he had felt the force of her ill will across the twenty or so yards that separated them. Callie dropped her gaze hurriedly but looked up again when she heard footsteps approaching. It was Miller. He paused and turned back to Jeffries, who was a few yards behind him, as if he had suddenly remembered something.

"Get uniform to pick up Jimmy Allen if they can find him, would you, Bob?" Then he turned back to speak to Parton.

"Is the Home Office pathologist on his way?" he asked.

"Yes, should be here within the hour."

Miller turned to Callie.

"No need for you to wait then, Dr Hughes. There's nothing more for you to do now. Professor Wadsworth will take over from here on in." He turned to leave and Callie could feel a flush of anger reach her cheeks.

"That's so kind of you," she muttered sarcastically to his retreating back. "Arrogant, patronising..." Callie was embarrassed to see that a female police constable standing by one of the police cars that had arrived with Miller and Jeffries had overheard her and was smirking in recognition of her description.

Callie stalked off towards the steps down towards the town, still angry at being so summarily dismissed without so much as a thank you. She knew it was silly, that she had merely done her job but done it well, and Miller was right, Professor Wadsworth did have to take over from here. Anything that she did or touched at the crime scene could cause contamination or a break in the chain of evidence, muddy the waters for any future prosecution, but he could have suggested that she wait for Professor Wadsworth and report her findings direct to him and then wait to see if he agreed, if her suspicions had been correct. After all, she had flagged the death up as suspicious in the first place. It would have been common courtesy to allow her to stay and hear the experienced pathologist's expert opinion, surely? She knew that she was being contrary, having wanted to leave a few minutes earlier, but that didn't change the way she felt. She had been disposed of as unwanted and unnecessary, and it grated.

At the top of the stairs she took one last look back towards the house and was interested to see Miller still watching her, obviously aware that he had irritated her. As she brazenly regarded him, he shook his head, as if giving up trying to work out why she was angry with him, and turned back to where Jeffries was busy on his mobile, probably urging his colleagues to rough up Jimmy Allen once they found him.

Callie practically stomped down the steps to where she had left her car, fuelled with righteous indignation. If he didn't know why she was upset, he couldn't be much of a detective. She decided to go home and clean the flat then take a shower; she didn't want to go food shopping until she had the smell of death, mixed with menthol and eucalyptus, out of her nostrils.

Chapter 13

Unsurprisingly, Callie was running late for her first patient of evening surgery and she hadn't even glanced at her paperwork – the pathology results, the repeat prescription requests, the hospital letters – let alone dealt with any of them. Up in the office, she rifled through the pile in her basket, trying to pick out anything urgent.

"Have we had Timothy Lockwood's results back yet?" she asked, knowing he was due in later.

Linda checked on his electronic record as Callie continued to sort through the paper copies.

"Yup. They're there," Linda told her and Callie came over to the computer screen to look at them. She frowned as she read them.

"Good thing he's coming in."

The phone buzzed, indicating an internal call, and Linda picked it up, glancing almost immediately at Callie, who was still engrossed in young Timothy Lockwood's blood results.

"Helen on reception says Mr Herring wants you to know that you are now four minutes late starting surgery and he is your first patient."

Callie groaned. Why did it always have to be him when she was behind?

* * *

Timothy was not looking well. Callie wasn't sure if she was seeing his complexion as sallow and jaundiced with the benefit of the insight that his blood results had given her or if she would have noticed it anyway. She pulled down his lower eyelids. The whites definitely seemed a bit yellow today and she knew they had not been before.

"Up on the couch, young man," she ordered, a smile taking any sting from her words, and turned to his mother as he obeyed. Mrs Lockwood was looking as expensive and immaculate as ever, with her perfectly polished and manicured nails, her thick, shiny, blond hair showing not one iota of the darker roots that Callie was sure would be more her natural colour, and with plenty of solid gold jewellery visible, for all her protestations of poverty.

"His test results are back and there are one or two abnormalities."

"And what does that mean? Do you know what's wrong with him?"

"His liver function tests are raised, which suggests that he might have a problem there."

"His liver? What do you mean, a problem?" She seemed more irritated than concerned, but maybe that was just the way she came across.

"The most common reason in boys his age is hepatitis A. A viral hepatitis that you can get from eating infected food, usually seafood, or from contaminated water. Has Timothy been abroad recently?"

Mrs Lockwood thought for a moment.

"We haven't been away since Koh Samui last year. Could it be from that long ago?"

"No. I don't think that's possible. Has anyone at his school been ill?"

"Not that I know of." Mrs Lockwood continued to think as Callie went over to Timothy and felt for his liver, sure now that it was enlarged.

"When we went away, we all had loads of injections. Isn't hepatitis A one of those?"

Callie turned back to Mrs Lockwood.

"Yes, but there's nothing on his notes about having had travel vaccinations."

"We had them done at a travel centre. It was more convenient."

"And he had the full course?"

"Just a booster that time, I think. We'd been abroad a few times; my ex-husband works in Hong Kong and we've lived there, off and on, until the divorce, that is, so he'd already had some of them. I can check his card."

"Please do. You can get up now, Timothy," she told the boy, before coming back and sitting at her desk.

"But what else could it be, if it's not hepatitis A?"

"That's a good question. I'll take some more blood." She saw Timothy pull a face. "Sorry, but it has to be done, I'm afraid."

Callie turned back to the mother. "I'll send it off for viral studies and antibodies, see if we can identify if it is that, or maybe another sort of hepatitis, and I think we should get him seen up at the hospital. As soon as possible."

"You'll write a letter?"

"I'll call, tonight or first thing tomorrow, get some advice from the paediatrician."

This, more than anything seemed to bring it home to Mrs Lockwood that there might be something seriously wrong.

"These other forms of hepatitis – some of them can be dangerous, can't they?" Mrs Lockwood seemed suddenly vulnerable, almost soft, despite all the expensive veneer and lacquer. Whatever else she was or was not, this woman was still a mother.

Callie stole a glance at Timothy, who was listening intently, a serious expression on his face. Callie didn't want to alarm him but, equally, she didn't want to lie. To either of them.

"They can be, as can hep A, but there could be any number of reasons why his liver is playing up; let's just try and find out why, quickly." She turned and spoke directly to Timothy, "Then we can get you feeling well again."

"Don't worry, darling…"

Callie was pleased that for the first time his mother was addressing Timothy directly.

"…I'll call your father as soon as we get home." She turned to Callie. "I'll tell him we need to go privately. There must be a decent hospital around here somewhere. Let me know what you've arranged as soon as possible. Hurry up, Timothy, it's already late in Hong Kong so I'll just have to wake your father up, won't I?" The prospect seemed to please her. "Goodnight, Dr Hughes."

She ushered her son out of the room, leaving Callie to sort out a private referral and ponder on how even supposedly amicable divorces seemed to turn into bitter wrangles over money, with children being used as pawns.

* * *

Callie had picked up the local weekly paper when she did the shopping in the Sainsbury's up on the Ridgeway on her way home. Sainsbury's was not actually on her way home, she had to admit; in fact, it was significantly out of her way but she had not wanted to go to Morrisons in case she bumped into the manager. Silly really. Much as she was curious to find out more about the body from the basement flat in Keyfield Terrace, she didn't want to be forced to talk about it with someone who probably knew less about it than she did and, selfishly, she didn't want to have to spend yet more time being sympathetic; she did far too much of that in her official hours to want to do it in her off-duty time. She was sure that the local paper would have a report on the death and she was not wrong.

Unsurprisingly, it was the lead story on the front page. "Supermarket checkout girl found dead" in large capitals filled half the page above what looked to be an old school photo of a plump young girl with limp mousey hair framing a plain face with a forced smile and a bad case of acne.

Poor girl, no wonder she developed a crush on her singularly uncharismatic manager, Callie thought, as she kicked off her shoes and settled on the sofa with a glass of wine to read the report. What she really wanted to know was if the police had anyone 'helping with their enquiries' as they liked to call it. In other words, had they picked up Jimmy Allen again?

The full results of the post-mortem would not be through for a while yet but she hoped that the police, Miller, that was, might have let something slip if they had had any kind of preliminary report. Was this a second strangulation victim as Callie thought or had she got it wrong?

She skimmed through the newspaper report once and then read it again more carefully. Nothing was said specifically about cause of death but the police were treating it as suspicious and they didn't have anyone in custody. Jimmy Allen was either guilty as hell and in hiding, or innocent and had decided that the best thing was to keep his head down, but Callie suspected that Miller would favour the first interpretation. A sudden thought hit her. Maybe they had found Jimmy Allen and he had a cast-iron alibi. That would seriously piss Miller off, she thought with a slightly mischievous smile, and resolved to ask him when she next saw him, more for her benefit than his. Much more.

The paper had dug up a bit more background on the victim, Denise. She was the eldest of four children – one boy, three girls –

from Croydon. Her mother was a school dinner lady, her father worked for the local authority parks department. A solid, unexceptional family, "devastated by the loss of their much-loved daughter and older sister", according to the report. She had apparently always loved Hastings after years of family holidays in the seaside town and had decided to move there soon after leaving school. Various old school friends were quoted as saying that Denise would be sadly missed, that she was a great girl, good fun. Maybe she should have stayed in Croydon, Callie thought, because she didn't seem to have had much of a life in Hastings. There was no cause of death noted or any similarities drawn to Jade Trent's death but the final line of the report mentioned the prostitute's unsolved murder so it was clear that the press were beginning to link the two. It was just a matter of time before the public would, too.

She put the paper down and went to pour herself a second glass of wine whilst she sorted out some dinner. Chicken fajitas. Quick, easy to cook, and not too bad on the healthy eating front.

As she thinly sliced the chicken and vegetables, Callie thought ahead to tomorrow night. Dinner with Jonathon. She was looking forward to it. He was, after all, good-looking and good company and very charming, unlike a certain detective chief inspector. Her few meetings with Miller suggested that he would be anything but good company. Going out with Jonathon would be good for her. He was a great catch, as her mother had pointed out. It had been a while since she had gone out with anybody other than Kate, and best friends didn't count anyway. She chucked everything into the wok to stir fry and surveyed the room. The flat was perfectly tidy and clean but maybe she ought to change the sheets tomorrow, just in case.

Suddenly there was a racket from outside, the sound of something ceramic being hit, or kicked, but not breaking. Flower pots maybe, or some bricks? A dog was barking and there were shouts of "Down!" and "Heel, boy". Callie looked out of the window and saw a man grabbing his snarling dog and putting it on a lead, literally dragging the animal away from the deeply shadowed recess where she put out her dustbin on collection days. Maybe the dog had found a cat and it was cowering in there terrified, or had jumped down into the garden beyond. Or maybe it was a rat. She would have to take a look, make sure there was no food or anything lying around that might tempt them to make it a regular haunt. But as she looked, she saw something move, something too big to be a rat or even a fat, pampered cat.

A fox maybe? she thought as she peered harder into the shadows and switched off the light to help her eyes adjust to the dark. There was some movement again, then nothing. Callie shivered and told herself not to be so silly. It was almost certainly just a fox. If she must live this close to open land it was hardly surprising that a bit of wildlife came round. She had read that foxes, increasing as they were in numbers, were getting more and more bold, moving further into towns and cities in their search for food. It wouldn't be anything to write home about if she had seen one in central London, let alone on the outskirts of Hastings.

That said, Callie closed the curtains before switching on the lights again. She had been unsettled by what she had seen because the shape had been big and bulky and she couldn't get the idea out of her mind that it was too big even for a fox and that the way it moved had been more human than fox-like. She kept seeing something that, the more she ran the pictures through her head, had looked like an arm moving to pull, what? A hat or a hood over its head. But maybe that was her imagination playing tricks. Maybe she was inventing it now, inventing the pictures to match her fears? Try as she might to get her thoughts back to Jonathon and her forthcoming date, she couldn't get rid of the feeling that there was a man out there, watching her. She would never be able to sleep.

Finally, telling herself that she was being very, very stupid, she grabbed a torch and coat and went out to see if there was anyone out there.

It was dark and damp as she crossed the road, clutching her coat round her and suppressing a shiver of fear.

"Come out, come out, whoever you are," she said, acutely aware of just how ridiculous she sounded as she shone the torch into the recess.

There was no one there but the top brick of the wall around the area had fallen. It had always been loose, she told herself; it could have been knocked off by a cat, or a fox, or a man, trying to get out of the way of a dog.

She hurried back to her flat, double locking the door behind her. She wished that it made her feel safer but it didn't.

* * *

He hurried along the road, anxiously checking behind him to see that he wasn't being followed. His heart was beating so fast he thought it must surely burst. How could he have been so stupid? He tried breaking into a run but his breathing was so laboured that he was almost sobbing in his attempts to drag air in and force it out. If anyone saw him like this they would know something was wrong and probably think he was having an asthma attack or something. The last thing he needed was to end up in the back of an ambulance. Not here. Not so close to her home. He stopped and gripped his side, bent double. A stitch, that's all it was, he knew, but that didn't make it any less painful. He forced himself to breathe slower, taking deep breaths, regular breaths, and slowly it worked, the sharp pain beginning to fade. He started to walk again, slowly. He'd so nearly been caught, concealed in the shadows by the dustbins and gazing up at her as she stood by the window, preparing vegetables. Slicing and dicing them like a surgeon. So cool, so calm. Oblivious of the fact that he was there, watching every move. Taking it all in, absorbing every detail. Didn't she know that anyone could see her? Or maybe that was what she wanted. Maybe she liked to be watched. He smiled and felt a small shiver of excitement run down his spine. They were made for each other, he felt sure. She was so still, her movements so small and yet so precise, and she liked to be watched. His perfect love. His soulmate.

A smile suffused his face as he remembered how she looked. A magic moment indeed, but he had been so caught up in watching her that he hadn't paid attention. It had been close, that fucking stupid mutt sniffing him out like that. If he did come back, he would have to be more careful. A lot more careful. Be better hidden and bring some pepper spray or something, something that would make the most inquisitive dog back off, howling. If he came back. When he came back.

Because he knew he would. Maybe next time he'd find a place to the side of the house, where her bedroom window looked out over the open ground towards the cliff top. Maybe he'd see her undressing. See her pale skin. He imagined the blue-veined whiteness of her breasts and the pink of her nipples, and he touched himself. Just imagining Callie undressing in front of an open window was getting him hard. He should get home now, didn't want to be seen like this, rubbing himself in the street, but he would return. He had to return. After all, it was what she wanted, deep down, he was sure. She was so much better than the others, the cackling hag, or the lump of lard. Much better. They were just rehearsals, practice runs. He needed to get everything ready, to prepare himself, and then one day, one day soon, he would be ready for the main attraction, the best: Dr Calliope Hughes.

Chapter 14

Callie had expected a bit of a wait when she turned up at police headquarters without an appointment but was still irritated that Miller kept her kicking her heels for more than half an hour before she was called through to speak to him. The detective constable who called her through was not anyone Callie had met before. She was an inconspicuously motherly-looking woman, with a homely face and a twinkle in her eye as she assessed her boss's visitor.

"This way, Dr Hughes. The DI can see you now." She led the way and opened a nearby door, ushering Callie into Miller's office, a light and airy room at the back of the building, with views over the town centre to the West Hill.

"Dr Hughes. Come in. Um, have a seat."

As she entered the room, Miller stood awkwardly, as if he was not sure whether he should do so.

He was dressed in a light grey suit, the jacket casually hung over the back of his chair, and his usual plain white shirt and a grey and blue flecked tie. Jeffries, lounging against the wall by the window, was wearing a pair of slightly-too-long black trousers, scuffed brown shoes and a blue checked short-sleeved shirt, no tie. No style makeover there then, Callie thought.

She sat down, careful to ease the fabric of her trouser suit over her knees so that it didn't get stretched, and crossed her legs, revealing the low-heeled shoes she always wore to work. Several years of experience as a forensic physician for the police force had taught her that skirts and high heels were not always practical when she did not know what she was going to have to do next. It had taken only one occasion, a body on a building site which she couldn't move because health and safety were on their way, to learn that lesson. She could clearly remember, as she leant over the half-built wall that had collapsed and trapped the victim, checking for the non-existent pulse, the chorus of wolf whistles that came from the scaffolders opposite. It might have been dubiously gratifying but it was hardly seemly, in the circumstances.

"What can we do for you?"

"I wondered if the post-mortem results for the body were in yet?"

"No, why?"

"I wanted to know if it was the same cause of death as Jade, the same killer."

"With respect, Dr Hughes, that's not your problem."

"It's part of my job, surely. After all, I was the person who spotted–"

"And I am indebted to you for doing your job, Dr Hughes, but I am very busy. I have a killer out there targeting prostitutes. Now, much as I appreciate your interest, is there anything else I can help you with?"

It infuriated Callie that every time she met Miller, he dismissed her and she wasn't going to let him do it again.

"Prostitutes? Plural? I thought it was just Jade who was a prostitute, the other girl, Denise? She was a checkout girl, wasn't she?"

Jeffries smirked unattractively.

"Didn't have the looks to make a full-time job of it."

Miller silenced him with a look.

"There are" – he hesitated delicately – "certain indications that she may have been supplementing her income."

"What indications?" Callie wasn't going to be fobbed off that easily.

"The Jolly Sailor is a well-known haunt for girls on the game," Miller explained.

"Is that all you're basing your theory on?"

"It's a knocking shop," Jeffries put in.

"It's also a popular pub and meeting place. It was karaoke night. Lots of single people were there looking for company and maybe more, but that doesn't mean they were intending to pay for it."

Callie stood, angrily.

"She was an ordinary girl, not a prostitute, and she was out that night looking for Mr Right. What she got was death and she didn't deserve that." She started to leave but then turned back. "And that doesn't mean that Jade did either." She corrected herself quickly. "I mean, she wasn't even working that night."

Callie left the room, head held high, but not before noticing that Jeffries had spotted her error, the subconscious suggestion that Jade might have got what she, in some way, deserved or, at least, would have deserved if she had been working. It took every ounce of her control to resist the temptation to slam the door behind her as she made her exit.

The motherly DC was sitting at a desk outside and raised one eyebrow at Callie with a wry smile of amusement.

"Goodbye, Dr Hughes."

Callie merely nodded in acknowledgement, hoping she wasn't too red in the face, and left.

* * *

Callie was walking fast and steam was practically coming out of her ears as she headed to the car park. Why did policemen have to be so sexist? It was such a cliché. And, more to the point, why did she have to accidentally suggest that Jade had brought her murder on herself? Got what she deserved? She didn't for one moment believe that one person's life was worth more than another. She didn't think that women were "asking for it" when they got attacked wearing short skirts or skimpy tops. She didn't think anyone deserved to be murdered, be they street walker or nun. And whilst inviting a stranger into your home could be considered to be taking a risk, it was also a risk to get behind the wheel of a car, or cross the road, even on a pedestrian crossing. Or to walk home alone, down dark alleys, late at night. Something that Callie often did.

That certainly gave her pause for thought. It wasn't far from the Old Town back to her flat but the shortest route, through the maze of unlit cat creeps and twittens, could hardly be called safe and even the longer route involved walking the last few yards along a dark lane. Her converted house was the last in the road and open parkland was all that stood between her and the cliff top, and then the sea. What had seemed secluded and scenic until now could also be seen as isolated and unsafe. Callie shook her head. This was no good. She refused to live her life in fear. She would not change her ways except, perhaps, to consider the option that she might be wise to invest in a good, strong torch, heavy enough to give someone a good clump if they decided to mess with her. Reassured by this eminently practical solution she got into her car.

* * *

Back at the flat, Callie held a dress up in front of her and looked in the mirror. She had a second outfit in her other hand and was alternating between the two. The red jersey wrap number or the little black dress? Both were subtle and expensive. Was red too daring? Or black too boring? It surprised her how much she wanted to make a good impression on Jonathon. She certainly didn't want him rushing off and leaving her in the lurch again. She held up the red dress again. On the plus side, it was a good fit, clung in all the right places and the crossover gave her a satisfyingly deep cleavage, but it was cut below the knee and her long, shapely legs were possibly her best feature. The black dress, whilst higher at the neck, was shorter and, with her ultra-high black heels, made her legs look like they went on forever. She held up the red again. Her legs would be under the table for most of the evening and her cleavage clearly visible, so she plumped for the red.

When she was finally satisfied with how she looked, every hair in place, her make up smooth, subtle and flawless, she picked up the matching red bag she intended to take for the evening and began to pack it with everything that she would need. She finally got to the torch. It was a small, powerful, handbag sized torch but it still was not going to fit in this bag. The red evening bag struggled to accommodate a purse, brush, makeup, keys and mobile – a torch was asking way too much of it. Callie dithered. She could take her black leather bag, which was bigger but less elegant, or she could leave the torch behind, which rather defeated the object of buying it. Eventually, she made a decision and left the torch. After all, she was having dinner with Jonathon and she was sure that he would see her safely home, whether or not he stayed. At least, she sincerely hoped he would.

* * *

Callie paused outside, hand on the restaurant door, taking a moment to compose herself. Her last-minute indecision had left her running slightly later than she'd intended and, although the taxi she had ordered so that she wouldn't have to teeter down the steep hill in stilettos had made up some of that time, she still felt a little rushed and breathless.

The Dining Room was busy but, unlike Porters, there was none of the noise, bustle or raucous laughter of people enjoying themselves audible from within. It was the sort of restaurant where the clientele spoke in hushed tones, either because they didn't want to disturb the other diners with loud conversation or because they didn't want to be overheard. The Dining Room was a serious restaurant, or at least it certainly wanted to be taken seriously. It was the sort of place that Kate always said made her want to shout out "Knickers" just to shake things up a bit.

Jonathon was sitting at the bar, and Callie quickly checked her watch as she pushed open the door. Five minutes late: perfect timing.

Jonathon looked up and smiled as he saw her enter. Sliding off his bar stool to greet her with a kiss on the cheek, he stood back and swept his gaze over her.

"You look wonderful," he said with genuine appreciation. She smiled back and thought that he did too. He had swapped his work day suit for cream chinos and a light blue Oxford shirt, open at the collar. The epitome of stylish smart-casual wear. She arranged herself on a stool next to his and, as he settled himself and signalled to the barman that he would like to order drinks, she was acutely aware that his knee brushed against hers. She hoped that he had been too.

They had one drink at the bar, ordering their food there before moving to a table. Callie wondered why they waited when another table was free, but it seemed that Jonathon wanted one particular table, to the right of the door, on its own. The secluded table was tucked in by the curtained window and set with linen napkins and silverware sparkling in the candlelight. Very romantic.

Their dinner was excellent: lightly seared scallops wrapped in bacon and set on a bed of rocket, rare fillet steak, sautéed potatoes and perfectly crisp vegetables, followed by an absolutely flawless crème brûlée served with fresh raspberries dusted with icing sugar, all accompanied by a smooth Sauvignon blanc and a mellow Chilean Merlot. Everything just as Callie liked it. Perfect, in fact. And Jonathon had kept her amused and interested with a raft of salacious and scandalous stories about colleagues and friends. Callie had had a wonderful evening and, as they lingered over coffee and Elizabeth Shaw bitter mints, she knew that she didn't want the night to end there.

Jonathon insisted on paying the bill and, for once, Callie didn't put up too much of a fight. She firmly believed that women had to pay their way if there was any hope of having an equal relationship but she also knew that Jonathon earned considerably more than she did and was old-fashioned enough to need to be led gently to the issue of equality. So, she let him pay. This time.

He helped her into the black pashmina which she had brought instead of a coat and opened the door for her to leave the restaurant. His manners were impeccable and as she stood in the pedestrianised road outside, looking up at the stars, she felt almost giddy with anticipation. Mentally she checked her flat, ticking off her usual failures. Yes, she had made sure that all the towels in the bathroom were straight and neat, yes, she had put away all the washing up and wiped the draining board and no, there was no underwear drying anywhere. She smiled and relaxed into him as he put his arm round her and started to lead her towards the main road where he had left his car.

"Are you all right to drive?" she asked, surprised that he was even contemplating getting behind the wheel of a car, knowing that he had drunk four or five glasses of wine during the evening. "We could walk back to my flat for coffee," she suggested.

He shook his head.

"Can't leave my car where it is overnight." He smiled meaningfully and she smiled back. At least he intended to stay the night, then.

As they walked along the street Callie let the slightly fuzzy feeling from the wine she had drunk envelop her and she leant further against him. He stopped and bent down to kiss her. A long, slow, delicate kiss. A tease. A taster. A promise of what was to come, interrupted by a gaggle of drunken youths falling out of a pub.

Callie pulled away from Jonathon, startled back to reality by the sudden noise.

"Come on," he said. "The car's just here. Let's continue this somewhere more secluded."

So, he led her over to the car park and opened the door of his top-of-the-range, racing green, S-Type Jaguar and, as she slid into the car and settled back into the champagne coloured leather seats, she felt a frisson of excitement and anticipation.

Chapter 15

It was early the next morning, a grey dawn seeping through the curtains, when Callie was woken by Jonathon slipping out of bed. She glanced over at the digital clock on her bedside table to see that it was only half-past five. She turned over and sat up. Jonathon leant over and kissed her.

"Sorry, tried not to wake you."

"Do you have to go?" She reached up and kissed him back, letting her hands stray down to the waistband of his boxers. He hesitated before removing her hand.

"Much as I would love to stay, I've got to do an early ward round before theatre."

She let herself drop back on her pillows with a sigh.

He pulled on the rest of his clothes and came round to her side of the bed for a farewell kiss.

"What about Saturday? Any chance of a repeat performance?" he asked between the light kisses he was planting softly on her lips.

"Mmm. I'll have to check my diary," she teased, "but I'm sure I could squeeze you in somewhere between the leg-waxing and the manicure."

He stood again and, despite the gloom, she could see he was smiling.

"How about a trip on my yacht? It's only small, a thirty-two-footer, nothing too flash I'm afraid, but easy to handle with just the two of us. Sailing is the best ever way of winding down after a long week, I find."

Callie was caught, still half asleep and unable to think straight. Before she knew it, she found herself agreeing.

"Yes, sailing, that sounds fun." She hoped she didn't sound too insincere but, whilst she loved to watch the sea from the safety of dry land, going out on it was another matter entirely. It was very hard to keep up a look of cool sophistication as you leant over the side, throwing up everything you had ever eaten. But if Jonathon had detected her less than enthusiastic response, he ignored it.

"Great. I'll check the weather forecast and tides and let you know what time I'll pick you up."

And with a final kiss he was gone. Callie closed her eyes with a groan and prayed for a hurricane on Saturday. Anything to get out of setting foot on board a boat. The trouble was, if sailing was so important to him, it was too early to refuse and risk scuppering things before they had fully got off the ground but, equally, letting him believe she enjoyed something she loathed was hardly building an open and honest relationship. Oh well, she thought as she snuggled back under the duvet, last night had been good enough to risk a little subterfuge. She'd buy some Dramamine at the chemist and try not to disgrace herself too dramatically.

* * *

The custody suite was quiet for once. Early Thursday morning wasn't known as a peak time for either brawling in the street or drink driving. It was just Callie's bad luck that one of the regular homeless people who committed petty crimes simply to get a bed for the night and what they, unlike the rest of humanity, considered a decent breakfast, had been taken ill in his cell.

The day shift custody sergeant turned out to be one of Callie's favourites, Jayne Hales. Jayne was in her late thirties, with a friendly face and a lovely smile. But it wasn't her looks that made Callie like her so much, it was her down-to-earth attitude coupled with a level of empathy uncommon in those who had been in the job more than a year or two.

"I'll take you down to him, if that's all right, only he's an awkward sod and he's really not looking too well."

"That's fine, Jayne. Lead on."

As Jayne led the way through to the cells, the duty inspector, a sour-faced man that Callie secretly believed must suffer from chronic dyspepsia, as there was no other real excuse for his bad temper, stopped them.

"You got rid of that dosser in cell nine yet, Sergeant?"

"Just getting him checked out first, sir. Fulfilling our duty of care and all that. Can't be too careful in these litigious times. Even dossers get legal aid."

"Quite so, quite so." He looked Callie up and down and nodded. "Carry on, Dr Hughes."

And he left them to it.

"Got to hand it to you, Jayne. You know how to handle the tossers of this world."

"Tossers or dossers, they're all the same to me," Jayne said with a smile and unlocked the cell door. "Doc's here to see you, George. Okay?"

George looked up from where he was curled up on a thin, plastic-covered foam mattress laid on the low concrete platform that served as a bed. He had wrapped himself in the well-worn blanket provided by the police and obviously still had on the several layers of grimy clothes that he habitually wore on the street. Even from the door Callie could see the sheen of sweat on his brow and the bouts of shivers that wracked his body at regular intervals.

"Can't you turn the fucking heat up? I'm frigging freezing in here," he said and covered his head with the blanket again.

Callie entered the cell, placed her doctor's bag on the floor near the door and opened it up to remove the electric thermometer. Taking out a fresh earpiece and going over to George, she bent down and pulled the blanket away from his face.

"Okay, George, I just want to take your temperature. I'm going to put this in your ear very gently, it won't hurt."

She could feel how hot he was even before the thermometer beeped and told her that it was 39.2 degrees centigrade. His breath was audibly rattling in his chest and she suspected that this was the cause of his fever.

"Can you tell me how you feel, George?" she asked as he huddled under the blanket again.

"Bloody awful," was all he replied.

"Do you hurt anywhere?"

The blanketed mound seemed to shake its head.

"A bit, in me chest, maybe."

"Have you got a cough?"

He seemed to give more of a nod this time.

"Can I listen to your chest, George?"

There was no reply for a moment, but the blanket came down and George looked out at her.

"Go on, then. Listen to it if you want."

"I'll need you to sit up, and maybe take some of those layers off. Can you do that for me?" Callie took her stethoscope out of her bag as Jayne helped George out of a grubby cardigan, which had been buttoned-up wrongly, a brushed-cotton shirt and finally a long-sleeved undershirt, leaving him in a filthy vest that looked as if it hadn't been taken off in a long time. Callie spotted something very small and black moving hurriedly out of the light and pulled out some gloves for herself and Jayne. Positioning herself as far from her patient as the procedure would allow, Callie slid the stethoscope up under the front of his

T-shirt and listened to the man's breathing before getting him to turn around so that she could listen to the back. Jayne was gingerly sorting through the man's clothing whilst she did this.

"I'll see what clothing we've got in the store in a minute, George," Jayne told him as she indicated some of his rags. "I think some of these have had it."

George turned back to face them, pulling down his brown-stained vest as he did so, and gave a sudden staccato burst of coughing. Both Jayne and Callie quickly stepped back out of range.

Callie turned to Jayne.

"He's got a nasty chest infection. I can prescribe him some antibiotics, but I'd really rather he was taken to the hospital for a chest X-ray. Any chance of him getting a lift? I don't think he'll make it on his own."

"He'd almost certainly forget where he was going," Jayne agreed and hesitated. "I'll have to call an ambulance to take him, is that okay? Only they won't allow us to take him in a squad car, not when he should really be being kicked loose."

"Besides which, it will mean de-lousing the car." Callie smiled and Jayne nodded, ruefully.

"I'd not be very popular, it has to be said."

"Okay, then," Callie said and turned to George who was back under the blanket. "We're going to organise some transport to the hospital, George. You'll be nice and warm there."

She got nothing but a grunt by way of thanks.

* * *

Back at the desk, Callie was just signing the forms the desk sergeant insisted on being completed when two uniform constables came in, laughing.

"Watcha, Sarge, you hear about Jimmy Allen then?"

Jayne looked at them.

"Please tell me it was nothing trivial."

"Not at all trivial, no." They could hardly contain themselves, they were so pleased with their news.

"He was picked up in Cardiff." The young, baby-faced boy telling the story put on a Welsh accent to add atmosphere to his tale. "Seemed like he'd done his usual, gone to see this Welsh prossie…"

"Was her name Dai?" his mate interjected.

"That's a man's name, you twat," the storyteller said, "and anyway, he tried to do a runner without paying, like."

"Only he made the mistake of not getting his clothes on first." The other constable cut in, again.

"So, this tart grabbed his todger, she did, and wouldn't let go, even when he punched her."

"They say he's going to need reconstructive surgery." Both men winced.

"Boys, boys, can you leave your organs alone for one minute, please?" Jayne had reached the end of her patience and both constables stopped obediently but seemed completely unembarrassed.

"Sergeant Jeffries has gone off down to Cardiff to pick him up as soon as he's bailed, Sarge."

Jayne was clearly delighted with the story.

"First bit of good news I've had all week. Fantastic. Seeing as George is on his way to hospital, we'll put Jimmy in his cell when he gets here."

"Shall we clean it out then, Sarge?" the baby-faced one asked, innocently. Jayne looked across at Callie and held her gaze with a mischievous smile.

"No, don't bother. I'm sure George didn't have anything contagious, like lice." And she grinned.

* * *

Callie felt really quite happy as she left the station, not just at the thought of Jimmy Allen catching lice from George, but also because he was off the streets of Hastings and that had to be a good thing for the safety of the female inhabitants. She just hoped that this time Miller and

Jeffries would play it by the book and get him off the streets for good.

She switched her mobile phone back on as she walked across the car park, and saw that she had a voicemail message. It was from Jonathon. Thanking her for a fantastic night and making a few suggestions for things they could try next time they spent the night together. Things that made her blush and look round anxiously, as if anyone else could hear what he was suggesting.

The sun was making a determined effort to break through the gloom and it looked as though it might be a nice day for a change. The only cloud on her horizon was that Jonathon mentioned in his message that his car had been scratched by some passing oik whilst parked outside her flat. She was surprised to hear this; not only had she never suffered anything like that in the two years she had lived in the house, but there was no reason for anyone to be passing. She was at the end of the street, on the way to nowhere. She shrugged and thought that it had probably happened whilst the car was parked in the car park by the restaurant and that they had been too preoccupied to notice. She smiled mischievously as she thought about it. They had both been in quite a hurry to get back to the seclusion of her home, and particularly her bedroom, as she recalled.

She was in such a good mood that she didn't see Miller until she was almost at her car, when she heard him call her name.

"Dr Hughes?"

She looked round, startled, and saw him standing by his car.

"Detective Inspector." She acknowledged him coldly, as he made his way over to her. Unsurprisingly, he was looking pleased with himself.

"I just thought I'd let you know, we've caught Jimmy Allen."

"So I heard. Although, technically, I think you'll find it was the Cardiff Police who picked him up." She couldn't help a little smile, not quite a triumphant one, but definitely a slightly self-satisfied one, as she turned back to her car and opened the driver's door, sliding into the driver's seat.

"Okay," he conceded, putting his hand on the door of her car so that she couldn't close it. She looked up at him, expecting him to be put out by her remark, but he was smiling, genuinely pleased. And it was a nice smile, she thought. "The Cardiff Police caught him, but the end result's the same. He's off the streets. Which should please everyone, Dr Hughes, including you."

He really had very nice eyes, with crinkles at the corners, Callie thought before she suddenly realised that she had been staring at him in silence and that he was probably expecting her to say something.

"Yes, indeed," she said sharply. How could she do something so embarrassing as look at him all gooey-eyed like that? She was so cross with herself. "And they even managed to arrest him without beating him up."

His eyes hardened and Callie looked away.

"I think he'd had all his fight squeezed out of him by the time they got there, or so I heard." He took his hands off the door and stepped back to allow her to close it.

"I've got to go," she said hurriedly but he had already turned and was walking away. She slammed the car door.

"Why does he always make me so cross?" Callie asked herself as she drove away with a little more aggression than was strictly necessary.

Chapter 16

The mortuary was quiet as Callie walked along the corridor but she could hear whistling from the storeroom as she passed on her way to Dr Dunbar's office. Someone was happy in their work.

Ian Dunbar was sitting at his desk, writing up a report on the computer.

"Calliope! What perfect timing," he said, looking up from his intense scrutiny of the keyboard. "Put me out of my misery and let me take a break from this wretched machine. I swear someone comes in at night and moves the keys around to confuse me."

Callie glanced at the keyboard.

"They all look in the right place to me."

"Hmmph." Dr Dunbar was unconvinced. "Have we got a case you're interested in?" He was looking puzzled. "I'm pretty sure they've all been referrals from the hospital the past few days."

"The girl found in her flat. I thought it might be strangulation? I know you won't have done the PM, but I thought you might have heard some gossip."

"Gossip? We don't indulge in gossip, here." Dr Dunbar pretended to be scandalised, before calling out to his assistant. "Dave? Have you got a mo? Only Calliope wants to hear all about that PM you assisted the prof with. The ligature strangulation."

"Dave assisted, did he?"

Dave came waddling in, surprisingly quick on his feet for such a big man.

"They needed an extra hand. It was great, Dr Hughes," Dave told her eagerly, "a bit pongy, but really interesting."

"And was it strangulation?"

"Yeah. The prof thought it was done with some kind of thin chain. Narrow. Killer must've taken it with him. He said you were pretty smart to have spotted it." He glowed with pride at the compliment bestowed on Callie by the Home Office pathologist.

"We don't need Wally Wadsworth to tell us that, Dave."

"No, Dr Dunbar," Dave agreed, before turning back to Callie and carrying on with his unofficial report. "And there didn't seem to be much trace evidence either, just like the last one. Vaginal swabs were negative. There was a bit of skin under her nails but Professor Wadsworth thought that might have been her own because she had scratched her neck, trying to loosen the chain, I suppose. He sent it off, anyway."

"So, do the police think it's the same killer?"

"Hardly likely to have two stranglers operating in a small town like this at the same time, are we? At least I certainly hope not."

Callie had to agree that it seemed unlikely.

"I heard they had someone in custody so I sincerely hope that will be the end of it," he continued.

Callie silently agreed.

* * *

Marcy was sitting slightly apart from the other patients, and her skin-tight, lycra leopard-print outfit, set off by incredibly high, fetish-style stilettos, was getting a fair number of disapproving looks, particularly from Mrs Lockwood, although Timothy was clearly fascinated by her. Marcy would never pass as a member of the general public, even to those with a high degree of myopia, and Callie couldn't suppress the smile that came to her lips. It always made her day, even though she knew that Hugh Grantham would prefer it if she moved her professional sex worker patients to another surgery. He didn't want them frightening the parents of young children and, given Marcy's outfit of the day, he had a point.

Callie hurried into her room and turned on the computer. She always liked to have a quick look through her list of patients before she called the first one in so as to prepare herself for any possible problems, even though that did mean the inevitable feeling of dread if she saw the name of any of her more obnoxious patients, like Mr Herring.

Timothy was her first and Marcy was fourth on the list, so she must have arrived early. Callie prayed it wasn't one of the days when Marcy was hyper and found it difficult to sit still. The last thing she needed was her creating a scene in the waiting room, especially dressed as she was.

Callie pressed the buzzer for Timothy and his mother to come in and took a moment or two to look at the latest blood results and the letter faxed through from the private paediatric consultant who had seen Timothy a few days earlier. It wasn't looking good. There was little doubt that the boy was in the early stages of liver failure and the cause remained unknown. The blood results had not revealed any infectious element and Timothy was being urgently referred to the specialist liver unit at King's College Hospital in London for their advice and treatment.

"Hello, Mrs Lockwood." Callie smiled encouragingly as the mother came in. She was surprised that Mrs Lockwood had come in alone, leaving Timothy outside, and waited whilst the woman settled herself and fidgeted about before getting to the point.

"What can I do for you?"

"I wanted to know what was wrong with Tim. The paediatrician told me but, you know, it all sort of goes over your head when they talk and it's only after you've gone home that you think of all the questions you should have asked. Philip, Tim's dad, is flying over to be here and I'll need to tell him what's going on."

Callie read through the consultant's letter again, which had been scanned into Timothy's computer records, and she pointed to it on the screen.

"Did you get a copy of this letter?"

"Yes, but I'm afraid it doesn't mean much to me."

"That's okay, I'll do my best to explain but basically all Dr Mitchell could say was that Timothy's liver isn't working properly and none of the usual suspects seem to be involved. He shows no sign of any infection and she did some tests to see if she could find any other cause but, so far, there's nothing showing up."

"But what other things could it be?"

"Well, there are quite a few substances that are toxic to the liver. Paracetamol, for example, and alcohol, of course, not that anyone's suggesting that Timothy's been drinking," she added hastily before Mrs Lockwood could protest. "But again, nothing specific showed up on the tests. Of course, it would take quite a while for the liver failure to show up, so the toxic substance causing the problem could have all gone, or they might not be looking for the right one."

"Paracetamol?" Mrs Lockwood had latched onto that, probably because it was something that she was familiar with.

"Is it something that you give Timothy? Or could he have got hold of some from somewhere?"

"I have it in the house, of course. Children's strength. But I don't think that any has been used. He hasn't had a temperature or been in pain. I'll check that Myra, the help, hasn't given him any, but I'm sure she would have said, asked me first, I mean."

"What about at school? Could they have given him some?"

"God no, they ring and ask for permission before they so much as put a plaster on a graze. They are absolutely paranoid about being sued, I think."

"It's understandable."

"I have to take Tim to King's College Hospital tomorrow with his father but can you tell me what's likely to happen, what they are going to do?"

Callie thought for a moment, not because she didn't want to tell the woman, but because it was hard to know exactly what would happen.

"As the failure isn't acute yet, I suspect that they will just monitor him for a while and do more tests to see if they can find a cause."

"And if they can't find one? If it gets worse?"

"Let's not worry about that just yet."

"I need to know, Doctor. I need to know what could happen."

Callie hated having to speculate like this, especially as what could happen was quite frightening, but she couldn't refuse to answer, not when she had been asked a direct question like that.

"Well, worst case scenario, if Timothy goes into acute liver failure, they will have to admit him and use supportive measures to do the work of the liver for him."

"And if that doesn't work? I mean, if his liver fails completely? They can't keep him on a machine, or whatever, for ever, can they?"

"If that happens, he'll need a transplant but let me stress, Mrs Lockwood, that he is a long way from needing that, okay?"

The woman nodded, frightened by the seriousness, but grateful for the small drop of reassurance that Callie had been able to give her. Callie hoped the woman believed her although, in actual fact, she wasn't really sure that Timothy was that far off needing a transplant. According to the letter, his liver failure seemed to be progressing pretty rapidly.

* * *

After a brief discussion with Helen, the girl at reception, Callie agreed to see Marcy next, because she was apparently pacing up and down in the waiting room talking to herself.

"Using the sort of language that upsets the other patients, not to mention Dr Grantham," she warned Callie, who groaned inwardly. Marcy had presumably fallen off the wagon. Big time.

Marcy came in and sat awkwardly on the edge of the chair, chewing gum and fidgeting. She moved her bag from one hand to another, adjusted her clothing, inspected her fingernails, picked up a paperweight from Callie's desk and put it down again; she could not sit still for a second. From checking her records, Callie could see that she wasn't due another prescription or check-up, so she took the bull by the horns and asked, "What are you here for, Marcy?" And prepared herself for a tirade.

"That DI friend of yours is a pillock, that's why. He's got it into his head that Jimmy Allen did it. That Jade picked him up in the vodka bar, 'cos they know that's where she was that night now but they don't know who with. What they're saying, guessing more like, is that it was Jimmy Allen and that she took him home like she was simple or something. No fucking way. She knew Jimmy Allen. She wouldn't have gone near him with a bargepole unless it was to hit him round the fucking head with it. She weren't stupid, unlike your mate Mr High and Fucking Mighty policeman."

Callie had spent years trying not to let bad language upset her but had eventually given up and now just concentrated on not allowing her face show any outward signs of distress or distaste. After all the practice in recent months, she was getting very good at it. Marcy had barely paused for breath and, although Callie would have liked to cut in to tell her that Miller was no friend of hers, she knew it was useless, Marcy was on a roll and quite obviously on something else too. She was high, no doubt about it. Callie looked her in the eye. Judging by her pupils it was coke or some sort of amphetamine-based drug. Whatever Marcy's choice of drug of the day, clean and sober she was not.

"Jade had dealings with Jimmy before, see, he'd done a runner on her, not paid. Gave her a split lip and all, a year or so back. She knew his rep. He's a vicious little fucker and she certainly wouldn't take him to her place. The pigs have got it so totally wrong, as usual, and you've got to fucking tell them. There's a killer out there, don't they understand that? And while I wouldn't put anything past Jimmy Allen, I got to say they're wrong here, he didn't kill Jade, no way, and what with all the time they're wasting trying to pin it on him, someone else is going to get killed. Tell them, go on, tell them they're wrong." She stood up abruptly. "Gotta go to work."

And she left. Callie hadn't even had time to argue. She sighed and rested her head in her hands for a moment or two, feeling one of her headaches coming on. There was a gentle knock on the door and Linda, the practice manager, poked her head in.

"It's okay. She's gone. And I don't think Hugh heard anything, so you're in the clear as long as none of his patients mention her visit to him."

Callie continued to massage her temple and closed her eyes.

"Want a coffee?" Linda asked.

"I think I need something stronger."

"A chocolate biscuit, then. Back in a tick."

Callie smiled in gratitude as Linda went off to fetch the required sugar shot.

"Please God, let the rest of the surgery be more straightforward."

Chapter 17

"So, come on then," Kate coaxed her, as she put the two glasses and a packet of plain crisps down on the table. "Tell me all about the amazing surgeon. Does he know his female anatomy or what?"

They were in their usual window seat in The Stag, although they had actually planned to go to an aerobics class. Kate's excuse this time was a bad knee, although Callie had seen no sign of it as her friend carried the drinks over from the bar.

"You are so crude, Katherine Ward. And anyway, how would I know?"

"You held out? But why?" Kate was surprised but she saw the little smile on Callie's lips and realised immediately that her friend was not telling the truth. "Liar. I knew you were too desperate to resist the advances of Dr Lurve." Kate opened the packet of crisps and split the bag the whole way along one side, opening it out on the table so that they could share the contents. She always did this, even though Callie rarely got to eat more than one or two because Kate moved so fast.

"I was not too desperate. I just didn't want to resist. There is a difference." She took her sip of her wine and picked up a crisp. The pile was already visibly smaller.

"Come on, come on, do I have to resort to torture? What was it like?" Kate was impatient to hear.

The smile on Callie's face said it all.

"I knew it. He's a sex god. You lucky, lucky girl." Kate emptied the last crisps and the residual crumbs into her hand and sat back, content.

"You are as bad as my mother," Callie protested.

"No, I am not. She wants you to get married, I just want you to get laid."

"Well, I did and very nice it was, too. Thank you very much."

"I want more detail."

"Well, you're not going to get it."

"I'm your best friend, Callie, you can talk dirty with me." Kate was teasing and Callie knew it.

"Absolutely not. You know I can't do it. It's just not me."

"God, you are hopeless, woman. How on earth do you talk to the prostitutes who are patients?"

"That's different, it's medical, and it's not like they discuss the sex bit." Callie could feel herself getting embarrassed just thinking about it. "Just the side effects."

"You are such a prude." But Kate was smiling as she shook her head in mock dismay. "When are you seeing him again?"

Callie grimaced.

"Saturday. We're going sailing."

Kate almost choked on the crisp crumbs she had just poured into her mouth, she was laughing so hard.

"Sailing? You? Are you mad? The relationship will be over before it's begun. You've got to get out of it somehow. Remember that gorgeous hunk who took you to Cowes week? Couldn't believe anyone could throw up that much?"

Callie looked miserable.

"Why are people, and by people I mean men, by and large, so obsessed with boats? If God had wanted us to go to sea, he would have given us webbed feet and stronger stomachs."

"It's not just men. Look at Dame Ellen Mac Thingy and the other one, went round backwards, you just think it's men because there's no way you would agree to get on a boat if a mere woman asked you."

Callie was about to protest but stopped. Kate was right.

"God, that makes me really pathetic, doesn't it? That I am willing to put myself through torture for a man?"

"It certainly does," Kate said.

They sipped their drinks in contented and companionable silence for a few moments, watching the flames of the open fire and contemplating life, the universe and men.

"So, how are things with you and your love life then? Anyone on the horizon?" Callie asked.

"Nothing interesting in absolutely ages. I shall either shrivel up or start stalking young boys if something doesn't come along soon, or maybe I should finally accept that I can only have a sex life vicariously through you, so you owe it to both of us to have a good one." Kate seemed happy enough, but there was a little sigh after her words and Callie wasn't taken in.

"Go on with you, what about that teacher? That was only a couple of weeks ago."

"And over so soon, I know. Let's just say he didn't live up to his initial promise. Personal hygiene issues."

"Too much information." Callie laughed. "I can't believe that here we are, two successful-ish career women, not too bad looking although admittedly in our mid-thirties, and we have such difficulty finding men."

"But that's the problem, isn't it? We've put our careers first and not snapped up the eligible men in our twenties.

All that's left are commitment-phobes, the frankly unloveable and recently divorced rejects."

"That is a very depressing view."

"It's the truth. Every bloke worth marrying is married before he's forty and stays married, unless he has honestly made a horrendous mistake, and those are few and far between. Divorcees of the masculine persuasion are, generally speaking, on their own for a very good reason. Believe me, I know, I've been a divorce lawyer, remember? You get a better standard of clientele in criminal law."

"At least we're not forty yet." It was a small consolation.

"But every year, month, week, day even, the number of unmarried men our age or older and under forty gets smaller. Think about that, but not for too long. It's a shrinking market."

"I've had lots of patients who have met new partners in their fifties or so and been very happy."

"Ah yes, but that's when they've accepted that all they want is companionship. Are you ready for that? No, let's face it, Callie, your surgeon might be your last chance. And me? Well, I might just have missed the boat."

"Rubbish. You are depressed, that's all. It must be lack of food."

Kate looked at her watch.

"You are sooo right, Doctor. And my stomach is saying another snack won't do, it's definitely dinner time. What do you want to eat?"

"How about we have a quick something or other and go to a karaoke night?"

Kate was more than a little taken aback. She couldn't remember Callie ever having suggested something like that.

"Karaoke?"

"You know, where they play the backing track of a song and you sing along?"

"I know what karaoke is, I just wondered if you had gone completely mad or if there was a reason behind your sudden interest in community sing-songs? Does this surgeon like it or something? Is he a closet Elvis impersonator?"

Callie spluttered at the thought.

"I have no idea but I can't see it somehow. He's got far too much dignity."

"And we don't?"

"Of course we do."

"So why are we going?"

Callie stood up.

"I have my reasons, as they say. Come on, we can stop off somewhere on the way up to The Jolly Sailor."

Kate began gathering her things. She could tell that Callie wasn't going to be talked out of whatever she was up to because she had grabbed her coat and umbrella and was already walking towards the door.

"We could pick up fish and chips. Eat them out of the paper as we walk there, if you like," Kate suggested, knowing that Callie would hate it but, after all, it was her own fault for dragging Kate off to a karaoke night in some dire hole of a pub which probably wouldn't serve decent beer.

Callie pulled a face. As Kate well knew, she despised the aggravation of eating out of the wrapper as you walked along the road. Bits of fish, or kebab, or whatever you were attempting to eat always ended up escaping, dribbling grease as it slid down your clothes so that you arrived at your destination smelling of your food rather than your expensive designer scent but, on this occasion, she was prepared to admit it was the most sensible option and, if it meant that Kate was willing to come with her, then it was a sacrifice that had to be made.

"All right, the Blue Dolphin chippy it is, then. Last one there pays."

They hurried out of the door, laughing and jostling for position.

* * *

Karaoke night at The Jolly Sailor had not proved to be as popular as the manager had hoped, but at least there were more people in the bar than on other weekday nights. Except for nights when the football was showing. That always drew in a good crowd. The place suffered from being one of those purpose-built pubs that supposedly catered to the middle classes. Large and spacious, clean, recently refurbished according to the chain owner's interior décor vision, the pub could have been anywhere. In a town full of local, character pubs serving good beers and only a short walking distance from their homes, who was going to travel further to a soulless barn of a place that sold freezing cold, fizzy beer and overpriced cocktails? Unless it was to drink said lager and watch the football. Or to find some easy company and maybe show off a bit, or embarrass yourself, depending on how you rated as a singer.

Callie and Kate pushed through the doors and looked round for a place to sit, preferably a quiet and unobtrusive place. Neither wanted to attract the attention of the single men hanging round the bar, drinking their pints of Stella and looking for someone, anyone, to take home for a shag. Kate indicated a free table in a dim corner and Callie nodded, it being hard to talk over the racket. The karaoke night was already in full swing and a man old enough to know better was busy massacring *My Way*. Callie pointed to the bar, meaning that she would get the drinks if Kate sat at the table to prevent anyone else taking it. Kate nodded and headed over there, unsurprised that she then saw Callie head straight for the ladies rather than the bar. She must have been desperate to wash her hands and get rid of the smell of fish and chips.

Once they were both settled with their drinks, Callie looked round and took stock. Four middle-aged men were leaning against the bar, trying to ignore a couple of women who were making eyes at them and giggling from a side table. A woman wearing far too much make-up and far too little clothing was perched on a barstool in the corner, nursing a coke and looking awkward and out of place. A group of teenagers were at a large table, talking loudly and excitedly about nothing worth hearing, and a single man in his thirties, dressed in jeans and a T-shirt, sat at another, smaller table. None of them looked like killers to Callie, but what did she know? The only killers she'd ever met were drunk drivers and arrogant surgeons and she was pretty sure she wasn't looking for either of those here.

A young girl hopped up from the teenage table and went up to Big Les – the Karaoke King, according to the poster on the amplifier. She was dressed in jeans cut low enough to show her ample love handles, and she pulled at her shirt, trying unsuccessfully to tug it down over them, as she told Big Les her name and what she wanted to sing.

"Please, God, let's hope no one decides to do *Bohemian Rhapsody*," Kate said as she took a suspicious sip of her beer. It could not have been too bad because she took another, longer drink. Callie had opted for a spritzer, so that it would not matter about the quality of the wine.

"Or that one from Grease, you know, *Summer Loving* I think it's called. Where John Travolta sings really high and everyone squeaks," Callie said.

"Oh, God, yes. Awful. I warn you now, one screech of a falsetto 'Mamma Mia' or a wella wella warm up will have me out that door pretty sharpish, so" – she gave Callie a long, hard look – "you had better tell me why we are here, Calliope Hughes. Right now, this minute. Tell me all and no bullshitting."

So Callie did. She told her about the two deaths and how Miller insisted that the killer was targeting prostitutes but that there was absolutely no evidence to suggest that

Denise was one. About how Jimmy Allen was in custody, being questioned by Miller about killing the two women, but that Marcy was adamant that Jade would never have taken him home.

"What if he's got the wrong man? All he seems to have on his suspect is that the man's been rough with prostitutes in the past, including with Jade, the first victim. But the moment you realise that the second victim wasn't on the game, it doesn't add up, does it?"

Kate looked around, took a long drink of beer and thought for a moment or two before answering.

"So, what's The Jolly Sailor karaoke night got to do with anything?"

"The police believe Denise met her killer here and took him home with her. Unfortunately, no one remembers seeing her with anyone that night."

Kate looked around and shuddered.

"You brought me to a place you think a serial killer might have picked up his victim? Really?"

Callie looked ashamed.

"Sorry, but you see why I didn't want to come alone. I just thought that maybe this was a meeting place for S&M enthusiasts or something."

Looking at the people around them, Kate couldn't stop herself from laughing.

"You know, this really doesn't strike me as a major hunting ground for sadomasochists. Not that I'd know one if I saw one, of course," she added hastily, "I mean, I've heard that Friday night's transvestite night at The Spotted Bull, but Karaoke and Bondage night at The Jolly Sailor?" She shook her head. "I don't see it somehow."

"The Spotted Bull?" Callie queried, "who would have thought?" She sighed and looked around again. "I've never really understood the attraction of inflicting pain on someone, let alone letting someone inflict pain on you."

"Me neither," Kate agreed.

Callie turned to the assembled men at the bar.

"Sad, desperate, lonely, yes, but nothing to suggest that any of them are pervs." A small, balding man, wearing a tracksuit for purely sartorial reasons, judging by his beer gut and double chin, caught her eye and winked. "Oh, God, I think I've pulled. Perhaps we should go."

They both snatched up their bags and hurried out of the pub before he could make a move towards them.

They were almost running across the car park, laughing and looking round to check that they were not being followed.

"Wait! I've got a stitch." Kate stopped and clutched her side, still laughing as Callie went back to her.

"See? You are so out of condition you couldn't outrun a couch potato, let alone anyone else. We really should have gone to the gym."

"Absolutely. The men are much fitter there, and I mean that in both senses of the word, though I wouldn't want to outrun them anyway."

Once Kate had recovered, they set off down the hill towards the Old Town and home.

"Seriously though, I think you need to tell the police about your concerns."

"I have thought about it," Callie said, "but they really won't want to hear that I think they've got the wrong bloke. They'll probably find out soon enough anyway."

"True." They walked in silence for a while.

The downward slope of the hill steepened and the damp pavement made the going more treacherous, particularly given the high heels Callie had put on as she wasn't on call, and she needed to concentrate to ensure she remained upright.

"You're sure Marcy is reliable?" Kate asked once the road had evened out a bit.

"No. In fact, I know the opposite. Marcy is hopelessly unreliable. But what she said had the ring of truth. Why would Jade go home with a man who had beaten her up and run off without paying her before?"

"But you don't think Miller will believe her? Or you, if you pass the information onto him?"

"No. It won't change his view at all. He's so rigid, so set on things being the way he sees them that he won't listen to anything else. He desperately wants Jimmy Allen to be guilty because it excuses hitting him before. At least, in his eyes it does."

"I would suggest that most policemen and a pretty hefty chunk of the general public would agree."

"I know." Callie sighed. "But I also know that two young women have died in a comparatively short space of time, and I think Miller is wrong to be so sure that Jimmy Allen is responsible."

"Then that is what you have to tell him. Convince him that Marcy is right."

"He's not an easy man to convince."

"But you will try?"

"All right. I will." Callie reluctantly agreed.

"And please tell me that you won't go off doing any more investigating on your own. Goodness knows what might have happened in The Jolly Sailor if I hadn't been there with you."

"I know, I could have ended up sleeping with a man in a nylon tracksuit."

Kate stopped and looked Callie firmly in the eye. "I am being serious, Callie. I mean, what if he was there? In the pub tonight? Looking for another victim?"

Callie smiled.

"No way. I wouldn't have risked going if I'd seriously thought that was possible. This man's much too clever to go back to a hunting ground after he's used it once successfully. I just wanted to get the feel of the place."

"And did you?"

"Yes. I realised what was going on almost immediately. The Vodka Bar and karaoke night at The Jolly Sailor are both regular singles' haunts. That's what Jade and Denise had in common. They were out on the pull. Looking for a man. The police need to concentrate on other singles venues because that's where he is, trawling for his next victim as we speak." Callie hurried on and Kate ran to catch up with her, grabbing her arm and forcing her to stop.

"Promise me you won't, Callie." Kate was frightened; she knew what her friend was like. "Promise me you won't go and try and flush him out yourself. Go to Miller, tell him what you just told me. He has to see it, has to realise that you are right."

"I will go and see Miller, I promise," Callie reassured Kate, but she didn't add that she was sure that he would not be convinced by her logic, and Kate was too relieved that she had agreed to go the police to notice that Callie hadn't actually promised not to visit singles bars herself.

* * *

They split up at the fork in the road, Kate heading further down the hill to her tiny house in All Saints' Street and Callie heading up to the top of the East Cliff and her flat. She was walking briskly, because the night was cold and she was feeling it, despite the several glasses of wine she had drunk during the evening. Whilst the days were still warm, if damp, the nights were beginning to get quite cold and wintry.

Time to get out the warmer clothes, she thought as she turned into the final stretch along the lane. Out of the corner of her eye she thought she caught sight of movement in the road below her and she turned quickly. There was nothing there. She listened for a moment but could only hear the distant noise of cars on the main road below. She turned back to the lane and hurried on, anxious to get home.

What was the matter with her? Imagining foxes were people. Thinking she was being followed. Perhaps she should lay off the alcohol she told herself, almost breaking into a jog as she kept checking behind her for any further signs of movement but not catching any. She was getting positively paranoid. Maybe a day out in the fresh air throwing up her guts into the sea would be good for her, help her to get her mind sorted out.

Only once she was back in her flat, with the door safely bolted and curtains drawn, did she admit to herself that what she really needed was someone at home, waiting for her to get back safely, or maybe walking back with her in the first place.

Chapter 18

Callie was back at the police station, sitting outside Miller's office, twiddling her thumbs as she waited impatiently for him to see her and thinking that this was a complete waste of time. She was about to get up and leave, promise or no promise, when the door finally opened and Miller invited her in.

"You're making quite a habit of dropping in, Dr Hughes."

"She must like us, guv."

Jeffries was lounging as far back as possible without falling off in an upright chair to the side of Miller's desk, leering at her. It was not an attractive sight.

Callie felt she managed to convey her actual feelings for the pair of them with a glare which left them pretty sure that 'like' didn't enter into it.

"Believe me, I don't want to be here," she added, just to be certain that they got the message, "but I feel I have some more information that may help you with your investigation."

"Our friend Marcy been bending your ear again, has she?"

Miller silenced Jeffries with a look of his own.

"Let the lady finish." He turned to Callie and smiled encouragingly. "Please, have a seat and tell us. What's she got to say this time?"

Callie was tempted to walk out. She wasn't sure which was worse: Jeffries' contempt or Miller's patronising tone. She took a deep breath and brought her temper back under control.

"Jade knew Jimmy."

They both sat forward: this was just what they wanted to hear, Callie realised, inwardly kicking herself. She wasn't there to reinforce their case against Jimmy but to destroy it.

"She had had dealings with him before. Professional dealings. He'd hit her and run off without paying. There is absolutely no way she would have taken him home with her that night. You've got to face up to it, you've got the wrong man."

Jeffries shook his head in disappointment and turned away, peering out of the window. Miller just stared at her as if he could not believe what she was saying.

"That doesn't fit the facts," he said simply.

"It doesn't fit your facts, which are wrong. Denise was not a prostitute, she was a lonely girl."

Jeffries snorted.

"Looking for love, was she?"

"As it happens, yes, that's exactly what I think she was doing."

Jeffries didn't look convinced but Miller at least seemed to be keeping an open mind, she thought, until he spoke, anyway.

"And exactly what evidence do you have for that?"

"If any," Jeffries added unnecessarily, and Callie could feel her face get hot. She just hoped she wasn't developing red blotches. She was particularly prone to getting them on her neck, she knew, and she pulled at her collar in the hope that it would cover any that might be appearing there.

She was acutely aware that Miller was watching her closely and that he was aware of her discomfort. What she couldn't work out was whether or not he was pleased to see her like this. Her instincts told her that he was not; indeed, he seemed more irritated by Jeffries and his withering comments than by her embarrassment, but her subconscious worked to destroy any confidence that thought might give her by insisting that he had been undermining her and patronising her from the moment she walked in the door.

She shot Jeffries another dirty look and spoke to Miller.

"Wherever Jade picked up her man—"

"We know it was the Vodka Bar, we caught her heading towards there on CCTV and the barman confirmed it."

"Ok," Callie was grateful that Miller had given her that news as it confirmed her theory.

"Not exactly the sort of place Jimmy Allen would use, is it?"

"He might do," Jeffries said.

"Unfortunately," Miller said, "we haven't got any coverage of her leaving."

"The Vodka Bar and karaoke night at The Jolly Sailor, they are both well-known places for singles to meet, right?" Callie said.

"As opposed to what?" Miller hesitated. "Working girls?"

"That's right." Callie hurried on before Jeffries could comment, "I know they can also be used by working girls, anywhere can, but they are primarily, well, pick-up places for single people."

"What's the difference?" Jeffries interjected unhelpfully.

"If you don't know the answer to that, you must end up paying for it more often than not." Callie couldn't stop herself from replying and was pleased to see Jeffries flush and, out of the corner of her eye, she thought she saw a glimmer of a smile from Miller, though it was gone before she could be sure, so she hurriedly continued.

"Look, I've got a theory. The killer isn't picking up prostitutes at all, it was just a coincidence that Jade was one. He's hanging round singles bars. I went to The Jolly Sailor last night and, apart from the singers, it's full of men picking up women."

"Did you pull then?" Jeffries was being deliberately offensive.

"No problem, you should try it, Sergeant. Maybe even you would."

"Enough!" Miller finally exploded, unable to contain himself any longer. "What the bloody hell do you think you were doing?"

Callie was taken aback.

"What do you mean?"

"You could have compromised a police investigation. Barging in with your mate. I presume you were" – he glanced at the notebook in front of him – "the two single ladies sat at a table at the back, pint of beer–"

"Not very ladylike."

Miller silenced Jeffries with a look, again.

"–and a white wine spritzer, who left after only a couple of songs."

Callie was embarrassed.

"I had no idea you had someone in there."

"My point exactly. Fortunately, it wasn't anyone you knew or you could have blown their cover. I mean, what were you thinking? What if the killer had been there?"

"He won't go to the same place twice. He's too smart."

"Really? You know that for a fact, do you? What are you, an expert on the criminal mind all of a sudden?"

"Amateur sleuth more likely. The Miss Marple of Hastings, only not as successful." Jeffries couldn't resist putting the boot in.

Callie was livid, embarrassed and confused all at once. She stood unsteadily.

"Right, well I'll leave you two professionals to it, shall I?"

"Please do, Dr Hughes, and keep well away from this investigation from now on."

"Don't worry, I will."

And Callie left with as much dignity as she could muster.

* * *

She walked straight to her car and got in, but didn't start it straight away. She was literally shaking with anger and humiliation. She leant back and tried to take long, deep breaths. In through the nose, out through the mouth. And again. Slowly, steadily, she got her breathing under control. How could she have been so stupid? She hit the steering wheel with a clenched fist and had to start all over again. In and out. Slow and steady. She leant her head against the side window and concentrated for a moment on the feel of it. The touch of cold glass on her burning cheek felt good.

Miss Marple, indeed. Compromising a police investigation? They wouldn't know how to conduct a proper investigation even if someone gave them instructions in triplicate. Their undercover officer must have been that really tarty girl at the bar, she thought. Not exactly discreet. If the killer had been there, she would have frightened him off. She took another deep breath and blew away the tension. She had stopped shaking. She was under control. She would show them. She would show them how wrong they were about her. She put the keys in the ignition and started the engine. She'd show them that they should listen to what she had to say.

* * *

What had started as a bad day got even worse that afternoon. Timothy Lockwood's report from the paediatric specialist was not good news. His liver was failing fast and they were going through the process of tissue typing in preparation for putting him on the transplant list. Even with the progress that had been made by splitting donor livers so that they could be used for more than one patient, they were still rare. No matter how small a piece of a liver might be enough for a young boy like Timothy it would still have to be a close match and if they didn't find one soon, very soon, it would be too late.

Callie went on to have a fractious evening surgery. It was just that sort of day. Every patient seemed intent on irritating her. Callie was relieved to get home though she didn't feel better knowing that her patients probably felt thankful to see the back of her too. Not to mention the receptionist and Linda, who had had to deal with the moans and groans and the formal complaint from her diabetic patient.

All she wanted, now she was back home, was to relax, have a glass of wine, listen to some restful music and prepare for her day out with Jonathon tomorrow. As she headed towards the kitchen, she took the packet of sea sickness pills out of her handbag in readiness and then noticed that the answering machine was blinking. She had messages. Her heart sank. She knew the messages wouldn't be good news, not on a day like today.

The first was just a hang up again, but the second was Jonathon, crying off their day out. "Pressures of work" he said on the message, and didn't manage to make it convincing even over the telephone line. She knew he would have been squirming if they were face to face. However, once he stopped giving his excuses, he begged her to call him to make another date; dinner, he suggested. Monday night. He should have finished the paper he had to write by then. As he finished with another "please call me" she was half convinced he wasn't dumping her politely. But not completely convinced. Pressures of work was so lame. Apart from the excuse he seemed genuine, but how was she to know?

The next message was another silent one. She pressed delete irritably, not even waiting the silence out to be sure no one finally spoke. She was going to have to do something about the silent calls, she knew, but she wasn't sure what.

The final message was from her mother, inevitably, fishing for news of the great romance.

"Some romance," Callie replied to the empty room. "He prefers writing papers on obscure surgical conditions to taking me out."

She went back to the kitchen, opened the fridge door and grabbed the open bottle of wine, knowing that she was being unfair. Jonathon was a consultant surgeon, and a young one at that. He was ambitious. He would want to make his mark. Maybe move onto a bigger hospital, a teaching hospital. That meant doing research, writing papers and getting them published. That meant working weekends, even when they were supposed to be time off. Even when you were supposed to be taking your girlfriend out. Girlfriend? Callie questioned her thoughts; she wasn't sure she qualified for that status yet but she sincerely hoped she wasn't just casual sex. That so wasn't her style. Maybe she should call him? Clarify the situation. She headed towards the phone and then stopped.

Her pride got in the way and dictated that she should wait for him to phone again, not rush to reply. She didn't want to seem desperate. He'd blown her out and, what's more, he'd left the message on her home phone at five thirty according to the machine. He must have known she would still be at work then. Evening surgeries were always packed. So, it stood to reason that he had not wanted to speak to her in person. And why would that be? Because he was lying through his teeth and didn't want her asking awkward questions, that's why.

She poured herself a glass of wine and took a sip, continuing the internal debate as she stared out of the window, watching the sun slowly sinking lower in the sky, dropping gently below the level of the West Hill.

Perhaps he just hadn't wanted to hear her whine about being stood up, even though he must surely realise by now that she wasn't a whiner. Or maybe he had heard about what happened at Cowes. Sailing people gossiped as much as everyone else, and she had been spectacularly sick. Maybe he had found another woman who liked sailing. Trying to look on the bright side, at least she wouldn't need the seasickness pills just yet. Callie could live with another woman in his life so long as he only went sailing with her.

She took another sip of wine. This wasn't getting her anywhere. The sun had almost disappeared behind the castle ruins. Call him? Or make him wait? Pride? Or pragmatism? It was time for a decision. She put the glass down, decision made. She wouldn't call him, she would make him sweat.

She put the bottle back in the fridge. She would call Kate and go to the gym. Make sure she was out if he called again. But as she picked up the receiver and went to dial Kate's number she had second, or third, thoughts. If he rang again and she was out he might think she was angry and not leave a message. He might decide she just wasn't worth it and give up.

She quickly started dialling, Jonathon's number this time, before she could talk herself out of it again. She was disappointed that his mobile went straight through to voicemail but told herself that he must switch it off when he was working. She left him a message.

"Hi Jonathon? About tomorrow? Don't worry about the sailing, I quite understand. Dinner Monday sounds good. Give me a call and let me know where and when. Bye."

She put the receiver down and tried to ignore the slightly sick feeling in the pit of her stomach. She had just done what she always swore she would never do, she had grovelled. Well, almost grovelled. She had let him get away with breaking a date at the start of the relationship and that, she knew, would probably set the pattern. She would always play second fiddle to his work. She closed her eyes. She was letting history repeat itself, she knew, but at least she had her own career, her independence, and any man she settled down with would have to accept taking second place to that too.

Chapter 19

Saturday brought that rare event, a bright and sunny autumn day, the sort of day that reminded Callie why she enjoyed living in Hastings. The seagulls were wheeling overhead, noisy and threatening, but she didn't care. What were the chances of being hit by a dollop of droppings? On a day like today? Low, she reckoned. At least she hoped they were low. She walked briskly along the promenade, dodging joggers and cyclists, letting the stiff breeze blow the cobwebs away, taking deep breaths of fresh air and feeling her spirits lift. Okay, so her love life and working life were both pretty crap at the moment but there was more to her than that, wasn't there? She didn't allow her pace to falter with that question but kept striding on, past the pier and on towards St Leonards. There was, had to be, definitely more to her. She was young – well, youngish – good-looking, fit and healthy. She might not be rich, but she was certainly not poor. She had some good friends and a loving, if irritating, family. Make that intensely irritating. She still had more than most and should be grateful.

She picked up a little more speed and headed for Bexhill. Her plan was to walk there and visit the modern art exhibition at the De La Warr Pavilion, then get the train back to Hastings in the afternoon. A good long walk would do her good and help her to sort out her head. Callie had always found that she thought better when she walked. Something about the background rhythm of keeping a steady pace seemed to help order her thoughts, and walking along the sea front going west, even though she still had to detour inland for a short section, had the advantage of no steep climbs or flights of steps, unlike all the walks going along the cliffs to the east.

Jonathon had not yet returned her call and, knowing that there was little she could do about that, she decided to put him out of her mind and concentrate instead on what she could do to convince Miller that she was right about the killer stalking single women. It was only a matter of time before he'd struck again. Callie did some sums in her head. Denise must have been killed between four and five weeks after Jade, and it was just over a week since Denise's body had been found and she had been dead two weeks by then, three and a half weeks since he last killed, as far as they knew. The killer would probably start looking for his next victim by the end of the week or early the week after – that was always provided he didn't speed up or slow down due to other factors in his life, like work or family. Callie knew it was never as simple as they made out in serial killer fiction.

As she walked, she pondered the other factors that might affect how quickly the killer got the urge to kill again, or even if he would. Was it possible that he would stop at two? No, she thought, this one's going to go on until he is forced to stop. She didn't know why she was so sure, but she was. And it didn't seem likely, somehow, that he would have a family. Callie couldn't imagine living with a killer and being completely unaware of it, although she knew that it could and had happened. There was no doubt that this killer had committed both the murders at his victims' homes, which might mean that he couldn't take them back to his place because there was someone else there. Maybe there could be a wife, or a girlfriend? What a horrible thought.

"No," Callie said to herself with some relief. *He doesn't take them to his place because he might be seen and also because he would have to move the body. That would be a terrific risk, so he goes to their place and leaves them there to delay them being found, not because of anyone else at his home.*

She got a strange look from an elderly lady walking in the opposite direction and realised that she might have spoken at least some of that thought out loud.

I hope she just thinks I'm a harmless loony or a crime writer planning her next novel, and not some kind of homicidal maniac, she continued, but this time she made sure that she kept her thoughts completely to herself.

As she came into Bexhill and saw the magnificent white Art Deco building that was the De La Warr Pavilion ahead of her, she had come to a decision. If the killer kept to his time scale, he would be beginning to scope out his next murder already. Choosing his location for the pick-up, if not his victim. And it would be a different location from the last two, she was sure of that. She had decided to visit some of the potential locations herself, although she had absolutely no idea what she was actually looking for, or what she could do if she saw anything suspicious. She could hardly warn the women who spent their evenings in singles bars not to take any strange men home with them, could she? It seemed hopeless and pointless but somehow better than doing nothing at all. Even if Miller had warned her off. In fact, especially as Miller had warned her off.

* * *

Callie wasn't sure exactly what she should wear. She had never, in her recollection, been out with the express intention of picking up a man in a bar. A school disco when she was in the fifth form once, yes, but not a bar. It wasn't her style and she didn't think she had the right sort of clothes. And anyway, she didn't really want to pick anyone up, she just wanted to look as though she did. There was a subtle difference. She wanted to talk to a few people, find out about the singles' scene: where it was at, how it worked. She hesitated. Perhaps she should get it deliberately wrong to make sure she wasn't actually approached, but she might be spotted as a fraud and then how would she find anything out? In the end she opted for jeans, a skimpy, sequined top she had bought to wear with her black silk evening trousers but decided was too glitzy, and high heeled sandals. She thought that she had probably got it about right and would just have to practice her best *get lost* look for any man who got too pushy.

Then came the question of what time should she go? She didn't want to start too early, as it would almost certainly turn out to be a very boring night and she would probably end up drinking too much. Not to mention that she might stand out like a sore thumb when she came into an almost empty bar alone. Equally, she didn't want to wait until the bars were packed and she wouldn't be able to get a feel for either the place or its clientele. She wished she knew about the etiquette involved. She had already decided that she would be visiting the town centre as the killer had not used a bar there, so far, and she knew there were several likely places she could choose from.

She started in the Sports Bar, two streets back from the sea front, at just after eight o'clock. Considering it was so early in the evening, it was surprisingly full. It didn't take long for Callie to realise that it was full because most of the men had been in there all afternoon watching some rugby match or other. And drinking. Heavily. Whilst they were a very happy, good-humoured bunch, presumably because their team had won, Callie quickly came to the decision that the killer would not pick a bar where the men outnumbered the women to such a degree. Besides which, after ten minutes she had had her bottom pinched twice, a scrap of paper with a man's mobile number scribbled on it thrust down her cleavage and beer splashed over her feet. It was time to try another bar. Fast.

Her next stop was another chain bar just down the street. It seemed a little less busy and there was a more equal mix of the sexes too. Callie went to the bar and got herself a spritzer and then found a quiet corner. At least, it would have been a quiet corner if such a thing existed in the place. The music was blaring at such a high level, bouncing off the bare walls and wooden floor so that it echoed and reverberated, that it would have been impossible to hold a conversation with anyone, even if she had wanted. Callie didn't even finish her drink. The killer would not be able to chat up his victims, unless he used sign language, so she didn't think that it would be here that he chose his next victim. Besides which, Callie's head was beginning to hurt.

At last she found a modern funky bar, brightly lit and woman-friendly, where the music was playing low enough to allow or even encourage conversation. There were plenty of single women in groups and one or two sitting alone or chatting to men at the bar. Several single men were at tables or perched on bar stools and they all looked up as Callie came in. She tried to look nonchalant and even smiled at one or two as she went to the bar and ordered her drink.

"Let me get that for you."

She turned to see a man beside her, having appeared out of nowhere, apparently. He was probably in his thirties, not bad looking and wearing some expensive designer gear a little too ostentatiously for Callie's taste. He was waving a twenty-pound note at the barman in a manner that Callie suspected would mean he might not get served too quickly, if at all.

"No, thank you. I prefer to pay my own way." She took the sting out of her words with a smile as she handed the barman the right money. "I hate to feel beholden to anyone."

"No problem. I like independent ladies. Bit of spirit."

Callie tried not to grimace.

"You on your own?" he asked.

She turned around and checked behind her.

"Looks like it. How about you?"

"Yes. Absolutely. Name's Simon. And you are?"

Callie resisted the urge to call herself something exotic knowing that if she started giving out false names, she would only tie herself in knots trying to remember what she'd used.

"Callie. Pleased to meet you, Simon." She compromised by following his lead and only giving her first name as she held out her hand.

"Good manners as well as good looks. I'm impressed," he said as he shook her hand and Callie wondered just how long she could take his appalling chat-up act. "Not seen you here before, have I? No, can't have, because there's no way I'd forget someone like you."

He answered his own question leaving Callie needing only to simper insincerely.

"It's the first time I've been in here." She looked around at the dimly lit décor. "It's nice."

"So, if not here, where do you usually hang out, then?" he asked. "Pissarro's? Yates's? The Vodka Bar?"

Callie mentally noted his suggestions as places she might visit, apart from the Vodka Bar, as that had been where Jade had met her killer.

"The Vodka Bar. How about you? This your regular haunt?"

"Yeah. Classy but friendly. Just like me." He looked as if he meant it to be a joke, but Callie wasn't entirely sure.

Callie smiled again and wondered how quickly she could leave.

"What about the others? Yates's did you say? And Pissarro's? What are they like?"

"Don't use them as much. Pissarro's is mainly couples and regulars, jazz bar, not my kind of music; Yates's tends to be so noisy you can't, you know, hold intimate conversations." He leant forward and his hand slipped onto her knee and rested there. Callie picked it up and put it back on his own knee.

"No offence, but I'm not that easy."

He held both hands up in the air in mock surrender and smiled to show that he hadn't taken offence, but Callie noticed his gaze had quickly shifted over her shoulder. She looked round and saw that another single woman had come into the bar. She was a little older than Callie, possibly a lot older, but careful make-up and well-chosen clothes made it hard to tell her age more exactly.

"Excuse me." Much to Callie's relief, her new acquaintance picked up his drink and sidled up the bar towards this latest entrant into the game of pick-up. Either Simon already knew her, or he reckoned that she would be less hard work than Callie. Either way she was grateful for the reprieve.

"Let me get that." She heard Simon suggest and smiled to herself. He must have a set routine, tried and tested, almost scripted and, judging by the swift acceptance he got this time, it obviously worked.

* * *

With Simon safely out of the way, and having finally got her drink, Callie spotted two women sitting together at the end of the bar, enjoying some banter with the barman. Maybe they would be more help than the testosterone-charged men that had proved so useless so far, she thought. So, she picked up her glass and went and sat with them.

"Do you mind?"

Both women, one blonde, one brunette, neither natural, were slim and in their early to mid-thirties, Callie guessed. They were dressed to impress the opposite sex, in high heels and short skirts, with plenty of cleavage on display.

"Well, I suppose it's okay. It's not like there's anyone interesting here at the mo." The brunette didn't exactly give Callie an enthusiastic welcome, but she pulled up another barstool anyway.

"Except Simon," the blonde said and giggled.

"I said interesting." Her friend corrected her and turned back to Callie. "You got rid of him pretty quick."

"Not my type."

"He's not anybody's." The brunette looked over to where Simon was clearly getting on like a house on fire with his latest choice. "Well, not twice, anyway."

Callie was immediately interested.

"Why? Is he, you know, into anything odd?"

The two ladies laughed.

"God, no. Unless you call finishing before anyone else has got started odd."

"Actually, that's pretty normal round here," the blonde woman said wistfully. "Not that I'd know, of course," she added quickly.

There was a moment's silence whilst Callie's two new friends thought about the sad state of their sex lives and Callie fleetingly recalled her more than satisfactory night with Jonathon. Would she have a second chance? Or was he giving her the run around because it was over? Maybe he hadn't been as impressed with their lovemaking as she was?

Callie's wildly spinning thoughts were thankfully interrupted by the brunette.

"I'm Louise, by the way, and this is Amanda."

"Callie," she reciprocated. "Do you come here often?"

"Not as often as we'd like, as you probably gathered." Louise grinned and both Callie and Amanda laughed, even though Amanda had probably heard that line a thousand times.

They chatted about men and their failings, where you could get a good waxing and the barman's cute bum. Callie was taking her time getting to the point of her visit; she wanted to establish a rapport before diving into the subject of the killer. She bought both ladies a vodka and coke and managed to get herself a sly sparkling water, with ice and a slice – that most helpful of drinks for a woman wanting to give the appearance of joining in whilst also staying sober.

Half an hour later, she knew most of what there was to know about the singles' scene in Hastings. The Vodka Bar was busy at weekends but, as it was also an internet café, tended to have more than its fair share of geeks and nerds during the week. Pissarro's was more of a niche market for the jazz aficionados and more intellectual sort of guy, or at least those that thought they were more intellectual. Yates's was strictly for the younger crowd, and those refusing to admit their real age. The Jolly Sailor was definitely for the lower end of the market, the blue-collar worker, otherwise known as a bit of rough. The Adelaide nightclub was the place to go when the bars shut and you were still unattached.

"You know you must be a real loser if you leave the Adelaide alone." Louise confided. "Helloooo," she added, looking past Callie to the door and automatically smoothing her already well-ironed hair.

Both Callie and Amanda swivelled to get a look.

"Don't be so bloody obvious, you two," Louise hissed as the latest prey approached the bar and looked around the room, checking out the available talent, his eyes resting on the trio of ladies at the end. He was a bit of a hunk, Callie had to admit, but she wasn't here to meet men and she felt she had probably learnt as much as she could without raising suspicions about her motive, besides which Louise and Amanda had suddenly looked at her and marked her out not so much as a sister, more as competition, so she excused herself and made for the door.

As she left, she saw Louise move down the bar, ostensibly to get the barman's attention but, more importantly, to put her within striking distance of the new man.

Callie smiled at the rather obvious move and headed off for the Vodka Bar. It may not be a future venue for the killer to pick up a woman but she might find out more about the sort of man that went there.

* * *

By ten o'clock Callie was ready to call it a night. The Vodka Bar was packed and spilling out into the pedestrianised street. She had spoken to a couple of groups of single women, both here and at another bar she had passed on the way which had looked a possibility, but had learnt little new. By judiciously ordering sparkling water more often than not she was still relatively sober and tired of the noise and pointless small talk. But had she learnt anything useful? As she went over every encounter and conversation, she rather thought not. There seemed to be an awful lot of sexually active single people in Hastings and they had peculiarly rigid routines and ways of getting together, which only meant that they probably met the same people over and over again. How was that ever going to work? The men, certainly, seemed only interested in getting laid but some of the women she had talked to, most of them in fact, were looking for a long-term relationship, although they knew very well that the men they met and went home with weren't, even if they ended up going home with the same woman more than once. Despite this clear difference in goals, the women, somewhat optimistically to Callie's mind, kept trying.

Callie wondered if she had the energy to stay up and try the Adelaide, last port of call for the desperate, but decided not. The Adelaide would have to wait. She wanted her home and her bed, even if she was the only person in it. Callie knew that after only one night of this treadmill she'd rather be single than go through it again. Maybe she would change her mind in a few more years, when the biological clock was ticking louder than ever.

As she walked up the steep hill towards her flat, she allowed her mind to dwell on her embryonic relationship with Jonathon. Maybe she should fight harder for this one, to stop herself from ending up like some of the women she had met in the bars during the evening. Maybe she should call, ask him over for a meal, brush up her cooking skills, or would he think that was too pushy, too early? Too desperate, even? But she knew, more than ever now, that she didn't want to be alone, she did want a partner, a family too, and she didn't want to leave it too late. Her mother was right, on that count, at least.

She checked her watch, it was early enough still, she could call him tonight, leave a message if his phone was off. Or maybe he had called and left a message at home. She quickened her pace but then slowed again. She mustn't be silly, build her hopes up. She was behaving like a lovesick teenager, and just because she was frightened, frightened of being a lonely old woman. She'd always thought it was better to be that than to be an unhappily married one but, after tonight, she wasn't so sure.

As she turned the last corner and started down the lane to her home, she saw that a car was parked at the end. Her end of the lane. A Jaguar, she thought, although it was too dark to be sure of the colour. She walked faster. It was definitely a dark colour and it could be hunter green. She hurried towards it – perhaps he had finished his work early, perhaps he had come over to see her and was waiting, but as she got closer she could see that it wasn't him, that it wasn't even his car. She was so disappointed, and angry at herself, that she slammed the door to her flat when she got in and then made herself take off her coat, go to the kitchen and pour a glass of skimmed milk before looking at the telephone. Nothing. No welcome blinking light. No message from Jonathon. She felt a huge surge of disappointment. So she took herself off to bed and gave herself a stern talking to: she didn't need to panic, she had years ahead to find the right man. Desperation was as off-putting as being standoffish, if not more so. It was better to be alone than settle for someone who wasn't right. She was an independent career woman, she didn't need a man. If only she believed it.

She sighed as she finished her milk and put out the light. A cat was definitely looking like a good idea.

Chapter 20

It was a pretty standard Sunday morning at the police station according to the whiteboard that covered most of the wall behind the custody desk. Five drunk and disorderlies had been brought in the night before, along with a couple of affrays, almost certainly the result of alcohol overindulgence themselves, and three soliciting, plus there was one shoplifting that was probably a hangover from Saturday afternoon. Callie had been called in to check a couple of them out; one of the D and Ds because he was still reluctant to wake up, and one of the affrays because he was complaining of pain in his groin. Callie checked the board, looking for any reference to Jimmy Allen, but his name wasn't in any of the spaces, so that meant that he was not being held in the cells, nor was he in the hospital having treatment. He must either have been released or remanded elsewhere.

Callie dealt with the D and D first, as he was the one who could conceivably be a serious problem but, thankfully, he was already beginning to come to in his cell, albeit reluctantly, which wasn't surprising given the hangover awaiting him. He seemed surprisingly unworried by the fact that he had woken up to find himself in a police cell, but this was explained once he admitted to Callie that it wasn't the first time he had done so. The fact that he was able to remember previous nights in the cells, if not what had happened to get him there this time, left Callie reassured that this was not a head injury masquerading as inebriation. It was a perennial worry for police and medical staff alike that they would mistake someone who had had a knock on the head for a common-or-garden drunk. It was notoriously hard to be sure which was which until it was too late so Callie was meticulous in her examination of him, checking and rechecking his vital signs until she was absolutely certain this was nothing more sinister than drunkenness, after which she spent even more time making careful notes of all her findings. Just in case.

As she waited for the groin pain to be brought into the treatment room from the cells, Callie nipped to the custody desk where Jayne was busy trying to keep up with the paperwork.

"What happened to Jimmy Allen, then?" she asked innocently.

"Remanded to Whiteleas," Jayne told her.

"They had enough to charge him?"

"Not on the murders, no, but there was enough other stuff, from Cardiff and that, to hold him; for a while anyway."

Jayne didn't look exactly happy with this state of affairs, making out she was busy checking a form and not looking Callie in the eye as she spoke, leaving Callie to suspect that Miller had concocted some holding charges.

"Miller still convinced he's guilty then, is he?"

"Seems like it."

"How about you?" Callie didn't want to let it go.

"Look, the bloke's no angel, that much is certain."

"That doesn't make him a murderer."

Jayne looked down the corridor. "Your pain in the bollocks is waiting for you, Doctor."

Callie diplomatically decided to leave it at that for now and returned to the treatment room. She was angry at Miller: he was still determined that Jimmy Allen was the killer after all she had told him, and as a result she was less than sympathetic to the young man with a bruised testicle.

"Next time you get into a brawl, wear a cricket box," she told him tersely after ascertaining that there was no permanent damage, and sent him on his way.

Jayne was on a break when she had finished, and Callie was pretty sure that she had timed it deliberately to avoid continuing their conversation, which told Callie all she needed to know. Jayne Hales didn't think Jimmy Allen was guilty.

Chapter 21

Monday dawned grey and overcast but Callie was almost humming with contentment as she parked her car in the cramped doctors' private car park at the rear of the surgery. Her Sunday morning might have been spent dealing with the usual bunch of drunks but she had come back from the police station to find that Jonathon had called her and left a message. It was just a brief message but full of nice words; kind, flattering, loving words, and fixing a definite date for Wednesday, with the promise that he would be able to stay over.

As she hurried down to her consulting room she was determined that, no matter what kind of day it turned out to be, she wouldn't let it get her down.

The first test of that resolve was waiting for her in the office: a letter from Timothy Lockwood's consultant. Things were not looking good. His liver function was pursuing a relentless downward path and his name had not just been added to the transplant list but marked as urgent too, in the sure knowledge that he was going to need one in the not-so-distant future, unless they discovered what was causing the problem and treated it successfully. The consultant wanted Callie to visit to make sure that the family were prepared for what the future was likely to hold for them. Suddenly, her day didn't seem quite so bright and shiny and lovely.

* * *

Timothy Lockwood's mother might have claimed poverty, but her house was hardly a hovel. It was a brand-new executive-style house, complete with double garage, on a recently developed site on the outskirts of town. Callie couldn't be sure from the outside, but she would bet that it had at least four bedrooms and probably as many, if not more, bathrooms to boot. There were two cars parked on the drive: his and hers Mercedes.

Callie locked her car and approached the front door. The garden was impeccably tidy, probably because all the bushes and plants had only recently been planted. They had that slightly isolated look of plants waiting to grow into the space they were in, so there had obviously been no time for them to grow straggly or die, or for weeds to grow rampantly between them like they did in the small communal garden at Callie's house.

She rang the bell and waited, listening to the sound of angry raised voices coming from somewhere deep inside the house. It was too faint to hear what was being said exactly but, once the door was timidly opened by Timothy, looking tired and frail, with eyes too big for his gaunt little face, she could hear it all too clearly.

"You haven't been here five minutes and you're already leaving."

"Do you blame me? I haven't been here five minutes and you've already had a go at me about money and women and–"

Callie cleared her throat and both Mrs Lockwood and the man she assumed must be Mr Lockwood turned and looked at her.

"Who the bloody hell are you?" he asked belligerently.

"She's Timothy's doctor," Mrs Lockwood explained belatedly, before turning and walking back towards what Callie thought was probably the kitchen. Callie put down her doctor's bag and held out her hand.

"Hello. You must be Timothy's dad." She gave him her best reassuring smile, and he hesitated only momentarily before taking her hand.

"I'm sorry, I don't know your name."

"Hughes. Dr Hughes. I'm a local GP. I've come to talk to you both about Timothy."

Timothy came and stood next to his father, looking awkward and more than a little lost, but Callie was pleased to see his father reach out and pat him reassuringly on the shoulder. Timothy could have been mistaken for being tanned and healthy if it wasn't for the yellowness of his eyes and the fatigue and lethargy that had replaced any childish enthusiasm and personality.

"What can we do for you?"

"His consultant asked me to pop in, have a chat about what's going on, make sure you both understood it all."

"We're not stupid, Dr Hughes. I've already spoken to his consultant and to other experts in the field, just to be sure. I think I can say that I'm fully informed." He turned to his son. "I'll see you later in the week, all right, Tiger? Be a good boy now." And with that he went out, leaving Timothy staring listlessly at the closed door. The sound of a car crunching across the gravel quickly followed his departure. Callie gave Timothy a reassuring smile but it didn't seem to have much effect.

"Has he gone?" Mrs Lockwood was standing in the doorway, a large glass of wine in her hand. Timothy looked at her, transparently disappointed by both his parents' behaviour, and slouched off into another room, to watch television judging by the sound of it.

"Come on through, Doctor." Mrs Lockwood turned and went back into the kitchen, calling over her shoulder, "Why did you say you were here?"

"Good question," Callie muttered under her breath as she followed. "To talk about Timothy," she said louder.

The kitchen was absolutely spotless. All bright and shiny stainless steel and black granite work tops. It didn't look as though it had ever been used.

"Can I get you anything?" Mrs Lockwood waved towards the fridge and Callie realised that the glass in her hand probably wasn't the first of the day.

"No. Not for me, thanks. I'm working."

Callie took a seat on a high stool at the breakfast bar, as Mrs Lockwood leant against the sink.

"It must be nice for Timothy to have his dad here."

"If you say so."

"A bit of support for you, too."

"Is that what you call it? Support? Huh. Swanning in here, laden down with expensive presents. Patting his son on the head and paying for doctor after doctor. He'll carry on, you know, getting more and more opinions until one of them tells him what he wants to hear. That's what he always does. He thinks money can buy you everything. Well, he's about to learn that it can't. Unless he can buy Timothy a new liver, that is, and I wouldn't put that past him."

She swallowed another gulp of wine. Realising that the contents of her glass were running low, she went over to the enormous American style fridge and took out an almost empty bottle.

"It really isn't possible to buy livers here. Apart from anything else, it has to be compatible," Callie told her.

"That won't stop him. He'll probably decide the doctors here aren't good enough and whisk Timothy off to Hong Kong. Prove to the world that he loves his son more than anyone else can and certainly more than me. And I couldn't fight him. Oh no, that would just show how selfish I was, wouldn't it? Putting myself and my needs first. Putting them before Timothy's welfare. Health. When, in reality, he doesn't care, you know, he doesn't give a toss about his son. All he cares about is getting one over on me. That, and impressing his clients."

Callie realised too late that Timothy was standing in the doorway, listening to every word. She hurried over to him and put her arm around his shoulders, whilst his mother looked on dispassionately, making no move to comfort her son.

"Come on, Timothy, Mummy and I are just having a quiet chat, you stay watching the telly for a while, will you?" Callie led him into the television room where he had been watching the cartoon channel on the enormous flat screen television hung on the wall directly opposite a cream leather sofa.

Timothy flopped on the seat.

"Why does it always have to be like this?" he asked Callie. "Why can't they just get on, like my friends' parents?" He sat on the sofa, looking small and lost.

She stroked his head.

"It's hard for you to understand, I know it is, but sometimes grown-ups can behave in a very childish way." She was glad that he managed a little smile at that. "It's just that they're both worried about you, you know." He didn't look convinced, so she hurried on. "It's not easy when your child is sick."

"No, I know that. When my eczema was bad, and I was all red and scaly, Dad really hated it. He wouldn't let me go out at all. He said it was because people might stare and I'd find it embarrassing, but I think he just didn't want anyone to see me like that."

"Must have been tough."

Timothy's attention had drifted back to the television so Callie gave him another pat on the head and went back to the kitchen.

Mrs Lockwood didn't look as if she had moved, except that her glass was almost full again, as was the bottle by its side.

"He's going to die, isn't he?"

Callie was thankful that she was at least speaking more quietly now.

"I can't deny that he's very sick, but if they can find out why his liver is failing or, if it comes to it, if they can get him a new one, then his chances are good." Callie went over to her and took the glass out of her hand as Mrs Lockwood started to cry. "He needs you to be strong."

"But what if I can't be?" A tear rolled down her cheek.

There was nothing that Callie could say that would help, she knew, so she just stood there silently, letting the poor woman weep.

* * *

After her heavy and depressing afternoon visit it was not surprising that Callie was left with a residual feeling of sadness. What would she be like if it was her child in that situation? Or who had been killed by a sexual predator? Or, probably worse than either of those, committed suicide? How could any mother, or father, recover from the devastating loss of a child? But many did, in time, on the outside at least. She knew that inside they were permanently changed, that they never forgot, but most got to the point where you wouldn't know about past tragedies to talk to them, unless the subject came up. They functioned as normal human beings, went out, had a laugh like everyone else, but deep down inside, there must always be a bit of them that had been lost. An empty space, with them until the day that they themselves died.

The only way to get out of this slough of despond, Callie knew from experience, was to exercise. Some might turn to the bottle, food, or simply choose to wallow in maudlin thoughts but she craved the instant lift of a hard, physical workout and went to the gym for the first time in several weeks. It was evenings like this that she realised that, however uneconomical being a member of a gym was, when one considered the all too infrequent visits that she made to it, it was still invaluable.

After an hour of the cross-trainer, treadmill, weights and some excruciating abdominal crunches on the mat, Callie felt hot, sweaty and exhausted and she ached all over, but more importantly, she was happy and relaxed. And smug.

"God, I hate it when you've been to the gym," Kate later complained. "You positively glow with self-satisfaction."

"Maybe you should try it sometime."

"It doesn't seem to have quite the same effect on me. I just feel knackered. And what's with the fizzy water and salad?" Kate indicated the offending articles in front of Callie.

"It happens to be a fact that after exercise you don't feel so hungry, until later anyway, and you feel thirsty, so alcohol isn't good enough."

"Unless it's by the pint." Kate tucked into her pizza with gusto. "So, what you're saying is: exercise and you not only use more calories and get fit, but you feel less depressed and actually crave a healthier lifestyle. Maybe you should get yourself a television slot, preach to the masses, or, better still, write a self-help book. But personally, speaking as one who has not yet been converted, it all sounds pretty depressing to me."

"Yeah, yeah, you might mock, but it's true." Callie continued to enjoy her grilled chicken and salad, but then nicked a slice of Kate's pizza. "No calories if it comes from someone else's plate," she explained.

"Hypocrite." Kate continued to eat. "At least your new hobby is healthier than your old ones. Hunting down serial killers can seriously damage your health."

Callie sighed.

"I wasn't getting anywhere with that, anyway."

They were in an Italian restaurant on the sea front, sitting inside and watching the world go by through the large plate-glass windows as they ate.

An elderly man was walking slowly along the pavement, pausing every few steps to catch his breath and let the pain in his legs ease. Two girls, probably foreign language students, underdressed for the weather, were walking by, arm in arm, laughing and giggling – English lessons forgotten as they spoke rapidly in Spanish. A lad, in T-shirt, denim jacket and low-slung jeans, turned to watch them walk by from under the brim of his baseball cap. A couple in their thirties, cheap clothes, tired expressions, one carrying a small child, the other pushing a buggy, stopped and looked in the window, longingly, before moving on.

"So, this health kick, nothing to do with your sex life, is it? Getting fit for Dr Love?"

"No," Callie said with exasperation. "Like I said, I was feeling a bit down, and needed to do something to get everything back in perspective."

"Has he dumped you?"

"No, he has not. We're meeting for dinner on Wednesday night. Firm date."

"Somewhere expensive, I trust, after letting you down on Saturday, although I imagine that was something of a relief."

"Mmm," Callie agreed. "But it's just a postponement, isn't it? There's going to have to be a time when he does find out I get seasick."

"Unless he dumps you first."

"You are such a pessimist, Kate Ward."

"I'm a realist."

Callie sighed. She wished Kate was wrong, but she had a sneaky suspicion that she wasn't.

"I think a pudding is called for."

"I knew it. The health kick was never going to last long."

But Callie ignored her and studied the menu instead.

Chapter 22

No one would have guessed that there was anything disturbing Callie's ice-cool exterior throughout Wednesday but inside she was alternating between excited anticipation and dread that something would happen again to scupper her date with Jonathon.

Her day had started early and after two packed clinics and four visits she almost fell into her flat, exhausted. It took a moment or two before she felt strong enough to look at her answer machine. Sure enough, it was blinking at her. She had a message, or rather two, the disembodied voice told her. She felt a sinking in the pit of her stomach. If Jonathon had cancelled again, that was it, she wouldn't give him another chance she decided. She really wouldn't. She held her breath as she played them back. One sales call, and Kate, advising her not to jump Jonathon until they had at least left the restaurant as she didn't want to come across as too needy. As if Callie would. She let out a long sigh of relief, Jonathon hadn't cancelled on her again – yet – and there were no more silent calls.

She was very tired, but knew that there was no way she would manage a quick power sleep or even a cat nap, not because she was too excited, because she was not an excitable person, but she was just too worked up and tense after a disturbed night and a busy day. At least, that's what she told herself. She was definitely not excited. She decided to try and relax with a long, leisurely bath and then promptly fell asleep in it. So much for excitement! As a result she found herself running behind schedule and in danger of being late. Fortunately, she had already picked out her clothes for the evening. Actually, she had picked them out several times, changing her mind as often as she had changed her underwear. Sophisticated but sexy was the look she wanted, hoping she'd managed to achieve it with her final choice: an embroidered chiffon jacket over a black silk camisole and wide-leg evening trousers.

They had arranged to meet at The Stables, a restaurant closer to the surgery than her flat, and she was supposed to be there at eight. As Callie adjusted her hair one final time and glanced at her watch, she realised that there was no way she was going to make it on time if she walked, or even if she called a taxi. She would have to drive and leave her car in the surgery car park overnight. She grabbed her keys and hurried out.

Jonathon had almost certainly chosen The Stables because, ever thoughtful, it was the sort of place where Callie would not feel uncomfortable if she arrived first, but there was little chance of that tonight. As she walked in, Jonathon was already there, sitting on a crimson velvet-covered love seat in the bar area, perfectly dressed as always, in chinos, sports jacket and open-necked shirt.

He looked up as Callie came into the anteroom and smiled, and at that moment Callie felt her heart lurch slightly. If her return smile was, as ever, small and controlled, his was a lovely smile, full and friendly, and he was definitely a very handsome man, she appreciated anew. He had such excellent manners too, so it was no wonder she felt this way, she justified her reaction to herself. He stood, helped with her coat, ordered her a drink and then not only asked her how her day had been, but seemed genuinely interested in her answer. Once they had ordered, they talked about life as a GP, her frustrations at the limitations of her job compared to his, and then they moved to a table and discussed her father's illustrious career.

They ate delicately stuffed mushrooms and carpaccio of beef as entrees, roast venison and grilled swordfish for the main course and, although she noticed that Jonathon turned every enquiry she made about his own family into a question about hers, or a story about his career, she didn't push him. He would tell her why he didn't want to talk about them in his own good time. After all, it was not as if she didn't have things to hide about her own family. She wasn't going to mention her mother, for instance, let alone her obsession with weddings. She did learn, however, that he had been to medical school at St Thomas's and had done both his houseman and junior registrar jobs there. He moved first to Brighton for a senior registrar position and then to a consultant's post in Hastings.

Over the grilled peaches and home-made vanilla ice cream that they both chose to finish the meal, they discussed music: Callie's love of oratorio and the baroque, Jonathon's love of jazz, and as they talked they touched each other, fingers stroking as they reached for their glasses, knees sliding against each other under the table, each not-so-accidental meeting of their bodies sending shivers of anticipation down Callie's spine.

He asked if she would like coffee and she was torn. She wanted to prolong the evening, the surreptitious touching was very erotic, but she was equally keen to go further, get closer, and they couldn't do that here.

"Perhaps we could have it at your flat?" he suggested, as if reading her mind, and she quickly agreed.

He paid the bill, waving away her suggestion that she pay, and again, she allowed herself to be over-ruled, thinking that now was not the right time to put the case for independence. Not when she felt this dependant. He helped with her coat and asked the waitress to call a taxi for them.

"I'm probably over the limit and anyway, I left my car at the hospital, I'm not going to risk leaving it outside your place again. Not after the scratch it got last time."

Callie smiled, but she was irritated; it had been an isolated incident, after all. Her car had never been scratched whilst parked outside her home and it wasn't as if hers was a wreck, it was just as smart as his. Well, almost, anyway. His comment, or her irritation with it, seemed to break the mood slightly and, as they waited outside in the cool night air for the cab to arrive and he put his arm around her she didn't lean into him, encouraging him to kiss her, as perhaps she would have done a few moments earlier.

"Is something wrong?" he asked and, as she thought about it, she knew there wasn't really, she was over-reacting, she told herself. Men and their toys. Cars seemed to mean more to the average man than wives, girlfriends and careers put together and there was little point trying to change that. Instead, she made a conscious effort to recapture the mood by sliding her hand along the side of his neck to the nape.

He responded immediately, reassured that she was still willing, taking her other hand, stroking her fingers sensuously, pulling her close and nuzzling her neck. Callie could feel he was aroused and that aroused her. She turned her head towards him and their lips met. It wasn't her fault that at that moment there was a couple walking along the street and the man called out to his wife to hurry up. There was something about the way he treated her, speaking to her in a slightly bullying way, that made Callie turn to make sure the woman was all right, which she was, in fact she complained to her husband about his nagging. The response to her distraction from Jonathon was an audible sigh of irritation.

"What is it now?" he asked impatiently, which irritated her again.

"Um, I'm sorry, but I just wanted to check she was all right."

"She's fine. You should worry about me," he said as he bent to kiss her again, running his lips up her neck, "You don't want to get on my wrong side, I might bite." He continued to kiss and lick her neck, working his way around to her most erogenous zone, her earlobes. She tried to let go of her irritation, but a burst of laughter down the street distracted her again and she pushed him firmly away, the mood totally broken.

"Oh, for God's sake." He seemed genuinely angry. "What's the matter now?"

"I just don't feel in the mood, at the moment."

"Come on, Callie, don't be like this, don't ruin my night, I've taken you to an expensive restaurant. Wined and dined you. You owe me a good night." He moved to kiss her but Callie was incensed.

"Don't ruin your night? Wining and dining means I owe you?" she hissed as she pulled away from him again. A couple came out from the restaurant and glanced curiously at them; other people's arguments are always fascinating when viewed from a distance.

"I am not so easily bought," she shouted and she almost went to slap him on the chest but he grabbed her arm and pulled her into a bear hug, forcing his mouth on hers so that she couldn't continue the argument. The couple hurried away, this was more embarrassing than a mere argument and they probably thought that this kiss was just a prelude to sex, even if Callie did seem to be struggling against it. She finally succeeded in turning her head away from his bruising lips, and dug the point of her elbow sharply into his ribs.

"Ow!" He still had hold of her wrist and Callie jerked that free, her bag going flying as she did so, the contents scattering across the pavement. "For goodness' sake, Callie. What's up with you?"

"Never, ever, do that to me again," Callie said with ice cold dignity as she picked up her belongings and thrust them back into her bag, not even bothering to close it properly in her haste to get away.

"Oh, come on, Callie, I had to stop you shouting like that, I mean in front of those people, it was embarrassing. Look, I'm sorry. I won't do it again but come on, get it in perspective."

But Callie was already walking away from him. He chased after her, grabbing at her wrist.

"Don't walk away from me!" He was angry now, as angry as she was.

"What are you going to do to stop me?"

"Don't be ridiculous." He was struggling to calm down, speak to her rationally. "Look, we've had a lovely evening, I'm sorry if I came on a bit strong. Now I know you don't like it, I won't do it again. I promise. Come on, Callie, we can get back into the mood." The taxi pulled up behind them, "let's just go back to your flat and—"

"I don't think so. Not now. Just, go, please, and leave me alone." Her tone was glacial and he must have seen from the expression on her face that he was not going to succeed because he let go of her arm and turned to walk back to the cab, but not before a parting shot.

"Fine. Whatever you want." He was so angry that he seemed to be speaking through clenched teeth. "But I don't pay out for expensive meals and get nothing back, so don't think you'll get another chance when you've changed your mind tomorrow."

"I wouldn't go out with you again if you begged me."

The taxi driver was sitting there, uncertain what he should do having arrived in the middle of what was clearly a domestic argument, but Jonathon got into the car and Callie carried on walking away.

"The hospital. Staff car park, off Regent Road." Callie heard him instruct the driver as the taxi door slammed and the car then drove off. She didn't turn and look as it passed her, just kept on walking, but she was shaking and she wasn't sure if it was from anger or fear. She stopped once she was sure that he was out of sight and leant against a wall, legs trembling, tears streaming down her face. Once she felt more under control, she walked on to the surgery car park and went over to her car. She was pretty sure she was still under the limit, as she had spent more time talking than drinking and anyway, the argument had sobered her. She looked in her bag for her keys. The light wasn't very good but she could quickly tell that they weren't there.

She groaned inwardly. They must have been lost when her bag went flying. She couldn't get into her car and, even if she got a taxi, or walked, home, she couldn't get into the flat. She was half-tempted to call Kate and ask her to come to the rescue. Kate kept a spare key to Callie's flat and Callie had a spare car key at home but it was late and it wasn't that far from the restaurant so she decided to go back and look for the keys. It was always a hassle getting replacements and the chances of them still being there in the morning if she left them on the pavement, or wherever they had fallen, were slim. It would be best to at least try and find them and if she couldn't locate them quickly, well, then she would call Kate for help.

As she walked back to The Stables restaurant she was consumed by righteous indignation at Jonathon and irritation at herself for being so misled by a man. How could she have got him so wrong? She began to check out the physical damage to herself. Her lips were sore from the way he had crushed his against them to stop her talking and her wrist was bruised from wrenching it free of his grasp, but that seemed to be all. She knew she had got off lightly, this time. If there was one thing that she could never forgive a man for it was the use of force, of his superior strength, on a woman. She had seen the aftermath of too many cases of domestic violence to fall for the age-old lies; that she had asked for it, that she had led him on, or that it was a one-off and would never happen again. A man that used force once would always use it when it suited him, when his twisted mind could justify it to himself, no matter how often, or how sincerely, he said sorry afterwards. And she knew the violence only got worse with time.

It was very late now, and there were few people around as she walked briskly along the quiet street to the restaurant, going over and over the incident in her head. There was no doubt the man was an arrogant bastard. He seemed to think she owed him. That she had to have sex with him just because he paid for the meal. Well, she had offered to pay. Maybe she should have been more forceful, maybe she ought to have realised what he was like earlier, but even if she had expected him to pay, he had no right to expect sex in return. That was little more than prostitution in her book.

As she neared the restaurant, she sensed that she wasn't alone. There were footsteps behind her but when she turned to look she could see no one there. It was just her imagination, she told herself, but she walked faster, not entirely convinced.

The restaurant was shut by the time she reached it and the lights switched off. She could only see small patches of the pavement in the pools of dim amber light cast from the streetlamps and those pools only deepened the shadow of the unlit areas. As she looked in the general direction that she thought her keys must have been thrown she heard the footsteps again, getting closer. She forgot her dignity for a moment and got onto her hands and knees, desperately scrabbling about on the pavement, feeling for the key ring in the dark. This had been a stupid idea, on her own, late at night, she told herself. She ought to have called Kate. Then it occurred to her that it might be

Jonathon following her; perhaps he had come back, feeling guilty at having deserted her, to check that she was safe, or maybe he had come back for another shot at her and was hanging around in the shadows to grab her any minute. She stood up.

"Come on then, show yourself. You fucking bastard!" she shouted at the shadows. There was no reply, but she could almost feel the shock in that silence. Whoever was out there, he hadn't expected to be confronted like that, just as she hadn't expected that sort of language to come out. It was a measure of how frightened she was. A light came on in a nearby house and the curtain was pulled back. A woman stared out at her and made Callie feel immediately safe and grateful. This witness obviously frightened the figure off as well because she heard his footsteps hurry away. In this new, added light from the window, she scanned the area and a glint from the gutter told her that the keys were there, half under a car. She bent down quickly and her hand closed on the set of keys. Hallelujah!

She stood up, clutching them, and waved at her saviour in the window, before hurrying back to the surgery and safety, holding the keys like a weapon, just in case. It was less than half a mile to the car park but it seemed to take her forever to get there. She stopped frequently to check for following footsteps but heard none and, once her destination was in view, she stopped in a shop doorway, watching to see if anyone was there, waiting for her, but it was quiet and still, and she could not sense any other presence. It was then that she noticed that her car was sitting differently, awkwardly. One side seemed lower than the other. She approached the car park to get a closer look and it became immediately apparent that somebody, some bastard, had let down two of her tyres. All her fear was forgotten in the wave of the anger that overtook her. How dare he? How dare Jonathon do this to her, just because she had turned him down? How dare he take out his sexual frustration on her car?

She almost laughed as she remembered that it was Jonathon's pride in his car that had started her irritation with him and here she was, acting in exactly the same way. She bent down and examined the tyres: they were undamaged but the valve caps were missing – someone must have removed them and pushed something into the valves to release the air. There was nothing she could do, she couldn't drive on tyres so totally flat and she had only one spare, so she couldn't change them both. She pulled her mobile out of her bag and finally called Kate.

* * *

Kate arrived only a few minutes later, coat hastily pulled on over her pyjamas, Callie noticed, as she sank thankfully into the front passenger seat.

"What the fuck's happened to your car?" Kate was too busy looking at the sad spectacle of the Audi TT to notice that Callie was looking far from her usual level of perfection.

"Someone let the tyres down."

"Kids, do you think?" Kate asked, unsure as she looked. "And where's your knight in shining armour, then? No, don't tell me, you sent him away in an effort to show your independence." She turned and looked at her friend and realised immediately that there was something seriously wrong. Callie's usually impeccable appearance was marred by streaked mascara, swollen lips, dirty hands and muddy, torn trousers.

"Callie, you look a state, what on earth's happened?"

"Thanks for telling me." Callie smiled despite herself and tried to check out her appearance in the vanity mirror.

"No, I mean–"

Callie held up a hand to stop Kate's apology.

"It's okay. I know I do. It's been a bloody, bloody awful evening."

"Jonathon?"

Callie nodded.

"We argued and, well…" she held out her arm for Kate to see the bruises developing there.

"He did that?" Kate was horrified. "The bastard. You should report him, Callie, you know you should."

Callie leant back in the seat, physically shrinking away from that decision.

"I can't face it, Kate."

"How many times have you told me that you wished more women reported domestic violence?"

"And now I will have more sympathy with the victims. Look, I just want to go home, lock myself in my flat, and sleep for a week, or at least until the bruises fade."

Kate started the car and began to drive away.

"We'll talk about it again tomorrow. I'll come over and take photos of the damage, the bruises will have developed properly by then and if you change your mind, at least you'll have some evidence."

When they got back to Callie's house, Kate insisted on coming in and making sure her friend was safe and secure.

"I'll make cocoa, or hot milk." She hurried towards the kitchen.

"It's okay. I don't want cocoa. I don't have any. Go home, Kate, I'm fine. And thank you for coming to the rescue, picking me up, you are a true friend."

"It was nothing. Honestly." She looked at Callie closely, worried. "Are you sure you don't want me to stay?"

"He's not going to come here."

"No, but–"

"Honestly, Kate, I'm fine. I'll double lock the door as soon as you've gone. Promise."

Kate finally left, and Callie watched out of the sitting room window. Despite her belief that Jonathon wouldn't come to the flat, that his anger and frustration would all have dissipated once he'd damaged her car, she checked that Kate got to her own car and drove away safely before closing the curtains and sinking onto the sofa.

The shock and fear of the evening had left her feeling exhausted, but she was not sure that she would be able to sleep, or even if she wanted to, and one glance into the bedroom told her that she certainly didn't want to sleep in her bed tonight. Her bedroom, normally the place she felt the most safe and secure, was now a reminder of failure. Made up with fresh sheets, candles placed around the room, flowers on the dressing table, in anticipation of a night of love. No, she didn't want to sleep in there tonight. Instead, she pulled her duvet off the bed, grabbed a pillow and settled on the sofa. Not the most comfortable of sleeping quarters, but better than waking in her abortive love nest. She switched on the television, tuned it to a twenty-four-hour news channel, with the sound barely audible, so that she didn't feel completely alone, and finally fell asleep to a discussion about world economics.

* * *

He knew that she would come this way, and he'd been waiting for her, thinking about what he was going to do, getting excited. The anticipation almost as good as the act itself. She was just a substitute, of course, he wasn't ready for his real victim yet. He needed more time to prepare and to practice. Angry as he was with her, Dr Calliope Hughes would have to wait, but this one, this one would keep him going. Help tide him over until he was ready.

She was young and pretty and pretty drunk. Too drunk to realise the danger she was in until it was way, way too late. Dressed for a night out, in a skimpy top and pelmet skirt. And having sex in the car the way she did, she was just another tart really, like them all, but still a good-looking one. She'd be dead pretty, he giggled to himself. Serve her right for treating him like shit, humiliating him in public, turning him down like she did. Like all women did. Well, he'd have the last laugh now, wouldn't he? He'd show her.

She walked down the narrow alley without even noticing that he had broken the security light or that he was hidden by the doorway into the incinerator room. And she dropped her bag as soon as he grabbed her, so she had no weapon to hit him with. She struggled a bit once the ligature was round her neck, biting into it, but the smooth rubber tubing was impossible to get hold of, to get her fingers round, when it was digging into her flesh the way it was.

She did manage to land a blow though, well, a kick rather than a blow, and she was wearing stilettos which hurt as she scraped the heel down his shin and pushed it into the dorsal aspect of his foot. It hurt like hell, even through his boot. He pulled his foot away, sharply. It was a good job her shoe fell off after that first struggle or she might have done him some real damage. And losing the shoe made her lose her balance too; she would have fallen if he hadn't been holding her up, by the tubing round her neck.

Chapter 23

Callie woke up in the living room and it took her a few minutes to remember why she was there. She switched off the television and swung her legs to the floor, assessing the damage. She ached in places that she didn't remember being hurt and thought that perhaps it was just the legacy of a night on the sofa. She certainly hoped it was, anyway.

She could see the bruise on her arm coming up, a livid purplish welt, with circular fingerprints around. She would have to wear something with long sleeves to cover it up. She padded into the bathroom and peered in the mirror. Her lips were slightly swollen still but it was not particularly noticeable. She would be able to cover the worst with some lipstick. Her clothes from the night before were just left in a pile on the floor and she wearily sorted through them. The knees of her trousers were beyond saving, crawling over pavements was not listed under the garment care recommendations, surprisingly enough. She balled the trousers and put them in the bin. Everything else she bundled into the linen basket for hand washing when she had time, even though she was tempted to just stick them all in the washing machine and hope they survived.

It was still early but she didn't want to hang around the flat so, once she was dressed, she called the garage and organised for someone to meet her at the surgery before it opened. She had picked up her keys and was about to leave when Kate arrived.

"The pictures will have to wait," she said, "I have to get to the surgery and meet the very nice man who's going to sort out the tyres."

"I'll give you a lift and we can do this whilst he changes them. I'm speaking as your legal advisor here, Callie, as well as a friend. Let me take the photos, even if you never want to use them, because at least they are there if you ever do, want to, I mean."

Callie had to admit that she didn't feel much like walking, and it was raining, so she agreed to be driven to the surgery.

As they arrived, so did Linda, always the first so that she could open up for the others.

"What happened to your car, Callie?"

"Just kids, I expect, serves me right for being lazy and driving down the hill instead of walking."

"Well, I think we should report it to the police, don't you agree?" She looked at Kate who looked as if she did.

Callie clearly didn't.

"I've got someone coming to change the tyres, Linda. If you call the police, and if they take any notice at all, which I somehow doubt, they'll want to see the damage and I'll end up being stranded. Not to mention that you will have a vandalised car sitting in the car park all day. I'm sure Hugh will love that. It's hardly going to give a good impression to prospective patients, is it? Honestly, reporting it will be more hassle than it's worth. I've got to get up to the hospital and then do my shopping and things. I need my car."

Linda looked at Kate, who was sucking her lip and looking disapproving. Linda threw up her hands in exasperation.

"Talk to her," she said to Kate, and went inside.

"I know. I know," Callie said. "I should report it. I should report Jonathon. But seriously, what's the damage? My pride's hurt more than my body and it's not as if he's going to come crawling back, begging to be forgiven. And believe me, I wouldn't forgive him even if he did. What can the police realistically do? We don't know he did this to the car so he can't be charged with criminal damage."

"And what about the damage to you?" Kate asked.

"If they charged him with actual bodily harm, I'd end up going to court for a couple of bruises that will be long gone by the time I get there, photos or no photos. He's a pillar of the community, a surgeon. He saves lives, for God's sake. The most he'll get, even if he's found guilty, is a conditional discharge. A don't-do-it-again slap on the wrist."

Kate kept quiet whilst Callie got all that off her chest.

"And in a year's time, when you read in the paper about him beating up some other woman, will you still feel the same?"

Callie was spared from having to answer by the arrival of the man from the garage and Kate, realising she was not going to get anywhere, left, calling over her shoulder.

"I'll give you a call tonight, see how you're doing." And she was off to her own workplace, a small and incredibly untidy office in the town centre, where the stacks of files and briefs in the corridors and landings threatened to topple and crush anyone silly enough to hang around there. Health and Safety would have a field day if they ever visited Harriman, Sydenham and Partners. Just as well Harriman and Sydenham had died many years ago; perhaps Kate could still pass the blame for the mess onto them.

* * *

Callie wanted to speak to Ian Dunbar about an elderly lady who had recently died and as she turned into the road that ran past the hospital she came up against a queue of traffic. In the distance she could see police cars, some with their blue lights still flashing, in and around the hospital car park as far as she could tell. As she inched closer she could see that a policeman was standing at the entrance to the hospital, stopping every car and turning them away, which was the cause of the queue. Callie pulled into a side street and found a more-or-less legal parking space. She grabbed her bag and got out of the car; it was going to be quicker to walk.

At the hospital entrance she stopped and tried to ask the policeman what was going on but he was too busy telling each car in turn that they couldn't come in, they would have to park elsewhere. They could probably see that but it didn't prevent them all from pulling up to him and asking anyway and then try telling him they had to come in because they couldn't walk and had an urgent appointment.

"I'm sorry, sir, there's been an incident, you will have to park elsewhere or come back another time."

He was going to be sick of saying it by the end of the morning, if he wasn't already.

Callie made her way across the car park towards the mortuary building, surprised to see that the area of most intense police activity seemed to be around there. A small crowd had gathered and she could see Sergeant Barlow, Jayne Hales and a couple of other uniforms trying to push them back and put a tape up to keep them away, further from the incident, whatever it was.

"Hi, Jayne. What's up?"

Jayne looked surprised to see her.

"Body's over there, Dr Hughes, I'm sorry, I didn't realise the guv had called you in." Jayne lifted the tape and motioned Callie through. Callie didn't really have time to say that she hadn't been called before she was on the other side of the tape and Jayne had turned back to the crowd.

Callie hesitated: should she admit she was uninvited? But Jayne had her hands full just getting people to move away.

"Keep back, will you? Or I'll do you for obstructing."

Callie wandered in the direction Jayne had pointed. She could see crime scene techies in their white suits and blue overshoes picking over the ground in a narrow alleyway between the mortuary building and the main hospital. They were looking for anything out of place, or otherwise, to put in their evidence bags. Every now and then there was a flash as the photographer took pictures of the scene, which seemed to be in a dim and damp recess off the alley. All Callie could see of the victim was a shapely bare leg, painted toenails on the exposed foot, and one stiletto sandal, lying on its side. Standing a little back, also suited and booted like the techies, was Miller. Callie was reluctant to go further without getting kitted up herself so she stopped and watched for a moment. There was something pathetic and sad about the lifeless limb and discarded shoe, speaking so eloquently of a life violently and suddenly cut short.

"Inspector?"

He turned and saw her.

"What are you doing here?"

"I was at the hospital for another reason and just wondered if I could be of any assistance?"

"No. Thank you. Professor Wadsworth's on his way. We won't be needing you."

"So it's another murder?" She was determined not to let his attitude get to her, and consoled herself with the fact that he had at least said thank you.

He ignored her question and she had to restrain herself from saying anything further.

"Guv?" Jeffries, looking like a refugee from a children's programme with his thin legs and beer belly cruelly exaggerated by the all-in-one suit, was holding a sequined evening bag in his gloved hand. "It was in a doorway just up from the body."

"Anything in it?" Miller seemed to have temporarily forgotten Callie.

Jeffries gingerly opened the bag and peeked inside.

"Make-up, hairbrush, a little money and this" – he fished out a cash card – "name of Caroline Sharpe." Jeffries was putting the bag and its contents into an evidence bag when there was a disturbance at the crime scene perimeter.

"Let me through, you've got to let me see her." They all turned and saw Sergeant Barlow trying to stop a young woman in nurse's uniform from getting under the tape. Jayne hurried over to help.

"You can't come thro–"

"It's Caro. I'm sure it is. I was with her. She's dead, isn't she? Oh my God." Callie was already hurrying over to the distraught girl as Miller hesitated and followed, pulling off his bootees and disposable over suit as he walked.

"Carry on, Bob," he called over his shoulder.

Callie reached the girl and put her arms round her shoulders. The small crowd were watching closely, relishing how close they were to a real murder, how they would be able to tell all their mates they saw a friend of the victim, that they were close enough to witness her pain.

"Come on, let's go somewhere quiet."

"I want to see her," the girl insisted.

"Not now. Later maybe, but you don't want to see her now," Callie said and started leading the girl gently but firmly towards the interdenominational and interfaith Chapel of Rest, situated on the ground floor of the mortuary building. The crowd parted reluctantly to let them through, and regrouped behind them, as if they were walking through some viscous fluid rather than people. Miller was closely following them and, as they reached the chapel, managed to scoot in front and open the door for them. Good manners at a crime scene – Callie had never encountered that before.

* * *

Inside, the chapel had been decorated blandly so that it could not possibly be accused of favouring or insulting any faith. No cross, no altar, no symbols of any kind. Just maroon velour and plastic flowers and abstract stained-glass windows. For all its political correctness, it was still a peaceful, contemplative place, a place for the bereaved and frightened to collect themselves and their thoughts in difficult times.

Callie led the girl over to the front row of seats and sat down next to her, taking her hand and stroking it, as Miller pulled another chair round and fished a notebook and pen out of his pocket.

"Perhaps you could start by telling me your name?" He smiled encouragingly at her, taking a closer look as he did so. She was small and dark, about twenty, in a student nurse's uniform; her hair tied back neatly. Neat actually summed her up: neat face, neat clothes, neat hair, neat hands, neatly manicured nails.

"Claire," she said hesitantly, "Claire Crehan."

"And you think you know who the, um, victim is?"

"Caro. Caroline Sharpe. When she didn't show up at handover, I thought she was probably just still a bit hungover. I didn't – I never thought–" She dissolved into tears again.

"Hush now. It's okay." Callie put her arm around her shoulders and stroked her back. "It's all alright." Claire cried for a few moments before straightening up. Callie had a tissue ready for her and was surprised that Miller waited until after she blew, noisily, before he resumed his questions.

"When did you last see her?"

"Last night. Well, could've been early this morning, actually."

Miller was interested.

"You'd been out together?"

"Yes. We went to a couple of bars and ended up at the Adelaide. We didn't stay too late, 'cos Caro and I were on earlies."

"The Adelaide?"

"It's a club, well, more of a late-night bar, really. Down near the front in the town centre, under the copyshop."

"What time did you get back here?"

"I'm not a hundred percent sure. We'd had a fair amount to drink. Sorry."

"That's okay. Don't worry about it, but do you have a rough idea?"

"I know the taxi dropped me off at my place in Bohemia Road about quarter past twelve and we dropped Caro off here first." She turned to Callie. "She only had to walk across the car park to get to the nurses' accommodation. It wasn't far. I should've stayed and watched, made sure…"

"It's not your fault." Callie tried to be reassuring, but Claire was going to spend the rest of her life thinking that she should never have left her friend to walk those last few yards home alone, no matter how short the distance or how supposedly safe the location, or the fact that Caroline had probably done it a hundred times before without problem. No one should live their lives expecting a homicidal maniac around every corner but Claire would from now on.

* * *

Later, Callie was sitting in the mortuary office, sipping her Lady Grey tea and talking to Ian Dunbar.

"Much as we are used to death and treat it as an everyday occurrence, this is different. For a young girl to be so violently taken, literally on our doorstep, it's just dreadful. Dreadful."

With a shock, Callie realised that Dr Dunbar looked old and tired. Despite his work, he had always seemed so full of life that it was easy to forget the fact that he was actually a year or two older than her father.

"Did you know her?"

"I doubt it. We get nurses down here quite often as part of their orientation or to deliver samples or collect reports but I wouldn't know any of them by name. It's not as if we tend to mix with other hospital staff. They regard us as a morbid necessity and, in some ways, a repository of their failures."

Dave came in with some paperwork for Dr Dunbar to sign.

"Did you know the girl at all, Dave? The one they found this morning?" Dr Dunbar asked him.

"Dunno, Doc. Do they know who she was?"

"I believe her name was Caroline Sharpe. Caro to her friends," Callie told him and he thought for a moment before shaking his head.

"Name doesn't ring any bells." He turned to Dr Dunbar. "I'm presuming it will be the Prof's usual arrangements, so I'm getting room one and a full set of instruments ready for him." Dave went out and Ian Dunbar scowled.

"That means I'll have to slum it in the small room as usual. Can't understand why Dave thinks he's so great. The man's a pompous ass."

Callie smiled. Ian Dunbar's nose was quite clearly put out of joint. He noticed her smile.

"I know, I know. I shouldn't let it get to me, especially under these circumstances." He reached for the delicate china teapot. "More tea?"

"No thank you." Callie looked at her watch. "I really ought to get going."

Callie stood as Dr Dunbar poured himself another cup, using sugar tongs to put in a fresh slice of lemon and a cube of sugar, before stirring vigorously.

"Do you know Jonathon Kane, at all?" she asked casually.

"Yes," he said casually, and paused before going on, "very competent."

"Anything else?"

"That depends on why you are asking."

"Just wondered if there was any gossip."

"Plenty. The best surgeons usually make the worst husbands. They think they're God and like to prove it not only by making decisions without even discussing it with their patients but also by exercising *droit du seigneur* over the nurses."

"Yup. That sounds like the Jonathon Kane I met," she said, and even managed a smile. But as she walked down the corridor to the exit, she pursed her lips. He did seem to think he was a god, and as for his *droit du seigneur*, it was her he'd exercised that with, not a nurse, and she wasn't about to forgive him for it.

Chapter 24

The press, understandably, really went to town on the story. Britain doesn't have many serial killers and, whilst the number of known victims didn't actually qualify this killer to be classified as serial just yet, the potential of one being at work in a picturesque seaside town was more than any journalist, self-respecting or otherwise, could reasonably be expected to resist. By the evening, outside broadcast vans had taken up residence in the streets around the hospital, making it almost impossible for ambulances to get in and out, and staff and patients were getting used to being stopped and asked for a comment, no matter how inane, and completely disregarding the fact that they knew nothing about the situation at all.

Immaculately dressed female presenters and scruffy male journalists addressed the camera or spoke into microphones, trying to fill the demands of their twenty-four-hour news channels. There were calls for more action by the police, calls for Scotland Yard to be called in, although it was many decades since that had been an option, and calls for women to 'Take care out there'. As always, there was an inversely proportional relationship between facts and speculation. The fewer the facts the more the speculation and the pressure on Miller to find the murderer, or at least someone to arrest and stop the mass panic, must have been immense. It hadn't escaped the press corps' notice, as it certainly couldn't have escaped Miller's, that Jimmy Allen was in custody at the time of this latest murder, meaning he really did have a cast-iron alibi this time.

Callie was sitting in her living room, curled up on the sofa, glass of wine on the coffee table beside her and only half-watching the news on her television as she sorted through Timothy Lockwood's previous notes which had finally arrived from his last NHS doctor in St Albans. She looked up briefly.

"Is this killer some kind of psychopath?" one journalist was asking.

"Is the pope Catholic?" Callie replied to the television before switching channels. If they'd sunk to that level of puerility it was time for a change, but the other channels were no better. Most seemed to have concluded that the killer was a man, which was a fair bet, but one reporter had gone further and apparently consulted an ex-FBI profiler and she was putting out a warning for the women of Hastings to beware of a man in his thirties or forties who probably lived alone, might have a dominant or dominating mother and who possibly had some sort of labouring or casual job or was unemployed. Callie burst out laughing. That description must cover a fair chunk of the men in Hastings and was almost completely worthless. She suspected that the enterprising journalist had put it together herself. As if any professional profiler would say anything with so little information available. It was ridiculous. She switched channels again, relieved to find a natural history programme about Africa. Nothing like a bit of death and gore in the Serengeti to take your mind off the death and gore in Hastings, she thought.

She went back to Timothy's notes. For someone so young, his file had a remarkable number of entries, all neatly summarised in a computer printout at the front: eczema, eczema and more eczema, with a little bit of hay fever mixed in for good measure. The boy was clearly severely atopic but there was little, if any, sign of the eczema now. What had happened to change it? She searched for more detail on the various treatments he had had and read through letters from his consultants, both NHS and lots of different private consultants, as if his parents or, as Mrs Lockwood had suggested, his father, had tried them out and then dismissed them and moved on to the next when they failed to deliver the cure he demanded. Timothy had certainly worked his way through every single medication and treatment for the condition that Callie knew. Some had worked for a while, some had not worked at all and, at the end of his notes, his eczema was as bad as it had been at the beginning, if not worse.

Callie went over to her desk and switched on her laptop. She signed in to a medical website and searched under eczema, then narrowed down her search to new treatments because she was wondering if he could have been given something new by a private doctor, something that she hadn't heard of but that worked. If so, she had several other patients who might benefit from it. She sent off some enquiries to a few medical chat rooms, hoping that someone had heard of a new miracle cure for eczema, and then wandered back to the sofa and switched the programme back to the news channel.

On the television, the studio presenter was halfway through an interview with a forensic psychologist who was desperately trying to sound knowledgeable in the absence of facts, when the host stopped talking, touched her ear to better hear what was coming through her earpiece and turned to face the camera.

"We're getting breaking news from Hastings General Hospital. We'll go over to Tom Almay, our reporter on the spot. Tom?" She turned back to address a static picture of the hospital, which suddenly changed to a real-time image of their reporter standing in front of the hospital entrance, looking pleased as punch that, at last, he had something to report. Callie stopped and watched, hoping this was more than just some minor revelation about the victims' sex lives, which seemed to have dominated earlier reports in lieu of anything more important. Perhaps they had found the killer; now that really would be a relief.

"Yes, Kerry, we've just been told that the police have a lead." On screen, Tom could hardly contain his excitement. "They've asked for the owner of a dark-coloured saloon car, probably green and probably an S-Type Jaguar, that was parked here in the hospital car park last night, to come forward."

"Have they identified the owner of this car yet, Tom?"

"Not yet, Kerry. But they have told me that after examining CCTV footage, they know that the driver was here, in the car park, at eleven forty-five, when the nurse walked back to the staff accommodation, and that he may well be a witness to the murder."

Callie sat down quickly, her legs were shaking far too much for her to remain standing, but she was no longer listening to what Tom and Kerry were saying.

Jonathon had a hunter green S-Type Jaguar. Jonathon had left her at the restaurant at about eleven thirty and had told the taxi driver to take him to the hospital where, presumably, he had left his car parked in the staff parking area just by the mortuary. Just by the alley where the body was found.

Chapter 25

The front reception area of any police station is a melting pot of people and emotions that can, at any time, threaten to erupt. Victims and witnesses waiting to be interviewed are left sitting next to the friends and relatives of those in custody, friends and relatives who may be desperate to get them out, certain that they are innocent or that their guilt has, at the very least, been exaggerated. To them, the victim is always a liar, their mate was provoked or misunderstood. The slightest word or look can trigger loud and often physical arguments, and Callie had been there on more than one occasion when a verbal dispute about just who had started a drunken brawl had escalated into violence and she ended up not just a witness to the assault, but also having to sort out the injuries afterwards.

Usually she knew she would only have to wait a minute or two before the custody sergeant confirmed to the desk that she was expected in the basement of the building, and she would be ushered through. With both the mortuary and the custody suite being hidden in the bowels of their respective buildings, it was no wonder she chose to live on the top floor of a house high on the cliff. The view through her home's tall windows was the antithesis of the claustrophobic, windowless rooms and the harsh artificial light she endured at her workplaces.

Tonight, though, she was unexpected, as she had come to give information rather than in response to a call, and everyone was busy so she had to wait her turn on a bad night to be hanging around the waiting area. The publicity around the Hastings killer had brought large numbers of the worried and lonely out of the woodwork, wanting to help but rarely able to do so, and most of them were in the front office with Callie, all queuing, like her, to speak to the increasingly harassed-looking civilian desk clerk.

As she stood in line, she wondered again if it wouldn't have been better to have called Miller but she knew she wouldn't be able to find out what she most needed to know in a telephone conversation. She needed to see Miller's face, to look for non-verbal clues when she asked him: was the man in the Jaguar really just a witness? Or was he a suspect? Did her argument with Jonathon wind him up to the degree that he took it out on another person? Caro? Could she, in any way, be responsible for the young girl's death?

The line edged forward as an anxious-looking man was told to sit down and wait for someone to come and see him. Callie sighed. She could at least have called to alert Miller to the fact that she was coming in to see him so that she wouldn't be kept waiting but in some way she needed this time of penance and preparation. Or perhaps she was just trying to put off the moment when she found out that if she had behaved differently, not fought with Jonathon, or had reported him to the police straight away and had him picked up at the hospital, Caro would still be alive.

So, she waited, whilst a shabbily-dressed woman told the young man at the desk that she wanted to talk to the detective in charge of the murder case, claiming that she had been the killer's first victim but had fought him off. She could give them a description, she said, in fact she could give them a name. As the lady, toothless and in her eighties, was a regular, repeatedly coming into the office to claim that she was a victim of every sort of crime and always naming her dead father as the culprit, she was well known to the desk clerk, who asked her to wait, in a resigned voice. Callie knew the old woman as well, she had examined her on several occasions after allegations of rape and molestation but had never found a mark or sign of trauma on her. No one knew what terrible crime her father had committed against her whilst he was alive, but it was clear she was never going to forgive him and that she remained determined that he would eventually be blamed for something, even if it was the one crime he hadn't committed.

Callie examined the posters stuck to the wall as she waited. There were the usual crimestoppers and neighbourhood watch ones, details of the nearest GUM clinics and drug and alcohol contact numbers, she was pleased to see, as well as several faded hand-written entreaties for information on lost cats, dogs, and even a stray hamster, the poster for which was written in multi-coloured pens and whose description – pale brown and answers to the name Fluffy – suggested that the distraught owner was likely still in primary school. Bored, Callie finally resorted to looking round at the other people waiting with her, making sure that she didn't catch anyone's eye. That was always a dangerous thing to do, as the paranoid would take offence, convinced that there was some sinister reason why she was staring at them, while the sad and lonely would take it as a signal that she was inviting them to start a conversation.

Fortunately, no one was looking at her as they were all far too preoccupied with their own thoughts and were themselves trying not to meet anyone else's eyes. They were probably old hands at visiting police stations too and had been caught out before. A scruffy man in the corner was muttering to himself and a young lad, clutching his vehicle and driving documents to show at the desk, kept glancing at the man's feet nervously, doubtless so as to be ready in case the madman sprang up and attacked him, or maybe concerned that lunacy was catching.

When at last it was Callie's turn to speak to the clerk she was recognised as quickly as the old woman had been but at least the young man at the desk didn't give her the bored and resigned look with which he had greeted the rest of his clientele.

"You been called in, Doc?" he asked her.

"No, I'm here to see Detective Inspector Miller."

"He expecting you?"

"No, but I have some information for him. I should have rung first, I know, but…"

"It's been a busy night; you probably wouldn't have been put through." The clerk told her. "I'll give him a buzz now. Take a seat."

"Thank you."

The only place to sit was a metal bench, bolted to the floor and apparently designed to be as uncomfortable as possible. Callie checked the seat carefully for deposited chewing gum before she sat down. She'd been caught out with that before now. She hoped that being known would mean that she would get shunted up the list of people waiting to be interviewed and that she would get to speak to Miller himself rather than one of the PCs in the incident room. But, while a steady stream of people presented themselves to the desk, she began to wonder if Miller was keeping her waiting deliberately, either to teach her a lesson, or because he just thought she was a time waster. It was already late, she had morning surgery tomorrow, and there was always the chance that she would be called out in the night as well.

Callie was fast coming to the earth-shattering conclusion that she was no longer as young as she used to be and that it was therefore getting harder to recover from broken nights. It had been a bit of a shock when she discovered that she could no longer rely on youthful vitality and enthusiasm to get her through the long nights on duty, as she had hoped that wouldn't happen until much later in her career and at a much more advanced age. Forty, at least. But here she was, in her early thirties and her body was already betraying her. Perhaps she should consider Dr Grantham's offer of a full-time job and a partnership at the surgery. At least her on-call would be limited to one or two nights a month with the local GP co-op. Or maybe she should consider training in pathology, become a nine-to-five body cutter? That would please both her father and Ian Dunbar, not to mention his assistant Dave Ball, if nobody else.

She had just decided to give up and come back after surgery in the morning when the door opened and Sergeant Jeffries leant into the waiting room, giving a jerk of his head to indicate that she should follow him. She stood up and did so hurriedly, only just catching the door as it was about to slam shut, and pursued the sergeant briskly in the direction of the incident room.

"Busy night," she said to his back as he went through another set of double doors and left her to catch them as they closed. No one would ever accuse Bob Jeffries of being an old-fashioned chauvinist for holding open doors for ladies. They could say he was a chauvinist for a whole host of other reasons, but not for that.

"You could say that," he replied. "Every nutter in the county's got urgent information for us," he continued. Despite the fact that Sergeant Jeffries was a small man, Callie was having to almost break into a trot to keep up with him, so she didn't have spare breath to ask if he included her as one of the nutters, although she had a sneaking suspicion that he did. Fortunately, they arrived at the incident room without her having to make any further conversation.

Despite the late hour, most of the desks were still manned and people milled around, consulting one another about leads and reports. Jayne Hales was sitting at a desk with Miller standing behind her and looking over her shoulder at a TV screen. Callie had the chance to watch him for a moment or two without him knowing that she was there. He looked tired, and the closest to dishevelled that she had seen him. He was not wearing a jacket and his tie had been loosened at the collar with the top button of his shirt undone and the sleeves rolled up to just below his elbow.

"There," Jayne said, pointing. "You can see that the security light's on by the reflection in the chapel window, until this frame" –

she checked the time on the image – "12:16 a.m. and then it suddenly goes out."

Miller looked at the screen intently, rubbing at his five o'clock shadow.

"So, we know exactly when he broke the light. Have you spotted the nurse returning yet? Or any other movements?"

"Still going through the tapes, guv."

He turned and, spotting Callie, self-consciously straightened his tie.

"Dr Hughes. What can we do for you?"

Callie hesitated. She had rehearsed exactly what she intended to say, over and over, in her head whilst she was waiting in the reception area, arguing with herself whether any of it was actually relevant, whether or not she should just go home and wait. Wait and see if there was a connection between Jonathon Kane and the dead nurse, if it was his car that was seen in the car park and if he was a witness or something more. In the end she had decided she had to speak out, tell them everything: about his car, about their disastrous date, his violent temper, but now that she was here she felt uncertain, her natural reticence coming to the fore. What he had done to her, hurting her arm, was hardly in the same league as killing someone, was it? Kate had said that she would regret not reporting

Jonathon at the time, and here she was, doing just that. Why was Kate always right?

She realised he was waiting; they all were, Jeffries, Jayne Hales, and Miller, waiting for her to speak.

"The car. Dark coloured saloon. Have you found out who owned it yet?"

"We have a list of possibles. We're going through them now. That's the staff parking area so we'll find it, I'm sure."

"Good, well, that's it then." She knew it was ridiculous to try and leave at that point, even as she was doing it.

"That's it?" Jeffries was, as usual, the first to say what he thought. "You came all the way over here, hung around in reception with all the loons and tossers for half an hour or more, just to say that's it?"

"Well, if you think you know who owns it… I mean, it might not have anything to do with this." She was suddenly acutely aware of Miller moving forward so that he stood, almost toe to toe with her, so close that she could smell the last, lingering traces of his aftershave. She had to tilt her head to look up into his face, and his expression was not what she expected. He didn't seem angry, irritated or even exasperated with her like he usually did. For a moment, he looked as if he was worried, as if he cared. He touched her arm, just where Jonathon had grabbed and bruised it, and she instinctively pulled her arm back, wincing and stepping away from him, but he moved forward again, real concern in his eyes. Jeffries cleared his throat and they both suddenly looked at him and then stepped back, startled by the realisation that for a moment, just a millisecond, they had been mutually attracted, to the extent that they had forgotten where they were and just how many other people were in the room. It was Miller who recovered first.

"If you know anything that might help, that might save us some time, even if it is irrelevant, Dr Hughes, now is the moment to tell us."

She knew he was right.

"Jonathon Kane, he's a consultant surgeon. He, um, has a dark green jaguar."

Jayne Hales checked down the list.

"Here, guv. S-Type, hunter green, six months old. That could be it."

Miller looked at Callie.

"There's more, though, isn't there? Something that made you connect him to this?"

"No, well... yes." Why couldn't she keep calm round this man? Be her usual detached, professional, self? "It's just that we went out, for a drink, dinner, the night of the murder, last night and he left in a taxi, about eleven fifteen, eleven thirty, and I heard him tell the driver to take him to the hospital because he'd left his car there."

"Had you argued?"

"No, no, nothing like that," she lied. "It was just a... a business meeting if you like, we were discussing a patient."

"Over dinner?" He seemed unconvinced.

"Yes."

"Where?"

"The Stables."

"Pretty flash for a business dinner."

"That's Jonathon. Flash."

"Know him well, do you?"

She managed to look him straight in the eye and, seeing his interest and irritation with her, tilted her head slightly, defiantly.

"You know how it is. Medicine's a small world, we all know each other."

"And you parted on good terms?"

She said nothing and was taken by surprise when he suddenly reached forward, grabbed her hand, and pulled her sleeve up with his other hand. They all stared at the bruises that were now fully developed, the purple prints of Jonathon's fingers clear where he had grabbed her wrist and twisted it trying to get her to go with him.

Callie pulled her arm back, away from him, embarrassed to have been exposed like that, not sure what she should or could say to explain. She glared at him but she could see that his eyes had darkened with anger, and when he spoke his voice was tight with the difficulty of keeping his emotions under control.

"That doesn't look like good terms to me."

* * *

When she finally arrived back at her flat, she was exhausted; too exhausted to go over what had happened or how she felt about any of it, but too wide awake not to. Jonathon was a bastard, and Miller, well, Miller was more complicated. Confusing. When she had finally made a full statement, telling them everything that had happened, he had been gentle with her, solicitous, coaxing out her memories, painful and humiliating as they were, getting the full story. He had seemed to care. About her, about what she'd been through. Then, as soon as she was done, story all told, he'd stood up, told Jeffries they were going to pick up Jonathon, and left her. Just like that. With hardly a backward glance. She groaned. He probably used that method on all the silly, girly witnesses who came to see him. All the battered women. Made them feel like he cared, got every detail that he wanted out of them and then, wham, bang, thank you ma'am, high-tailed off to arrest his suspect.

Callie looked at the half-full wine glass on the table and then headed into the bedroom. She desperately needed to go to bed and get some sleep, even though she knew that that was probably the last thing that was going to happen.

Chapter 26

She was finally woken by the telephone ringing and the vague feeling that it had been ringing for some time. She reached across the bed and grabbed the receiver, just in time to hear a click and then the dial tone. Seconds later the start of a Mozart piano concerto told her that whoever wanted her was trying her mobile number. So, at least it couldn't be her mother.

Callie got out of bed and went searching for her mobile. It was in her bag where she had left it when she got in last night. By the time she extracted the phone out from the depths of her bag the ringing had stopped. Ten missed calls, half from Kate and half from the surgery. Her home phone started ringing again and as she leant over to pick it up, she glanced at the clock on the mantelpiece. Nine o'clock!

"Yes, yes, Linda, I know I'm late and I'm really sorry. I must have slept through the alarm – I'm on my way, okay? Just pacify my patients, apologise to them, give them tea and biscuits or something. I'll be there as soon as I can."

She slammed the phone down and charged through to the bathroom. Nothing, but nothing, was going to stop her from having a shower, no matter how late that made her.

* * *

As she drove, just about within the speed limit, down the hill to the surgery, she talked to Kate on hands free.

"I know. When I left the police station last night, they were on their way to question him."

"They said on the radio that they had actually arrested a doctor, a surgeon, Callie. That must mean that they suspect he was more than just a witness. Did you tell them about him hurting you?"

"Yes. I did, promise. They even saw the bruises, okay?" Callie didn't mention the fact that she hadn't initially volunteered the information. "And I admit it. You were right. I should have reported him at the time, it would have saved me the humiliation of having to tell Miller last night."

"Not to mention that it might have saved that nurse her life."

"Look, you've every right to be angry with me, Kate, but you can't lay that guilt trip on me. I honestly don't believe that Jonathon killed her. Maybe for a while last night I did but in the cold light of morning? No. I'm sorry, but it just doesn't ring true, and that's not just me trying to feel better about it and making excuses. Look, I'm at the surgery and I've got a waiting room full of irate patients, I'll speak to you later." She disconnected, parked the car and took a deep breath before getting out and striding into the surgery, ready for whatever was waiting there for her.

Except for what was actually waiting for her after her surgery finished. Detective Inspector Miller was sitting outside her consulting room and Callie silently gritted her teeth. The receptionist really should have warned her. He smiled and she frowned.

"I take it you're not pleased to see me?" He seemed a little put out by it.

"It's nothing personal, Inspector, it's just that I've had the surgery from hell this morning and then got a ticking off from the senior partner for being late. I am absolutely starving and I have precisely forty-five minutes to eat and get my paperwork done before I have a baby clinic. Three hours of screaming infants. I really don't have time to speak to you."

Miller stood up and she looked at him more closely. He had a slightly swollen and split lip and she wondered if he had upset Jonathon to the extent that he'd taken a swing at him. If so, she hoped Miller had hit him back. Then she suppressed the thought, shocked that she was musing about violence with approval. Even against Jonathon.

"There's a really nice café just down the road, so you can talk to me while you have your lunch. Kill two birds with one stone. And you never know, I might even pay. This way."

He led the way to the door and, too hungry to argue, she followed.

The café was not what she had expected from Miller at all, being a vegetarian, whole food establishment.

"Not that I'm a vegetarian," Miller assured her, "but they do lovely falafels, stir-fries and salads. Is it okay with you? Only it's not really the sort of place I can take Sergeant Jeffries."

Callie smiled.

"No, I wouldn't imagine you could. He's definitely the full English breakfast type of man."

"Not at all," Miller said. "I've seen him eat steak pie and chips on a number of occasions."

"I hate to think what sort of state his arteries are in." Callie laughed. Miller constantly surprised her. Just when she thought she had got him pegged he went and did something else that turned her opinion of him on its head.

Miller ordered a stir fry from the young, fresh-faced waitress and Callie asked for a hummus and salad-filled pitta bread.

Once the waitress had left, Miller looked at Callie, a serious expression on his face.

"I wanted you to know before you read it in the newspapers." He hesitated.

"I know that you have arrested Jonathon but I'm guessing that's just because he's being uncooperative."

From the look on Miller's face Callie knew that it wasn't just that.

"What?" she asked him, "don't tell me you're serious about Jonathon? That you really think he killed that girl?"

Miller flushed slightly, irritated that she wasn't taking this as seriously as he did.

"We certainly can't discount him. We suspect the killer is involved in medicine in some way, for several reasons."

"Like what?"

Miller was clearly reluctant to say but equally he wanted to convince her that Jonathon was a viable suspect.

"Fibres found at the scenes have led us to believe the killer is wearing hospital theatre greens to keep the trace evidence to a minimum. Also, who would notice a set of bloody body fluid stained scrubs going through the hospital laundry?"

Callie had to concede he had a point. If that was what the killer was doing, then it was a brilliant idea.

"Also, the ligature this time was probably some sort of rubber or plastic tubing; it could be surgical in origin."

"So, you are serious about Jonathon as a suspect?"

Miller nodded.

"But what I wanted to warn you about is his alibi."

"Alibi?"

"He admits he went to the hospital to collect his car after he left you at the restaurant, although he denies laying a finger on you."

Callie snorted in disgust.

"Yes, well, I didn't say I believed him, did I? Anyway," Miller continued, "he also admits that he picked up the nurse, took her 'for a spin in his car' before dropping her back at the hospital, although he didn't take her all the way into the car park, just dropped her at the entrance."

"What a gentleman." Callie sounded bitter, even to herself. "I take it that 'for a spin' is a euphemism?"

Miller was looking uncomfortable.

"Yes. He did finally admit to having sex with her. Just 'a quickie' as he put it."

"And to think I…" Callie stopped as the waitress arrived with their food. It looked lovely, which was a shame, because Callie suddenly seemed to have lost her appetite. She pushed the plate away and massaged the spot between her eyes that was the focal point of the tension that was building, making her feel as if her head was about to explode.

"You have to eat." Miller's voice was solicitous, gentle even.

"I'm really not hungry." She looked at him, saw the hesitant look on his face. "Don't tell me there's more?" She thought for a second. "You haven't got to whatever his alibi for the murder is yet, have you? Well, I can assure you he wasn't with me."

"No, I know. He says he was with his wife."

Callie felt all the anger and humiliation inherent in those words wash over her. She had been used, there was no other word for it; he was married all along and she was little better than some girl he took out for a 'quickie'. She felt hot and then cold and clammy; her breaths were too fast and shallow but she couldn't seem to slow them down, make them deeper, her head was spinning and she felt dizzy. Then she heard the sound of Miller's chair scrape as he stood up rapidly and pulled her chair round.

"Put your head between your knees. Now!"

Too dizzy to object, she did as she was told and the swimming feeling in her head slowly abated.

"Come on, deep breaths. Nice and slow now."

Callie would have liked to ignore him; it went against the grain, taking medical advice from a policeman, but there was no getting away from the fact that he was telling her to do exactly the right things. So, she did as she was told and eventually managed to get her breathing under control.

"Is she all right?" The waitress seemed to be asking from a long way away.

"It's okay," Callie said. "I'm fine, absolutely fine, just a slight dizzy spell." And she lifted her head to see Miller, crouched on the floor in front of her, looking concerned.

"Take it slowly. That's it." He was watching her closely for any signs that she was still feeling faint. "I should have waited until you'd eaten." He turned to the waitress. "A cup of tea, with sugar." And she scurried off, glad to have something to do to help.

"I don't take sugar," Callie told him.

"You will today," he told her in a voice that said he was not going to take any argument from her. The sort of voice that she would normally have argued with for that very reason, but not today. Today, she really wasn't feeling strong enough.

The waitress reappeared with her tea and Callie sipped it, obediently.

"I didn't know," she told Miller.

"I didn't think you did. You're just not the sort of woman who would have an affair with a married man, are you?"

"Not knowingly, no. I'm sorry about that, coming over all dizzy on you. The number of times I tell my patients not to skip meals." She could tell he wasn't completely convinced that a lack of food was the sole cause of her faintness. How could she have been so stupid? She took another sip of tea; she was beginning to feel better for it already and beginning to allow herself to get angry again.

"Do you believe his alibi?"

"No."

"Is she, I mean, is his wife the sort of passive woman who would say whatever he tells her?"

"She's the sort of ball breaker who would happily lie, die for or, better still, kill her husband rather than let him cause any kind of a scandal that affected her standard of living. My only consolation now is that she's giving him a far worse time than PACE would ever let me give him."

Callie smiled and had more tea.

"That's better," he said. "At least you've got a bit of colour back. Now, how about some food?"

She took a tentative bite of her pitta bread, as he went back to his chair and tackled his stir fry.

"What about the other murders? Do you honestly think he could be responsible?"

"His wife is his only alibi for all of them and, as I said, I don't place much stock on her truthfulness."

"I just can't see it somehow. I know he's a, a—"

"Shit?" Miller interjected helpfully, as she was clearly struggling to find the right word.

"Over-sexed, two-faced adulterer," she corrected him and he smiled. "But that doesn't mean he is a serial killer or that he behaves in the way that the killer did when he picked up his first two victims from the singles' scene. That's really not Jonathon's style."

"Yet he fits the description of one of the men who was in the Vodka Bar the night Jade was there."

"Really?" She was genuinely surprised. "Has he actually been identified? Or is it one of your leaps of deduction?"

Miller bristled.

"And that's always supposing I agree with your half-baked theory about the singles' scene."

"Half-baked?" Callie counted off the murders on her finger as she spoke. "Jade met her killer in a singles' bar, Denise at a karaoke night, and Caro—"

"Met hers in a car park," he finished for her.

"Having just come back from the Adelaide, last resort of the desperate in singles' scene terms, or so I've heard."

"And you'd know, of course."

Callie flushed and Miller was suddenly apologetic.

"I'm sorry. I shouldn't have said that, it was unforgivable." He looked round and realised that the waitress was listening open mouthed to every word before continuing quietly.

"Look—"

But Callie had glanced at her watch and she leapt up in a panic.

"I'm going to be late again, twice in one day." She flung some money on to the table and rushed out.

"Wait!" But by the time he had paid the bill and hurried after her, she had gone.

Chapter 27

It wasn't until late afternoon, after the last baby had been weighed, measured and jabbed, that Callie was able to get away and at long last go to the mortuary to try and find out what the hospital gossip was saying about Jonathon's arrest.

As she slowly circled further and further away from the hospital, she wondered how long the car park was going to be taped off as a crime scene; at this rate she would have been better off getting a taxi. She finally found a legal space she could squeeze her car into about a quarter of a mile away and began the trek back to the hospital. At least she wouldn't need to go to the gym to get her daily exercise, she consoled herself, it was just a shame that it looked like rain and she hadn't brought an umbrella. If she had to run back to the car later, she'd get drenched.

She found Dr Dunbar in his office, once again attempting to edit a report on his computer.

"Why don't you get your secretary to type it up for you?" she asked as she cleared a pile of reports from the only other chair and sat down.

"Because some bloody administrator with two PAs and a receptionist says I don't need a secretary anymore. I told him that I have much better things to do with my time than struggle with this infernal machine and he had the cheek to offer to send me on a course. Bloody whippersnapper. I've a good mind to get him in here and ask him to do the damn reports himself." He sat back and looked at her closely.

"Much as I am always happy for tea and chat, have you come to see me for a reason?"

"Yes, I wondered if you had any interesting news about the murdered nurse?"

"Hmm." Dr Dunbar hesitated. "Just how well do you know our Mr Kane?"

Callie flushed.

"Well, let's just say better than I would like."

"Yes, all right, I'll accept that and pry no further, but you should know that he's involved."

"I, um, do know about his involvement and I've been questioned by the police, Ian, so you don't have to worry about all that. Jonathon Kane was having dinner with me earlier in the evening, and then came back here to pick up his car and, how can I put it, meet with Caro Sharpe."

Dr Dunbar looked relieved.

"I didn't want to break it to you that our Mr Kane is a bit of a ladies' man, and a bit of a bastard about it if the rumour mill is to be believed."

"I think I can vouch for both charges being true and no, I didn't know he was married."

"I'm sure you didn't, Calliope. There's very little else I can tell you about the murder then. Old Wally Wadsworth is keeping his findings very close to his chest, but according to Dave, who is being irritatingly tight-lipped as well, it does look as though she's linked with the other two."

Dr Dunbar was all brisk efficiency now that he knew he wasn't treading in delicate waters.

"Thanks, Ian, I—" she stopped and looked up, suddenly aware that someone was standing in the doorway, listening to their conversation. It was Miller, leaning nonchalantly against the doorpost, politely waiting for her to finish. She blushed and was immediately irritated to have done so.

"Carry on, please, don't let me interrupt. I've only come to collect a couple of samples that need to go to forensics." He smiled, knowing that they all must know this wasn't true. The chain of evidence meant that all samples taken during the autopsy, as well as the victim's clothing and belongings, were bagged and tagged during the procedure and sent direct to the forensic laboratory.

"No, no. I've finished here." She stood up quickly and turned to Dr Dunbar so that her back was to Miller, in the vain hope that she could get her colour under control before having to speak to him again. She was even more irritated to see an amused expression on Dr Dunbar's face. He had always read her far too well. "If you could just send me the report, Dr Dunbar."

"Of course," he said and also stood.

"Reports!" Miller almost snorted. "Your Professor Wadsworth is impossible. Hardly says an intelligible word during the PM and then sends me a report where he never knowingly uses one word when two, particularly two in a foreign language, would do."

"Ah, that's Wally Wadsworth for you. He relies on people thinking he's intelligent simply because they can't understand what he's saying." Dr Dunbar was clearly pleased to hear criticism of his bête noire. "I'd be happy to take a look at those reports for you, Detective Inspector, see if I can translate them into the English language for you."

Miller smiled and whipped out a couple of folders from behind his back.

"These are the first two done by Professor Wadsworth." He handed the folders to Dr Dunbar. "I'll drop off the report on Ms Sharpe as soon as I get it."

He stood back to allow Dave to come in.

"The stock order, Dr Dunbar." He held out a form.

"Just put it on the side will you, Dave?" Dr Dunbar was already flicking through the folders. "What about the independent PM on the first victim? Have you got that?"

"At the office. It's a lot clearer but if you think it would be helpful to see it, I can drop that off as well."

"I think it would be good to make sure that they both marry up. Nothing I'd like better than to catch Wally out, find something he'd missed." Dr Dunbar had a mischievous twinkle in his eye. As he leaned across Callie to put the stock request form on the side, Dave managed to brush some bits of paper onto the floor. He bent down to pick them up and Callie moved to the side in an attempt to get out of his way but the room really wasn't big enough for the four of them, particularly in view of the fact that Dave was by no means compact. Callie edged past him towards the door.

"I'll say goodbye then."

"Bye, Callie." Dr Dunbar was already engrossed in the autopsy reports and barely looked up.

"I'll walk out with you." Miller stepped back into the corridor.

"I thought you had some samples to collect?" she said as coolly as she could as she walked towards the lift.

"I think we both know the purpose of my visit was to get Dr Dunbar to decipher those ruddy reports for me."

"It was a bit obvious," she agreed, with a smile.

"I'm glad I bumped into you, though. Make sure you're okay."

"After I made such a spectacle out of myself, you mean?"

"Not at all. You hadn't eaten and you have had a difficult couple of days."

"Nothing I can't handle, Detective Inspector." She was damned if she was going to encourage his solicitousness; she was a strong independent woman, after all, she told herself, not some flaky neurotic. She punched the lift call button, the doors slid immediately open and they both got in.

"I'm sure. But–"

"No buts. I admit to an error of judgement in going out with Jonathon Kane but that's it. We only went out a couple of times and he proved to be unacceptable. End of story. Okay?"

"Unacceptable?" Miller wore an amused expression on his face.

"Yes, unacceptable," she snapped as the lift doors opened onto the ground floor corridor.

She marched hurriedly away, pleased to see through the windows that at least the rain seemed to be holding off.

* * *

Back at her flat, there were fifteen messages on her answer phone. One from her mother, sympathising and offering support, one from a reporter who must have heard something about her and Jonathon, however vague, and was fishing, and twelve hang ups. Callie dialled 1471, but the number was withheld every time. They were probably all from the reporter, checking to see if she was home yet, Callie thought, inwardly groaning. That was all she needed: her unsuccessful love life splashed all over the front pages. She would never be able to go out again.

As Callie was brushing her hair, getting ready for bed, the phone rang again. Nervous in case it was the press again, Callie left it for the machine to pick up.

She listened as the message kicked in asking the caller to leave a message after the tone. There was a bleep and then nothing.

Callie stopped brushing her hair. She could feel the hairs on the back of her neck stand up and a shiver run down her spine as the silence went on. She put down the brush and went through to the living room, standing next to the phone, listening. There was nothing but the faint sound of breathing.

In a sudden rush of anger, she picked up the phone and shouted "Go away!" into the receiver, slammed it down, and pulled out the plug.

She didn't know what the person at the other end thought of her outburst, but it certainly made her feel better.

* * *

He smiled. He was getting to her, he could tell. He had known she was home. Standing where he was on the cliff top, he had seen the light come on in her living room when she got back. She shouldn't have answered but she couldn't resist it. Couldn't resist him. He dialled again, withholding his number like before, but there was no answer, not even the answer phone message.

He was disappointed. He wanted to hear her voice again. She was such a whore, such a cock-tease. She probably had hundreds of men at her beck and call.

He tried again without getting through. She must have unplugged the phone, but she couldn't do that forever. He would catch her out again, he just needed to keep trying, then he would hear her voice and maybe next time she wouldn't be angry. Maybe next time she would be frightened.

Chapter 28

The next day, Callie deliberately didn't put the TV on and, when she drove to work, she didn't listen to the radio and even avoided looking at the newsagent's hoardings which she was sure were full of the arrest of a certain surgeon. She no longer wanted to know what was in the news because it was bound to be bad. Miller had rung her on her mobile first thing that morning to inform her that Jonathon Kane had been released on bail the night before. He wanted her to know in case Kane tried to contact her. Once she knew he had been allowed out of custody she was sure that last night's batch of silent phone calls must have come from him, not a journalist as she had suspected before. He was obviously trying to frighten her because he blamed her in some way for what had happened to him. Well, she wasn't to blame – for the row, for him hurting her, or for him picking up a nurse who was later found dead – he was the one who was to blame, and there was no way she was going to allow him to intimidate her.

As she unlocked the door to her flat and placed her doctor's bag neatly in the small cupboard in the hallway, the first thought on her mind was how to get to the kitchen for a glass of wine without even looking at the phone but it was hopeless, her eyes were automatically drawn to it as she crossed the living room. She stopped dead in the centre of the room, the answer phone light wasn't flashing, in fact it wasn't even on. Then she remembered: she'd left it unplugged last night. Fantastic! What a stroke of luck, there wouldn't be any messages from her mother or reporters, or long silences from Jonathon Kane; she had nothing to dread hearing after all.

She was inordinately pleased with herself for not plugging the phone back in, even though it had been forgetfulness rather than a conscious decision to avoid unwanted phone calls. No matter the reason, it made for a much more relaxed evening as she settled down to a chicken Caesar salad that she had bought in M&S on her way home, followed by a real treat: a slice of chocolate cheesecake, all washed down with a glass of chilled Pinot Grigio. She felt she deserved to be spoiled after the events of recent days. It was only after she had eaten the last crumb, drunk the last drop of wine, and made a pot of coffee that she allowed herself to think about the day and its problems.

* * *

She really didn't think there was anything more she could do about Jonathon except avoid all contact, so she decided to see if she could find out any more about Timothy Lockwood's mystery illness. She plugged in her laptop and checked her mail. Apart from a large number of offers to enlarge the size of her organ, supply her with cheap medication – more slimming pills than Viagra these days she noted, the cheeky beggars – or congratulating her on winning lotteries she had never entered, there was little of interest so she deleted everything and logged onto the medical chat room-cum-bulletin board she had been on before, asking questions about new cures for eczema.

She was surprised by the number of answers she had received to her initial inquiry; there were obviously a lot of doctors out there with nothing better to do than hang out in chat rooms. A whole conversation seemed to have taken place while she was out of the room, so to speak, so she skipped forward to the conclusion: Chinese herbal medicine used to be excellent but didn't work so well now. Most of the correspondents thought that it had never really worked or that patients probably became immune to it, in a similar manner to the way they became resistant to steroid creams and other mainstream treatments. There was a lot of discussion about alternative therapies in general with the participants split into two distinct camps: those who couldn't see the harm and those that could, and things were getting really quite heated.

Herbs, that old chestnut, she thought. There had been loads of activity in that area in the eighties and nineties, with even some respected hospitals running pilot schemes to assess various concoctions on eczema but, as far as she knew, the interest in it had died out. She typed in a query, asking if anyone knew why Chinese herbal medicine had stopped being so fashionable, was it just that it stopped working after a period of time or was there something more? And then she waited to see if anyone was currently online. Their use would explain the improvement in Timothy's health whilst he was in Hong Kong with his parents. Maybe they had seen a herbal specialist over there? She was surprised at the speed of the response. Dr D told her that one of his patients had done wonderfully well ten or more years ago and had been distraught when the particular blend of herbs she used were withdrawn for safety reasons. The mix she had used had subsequently been banned in this country.

Callie asked him what were the safety reasons that led to the herbs being banned and the response came quickly: dangerous side effects, although his patient hadn't suffered any, he hastened to add.

Callie thanked him and went back to med-online, searching on Chinese herbal medicines and side effects.

There were numerous results and she slowly started working her way through them, but a pattern soon emerged. Mixes containing aristolochic acid obtained from the herb Mutong were associated with some cases of renal failure. Well, Timothy's kidneys seemed to be working just fine, so it wasn't that. She read on and finally found an article that caught her attention: Chinese herbal medicine used for eczema was thought to have caused acute hepatic necrosis in six cases in one study, and two in another, although which of the commonly used herbs and alkaloids in the mix actually caused the problem was unknown. Dictamnus and Paeonia were concluded to be the main suspects, either on their own or in combination.

Callie knew that the liver was vital in detoxifying alkaloids and the report seemed to think that abnormal liver enzymes in some people might predispose them to acute reactions to certain alkaloids found in these herbs. This seemed not to be a problem in China or for people of Chinese ethnicity so the article postulated that it could be a western liver enzyme variant that caused these acute toxic reactions. Whatever the cause, the result of these cases, and several other side effects from herbs used for sleep problems, had led to a severe clampdown on what was allowed, with some herbs and herb mixes being banned outright and others having their use severely restricted. The result meant that Chinese herbal medicine was much safer now but, in some cases, also much less potent and it followed on that they were also not so effective. So, that was why they became less fashionable, in eczema at least.

Callie sat back and thought about this and what it meant in relation to her patient, Timothy Lockwood.

She didn't believe for one moment that the fact that his eczema cleared up whilst he was in Hong Kong and his parents would have easy access to herbal remedies that were banned in Europe was a coincidence. Callie looked at the carriage clock on her mantelpiece. It was eight o'clock and, it seemed to her, as good a time as any to visit the Lockwoods.

* * *

There were few lights on when Callie drove onto the gravel driveway and parked behind one of the two cars already there.

Good, she thought, they must both be in. She rang the bell quickly, not giving herself a chance to change her mind.

The door was opened by Mrs Lockwood, looking rather bleary-eyed and dishevelled, a large glass of wine in her hand as usual.

"Oh, it's you." It didn't seem to occur to her that a doctor visiting late at night without having been called was strange, and she held the door open wide for Callie to come in.

Philip Lockwood was in the living room, a half-empty whisky bottle open in front of him. They had clearly been drinking for quite some time.

Mrs Lockwood flopped into an armchair and indicated vaguely for Callie to follow suit.

"Would you like a drink?" His voice was slightly slurred but, thankfully, he still seemed to be in control.

"No, thank you, I wanted to ask you some questions about Timothy, if that's okay?"

"Fire away, if you really think it will help."

Mrs Lockwood hiccupped and took another sip of her drink.

"They said he probably isn't going to make it," she explained with a sniff. "Can't find him a new liver in time they said, as his own one's stopped working pretty much completely. They'll try but–"

"I'm sorry to hear that, Mrs Lockwood." Callie turned to her husband, "and Mr Lockwood, but what I wanted to ask about was Timothy's eczema."

"Didn't you hear what my wife just said, Dr Hughes?" Philip Lockwood was at that slightly belligerent stage of drunkenness that warned Callie that she would have to tread carefully, "Timothy is dying, as good as dead already, and you're worrying about his eczema? Believe me, it's not going to be a problem once he's been cremated."

Mrs Lockwood began to quietly cry.

"Pull yourself together for God's sake, Victoria." Her husband was less than sympathetic with her and then turned to Callie. "This isn't exactly helping, you know."

Callie bit back a retort that it was his attitude that was causing most of the problems and tried to be more diplomatic.

"I understand, Mr Lockwood, but bear with me a moment, it honestly might help." She took a deep breath and started again. "Now, Timothy had really bad eczema and all the conventional treatments didn't seem to work, right?"

"It was awful." Mrs Lockwood fished a tissue out of her sleeve and wiped her nose. "He had these red scaly patches all over. He was teased terribly at school."

Philip Lockwood poured himself some more whisky, sighed and looked at his watch pointedly. Callie ignored him.

"But it cleared up when you went to Hong Kong?"

"Yes, we went to a lot of doctors—"

"The best in the world. Cost a lot but they found it, the treatment that worked," Philip Lockwood cut in. "You should have seen him before, covered in all these oozing scabs, it was disgusting, I couldn't bear to be seen with him."

"You never were seen with him. Wouldn't have let him out of the house if you'd had your way."

"And who could blame me?"

"And what treatment was it, the one that worked?" Callie tried to stop the bickering.

"A herbal tea," Mrs Lockwood carried on, "tasted disgusting but it was like a miracle."

"And is he still using it?"

Even though Callie was addressing her remarks to Mrs Lockwood she could feel the husband tense at this question.

"Oh no, we stopped it once we left Hong Kong. The doctor there said he'd been on it long enough but we could have it again if Tim really needed it, once he'd had a break. But the eczema didn't come back. He'd been cured."

"He didn't give you a supply to bring back here with you?" Callie was puzzled.

"No. But I was up in London and took the prescription into a shop in Chinatown, I thought I'd get some just in case, but they said they couldn't fill it, something about some of the ingredients not being allowed in this country."

"So, you knew he couldn't take it over here?"

"Stupid red tape. Just because it comes from outside the E.C. or something like that. No real scientific reason not to allow it here, just bureaucracy."

Philip Lockwood gave her a look that challenged her to disagree, so she did.

"Actually, some Chinese herbal medicines were banned in this country a few years ago because of toxic side effects. Particularly liver toxicity in eczema remedies."

Victoria Lockwood looked closely at Callie, trying to focus her befuddled mind and work through the meaning of what she had just said.

"What rubbish." Philip Lockwood was less slow to see where she was heading. "It's just a few herbs."

"Deadly nightshade is just a herb, Mr Lockwood, belladonna, hemlock, strychnine: just a few herbs. That's why we insist on everything being tested. To make sure that it is safe."

"Yes but—" he was about to bluster but his wife cut in this time.

"Does it matter, anyway? Tim hasn't taken the tea since we left Hong Kong so, if it was the herbs that caused it, his illness, why did it take so long?"

Callie looked at Philip Lockwood and said nothing. The silence stretched on with Mrs Lockwood looking from one to the other until the penny dropped.

"He's still taking it, Philip?"

Philip said nothing.

"His night-time drink. He always makes his own night-time drink." Her voice was rising in volume and tone as she got into her stride. "You've been sending him the medicine and he's still taking it? Even when the doctor over there said not for more than six months? Philip, how could you?" She launched herself at her husband, fists flailing at his chest, her glass of wine, his whisky and the bottle all sent flying. She was shouting now, almost screaming at him.

"You've killed him, you've killed my son."

Callie pulled Mrs Lockwood back and held her as she sobbed, helping her back into her chair.

"There, there, now. It may be okay, if he stops taking it. His liver may recover." She glared at Philip. "I hope he's not got it with him in hospital or that, if he has, he can't make it for himself in there."

Philip Lockwood continued to say nothing.

"Where is it? What have you done with the tea?"

"I didn't know. I swear."

"Where is the tea?" Callie was not going to let him off the hook. "You can't seriously prefer your son to be dead than have eczema?"

Philip Lockwood seemed to sag as the full enormity of his actions began to get through.

"I made some up and put it in a drinks bottle for him, but he's so sick now, he's probably not drinking it anyway."

"Well, you'd better ring the hospital right now." Callie was tight-lipped with anger. "And tell them exactly what you've done, Mr Lockwood, and you'd better hope and pray that the liver damage is not irreversible. If your son dies, I'll make sure the coroner knows exactly why he did. He died because you couldn't bear to be seen with a scabby son."

Philip Lockwood looked as if he was about to argue but Callie was having none of it.

"Call the hospital, now!"

Obediently, he reached for the phone.

Chapter 29

First thing the next morning, Callie called the liver unit at King's College Hospital and spoke to the ward sister. Tim had lapsed into a coma, but she confirmed that Mr Lockwood had confessed to having been dosing his son with herbal tea and that the tea had been sent for analysis, although the mother had also given them the prescription, as written by the Chinese doctor. It certainly contained some herbs that had been withdrawn from use. However, they weren't hopeful that the liver would recover because even though, according to Philip Lockwood, Tim hadn't had any of the tea for several days already, his condition was still deteriorating. It was the consultant's opinion that it was too late to save him.

Callie put down the receiver and closed her eyes. It was a real blow that the hospital didn't think Timothy was going to pull through. Overnight she had managed to convince herself that he would get better. If only she had realised the problem earlier.

"Looks like you are in urgent need of some chocolate." Linda interrupted her thoughts and Callie opened her eyes to see her holding out the biscuit tin.

"Somehow I don't think that's the answer."

"No, but even if it doesn't help, it doesn't hurt, either."

Callie took a biscuit and Linda put down the tin and sat next to her.

"It's not your fault, Callie."

"Isn't it?" Callie was feeling really miserable. "I'm beginning to think Hugh is right. By trying to do two jobs, I'm not giving either one the time and commitment they need."

"How would you being a full time GP have helped the boy?"

"I would have spent more time trying to work out what was wrong with him and maybe I would have come to the right diagnosis earlier, in time to save him."

"And some GPs would have never bothered to look for the cause once they'd referred him on and others could have spent from now until next year checking out the internet or their textbooks and still never got there."

"I know, but I" – she jabbed a finger at her own chest to emphasise her point – "I would have got there earlier if I hadn't been distracted by other things and that's what's important. I know I failed Timothy because of my other work and that's what I have to live with."

There wasn't really anything else Linda could say to make it better so she withdrew and let Callie sit there feeling guilty. The office phone was constantly ringing with people trying to be fitted in to morning surgery or asking for visits, and the post had arrived and needed sorting. Life had to go on, no matter what: there would always be more patients needing help and she knew that Callie would snap out of it as soon as she was faced with another sick child, or adult, who needed her attention.

* * *

She knew she shouldn't be here, standing outside Jonathon's home, it was the sort of thing that the worst bunny boilers did in films. It hadn't been hard finding out where he lived – if it had meant having to break into personnel and steal his records she wouldn't be here – but she found the address on the electoral roll in the library. As simple as that. Callie had to see him, tell him what she thought of him. She could have accosted him at the hospital once, *if*, he'd gone back to work, but the thought of a scene, in front of people she might have to work with again, would be far too embarrassing. She just wanted to say a few choice words and go, although she rather hoped that his wife would be there to hear it and, as there were two cars parked outside the elegant Victorian home, it looked like she might be in luck. Callie took a deep breath and pressed the doorbell. After a few moments, during which Callie began to change her mind and wondered if she could do a runner, the door opened and Jonathon stood there, expression changing from mild irritation to fury very quickly.

"What in God's name are you doing here?" he hissed.

"Who is it?" a voice asked from inside the house.

"Just someone from work," he called back inside, before pulling the door closed behind him and taking a step towards Callie.

"Go away, for Christ's sake."

Callie stood her ground.

"I wanted to tell you just what a sad, despicable excuse for a human being you are. A two-faced, violent, arrogant, bastard." Even Callie had to admit that bad language had its place and, mild as her language would seem to many, she could feel it help release her anger and let it go. "You led me on, letting me believe you were single–"

"Are you trying to say you didn't know I was married?"

"I don't go out with married men and you didn't exactly go out of your way to make the position clear, quite the opposite in fact."

"It's never polite to mention the wife to the mistress."

Callie flinched at hearing herself described as a mistress. It was an almost physical slap in the face. She would never allow herself to be one, not knowingly.

"Well, excuse me for not knowing the etiquette in extra-marital affairs, it is not a situation I've been in before."

"Don't tell me you actually thought our little fling was serious?"

Callie flushed and he laughed at her.

"You did, didn't you? You probably even had visions of white weddings and heard the patter of tiny feet. God, you're pathetic."

He hadn't noticed the door behind him open as he spoke and Callie was delighted to see the hard-faced woman behind him was not happy, not happy at all. Suddenly Jonathon realised that Callie was looking over his shoulder, or perhaps he had felt the sudden drop in temperature as the ice queen came out of the house, but he turned around and visibly paled.

"I'm sorry, dear, let me introduce you to Dr Hughes, from the hospital, she was just asking advice—"

"Get rid of the whore and come inside, Jonathon," was all she said before going back inside, but the look of disgust she gave her husband and the cringing fear on his face was a joy for Callie to behold.

"You'd better do as your beloved wife tells you," Callie said and walked back to her car smiling to herself. They deserved each other and she sincerely hoped that they would both be truly miserable together but now she felt she could move on. Jonathon was history.

* * *

Her feeling of elation at causing a certain amount of friction in Jonathon's marriage didn't last long. He might be in the doghouse for a month or two, but she had no illusions; he would be out and about, having affairs again before too long. His wife probably knew that too. After a busy evening surgery, and having heard that there was no change in Timothy's condition, Callie decided the only way to lift her looming depression was exercise. She rang Kate, and after much cajoling and promises of a decent dinner afterwards, managed to persuade her friend that it really was a good idea to meet at the gym. Callie knew she herself hadn't been all that regularly, only once in the last couple of weeks but, judging by the fact that Kate didn't seem to remember how to sign in, or even where to find the changing rooms, Callie thought it must have been considerably longer since she last went.

The gym echoed with the noise of metal weights crashing against metal rests, the grunts of the more serious body builders and fitness fanatics and Kate moaning about how tired she felt as she ambled into the cardio section behind her. The air-conditioning was set low, causing goose bumps on Callie's arms as soon as she stepped out of the changing room in her T-shirt and joggers, but she knew it was only going to be for a short time; she expected to fully warm up in a matter of minutes so she tried to position herself as close as possible to one of the vents for maximum cooling effect.

After twenty minutes on the cross-trainer, Callie used some free weights and then moved onto the rowing machine. She noticed that Kate seemed to have disappeared; she certainly wasn't in the cardio section. Callie looked round and quickly spotted her, chatting to one of the fitness instructors. One of the young, male fitness instructors. He didn't look much over twenty-one and was busy apparently showing her how to use one of the weight machines, but Kate wasn't looking at the machine and neither was he much. Callie smiled, that was so like Kate: Callie would leave the gym exhausted but virtuous and Kate would leave with a date.

After an hour, Callie decided she had tortured her body enough and she went back to the changing rooms to shower. Kate was already in the crowded locker room, drying off her voluptuous naked body with a lack of self-consciousness that Callie had never managed to achieve. She always used the curtained-off changing cubicles, or wrapped her body in a towel as she awkwardly pulled clothes on or off, even though her figure was nothing to be ashamed of. There was no way she could be like Kate, who seemed to have no qualms about walking around the room completely starkers and often teased Callie about being a prude.

"Go on, strip off. Let everyone look at you. If I had a body like yours I'd want everyone to see it and weep," Kate would tell her, but Callie just couldn't bring herself to do it.

Callie was still dressing after her shower when Kate was ready to go.

"I'll meet you in the bar next door," she called as she hurried out, clearly having arranged to meet somebody and leaving Callie to worry about playing gooseberry for the rest of the evening. She took her time dressing, to give Kate a bit of a start, and decided that if it was clear her friend was interested in the man – and when was she not? – she would politely make her excuses, plead work pressures or some such, and beat a hasty retreat. However, when she got to the bar, Kate was there, nursing a pint and a half-eaten packet of crisps, on her own.

"What's happened to him, then? Blown him out already?" she asked.

"Working. He joined me for his fifteen-minute break but he doesn't finish until ten and then he's going to take me for an Indian. So" – she looked at her watch – "you've got to keep me company for another hour and a half. What are you drinking?"

"What about food for me? I can't drink for an hour and a half and not eat, and I'm certainly not going to go with you for an Indian meal at that time of night. I wouldn't get a wink of sleep."

"One: you weren't invited anyway."

"Charming." Callie pretended to be hurt.

"And two: I certainly hope I don't get a wink of sleep." Kate grinned and Callie couldn't help laughing.

"You are such a—"

"Slut." Kate finished for her. "But you love me, really." Kate grabbed a menu from the bar and passed it to Callie. "If you're starving they at least do food here and I promise not to pick at your plate, well, maybe a bit but that rather depends on what you choose." Kate leant over and peered at the menu as Callie read it. The girl behind the bar came over, expectantly.

"I think I'll have the chicken fajitas with salad but hold the spicy potato wedges." Callie decided.

"Don't you dare!" Kate interjected and turned to the barmaid. "Make it a large portion of wedges, I'm starving, and how about a drink?" she asked Callie.

"Fizzy mineral water with a slice of lime," Callie told the girl. "I'm driving," she added as Kate looked aghast.

"You are way too healthy, you know."

"I'm a doctor, I have to lead by example."

"Quick! I need a doctor who smokes, drinks and is morbidly obese."

Callie laughed, although she could think of quite a few colleagues who would qualify.

"Did you really go to that slime-ball's house and give him the what-for?" Kate asked.

"Yes, although you probably wouldn't rate it as a what-for, just a bit of a telling off. Still, it made me feel better, particularly the look on his wife's face when she saw me."

"I'll bet. I hope she makes his life hell."

"So do I. He certainly wouldn't want to risk losing all the status and money she brings to their marriage." Callie's drink had arrived so they clinked glasses and she spent a moment or two savouring the thought of Jonathon being made to beg forgiveness.

Once Callie's meal arrived they talked of Timothy's chances but, whether it was Kate's cheerful common sense, or the endorphins released from exercising, Callie no longer felt quite so down about life.

"I'd hazard a guess that it's not been the best week of your life, what with that bastard Kane and everything." Kate spoke between mouthfuls of slightly soggy, and not very spicy, potato wedges.

"That is an understatement." Callie conceded.

"Have you heard anything more about the murders?"

"Not really. Obviously they know that Jimmy Allen can't have done them, seeing as he was in custody at the time of the last one, but their new obsession seems to be Jonathon and I just can't see it."

"Be nice to see him banged up for life, though, wouldn't it?"

"Yes, but it won't stick, I'm sure. I know they're going through all the CCTV footage: they had been concentrating on Jade's usual haunts around town but they've collected everything from the Old Town as well, now that they know she was there, although a lot of it has gone, been recorded over."

"What about on The Priory Estate? They must have cameras there."

"All moved to watch over where the renovation is taking place to catch people walking off with the building materials. So, nothing covering Jade's block or her way into the estate."

"There are loads of cameras around town, if they're going to cover the other girl, what's her name? Denise? Her route back from the karaoke, and the hospital as well, they've got tons of cameras there, they must have teams of people checking the footage."

"No, that's the problem, I think they've left most of it for poor Jayne Hales. She's been seconded into the team to help and has been given all the boring jobs. She'll be completely boss-eyed at this rate. It will take her months to get through the relevant tapes, by which time the real killer will have disappeared."

"It's spooky, isn't it? To think that somewhere there's a CCTV camera watching you."

Callie pushed away her plate and let Kate finish the remaining wedges, which were now tepid as well as soggy.

"But they are what catches criminals, and will probably be what catches this man, rather than old-fashioned detecting. And if they concentrate on the hospital pictures, they should catch him soon." Callie wasn't sure who she was trying to convince, Kate or herself.

"Question is, how many more girls will he have killed in the meantime?"

And that, Callie knew, really was the issue.

Chapter 30

It was mid-afternoon and Callie was having a cathartic sort out of her wardrobe, trying to keep her mind off the terrible state of her love life. If she was to rate her recent affair with Jonathon on a scale of one to ten, it would definitely be a minus figure, she thought as she looked at the flimsy low-cut sequin covered top that she had worn on her trawl of the singles' bars. She was about to consign it to the charity bag when she stopped.

It was a Saturday night and she didn't have a date.

Nothing new there, she thought.

Kate was out with her new man, the fitness instructor. Callie was going to spend a night in, with just a baked potato and the television for company. She was a sad excuse for a human being who would die alone and single if she didn't do something desperate.

But just how desperate was she?

* * *

The Adelaide, last resort of the desperate, had an entrance that looked as though it was quite used to disgruntled customers kicking it on the way out. Callie assumed it was on the way out, because she couldn't imagine that anyone would be mad enough to try and kick their way in to the place.

Inside, the actual club was down a steep flight of stairs, and was dimly lit, presumably so that the customers didn't notice that it was in dire need of refurbishment or, failing that, at least a good clean. Callie approached the bar, perched on a distressingly sticky, vinyl-covered bar stool and surveyed the scene. It was still quite early, only eleven o'clock, and not many people had reached the level of frustration needed to end up here.

In planning how to play the evening, Callie had decided that getting there early would be a good idea and that had been pretty much the extent of her strategy. She had little idea of what she was going to do, just that she wanted to check the place out before many people had arrived and have a chat with the staff about last Saturday night when the latest victim, Caro the nurse and her friends, had come to the club. Eventually, having waited at the bar for what seemed like an eternity, a bored young man dressed in low slung jeans and a T-shirt declaring that he was a sex god in training came over to ask for her order.

Callie asked for a white wine and soda and attempted to engage the barman in conversation as he mixed her drink.

"Is it always this quiet in here?"

"Till late, yeah."

"How late?"

"Late late, when everywhere else is closed, right?"

"Get a lot of nurses in, do you?"

He looked at her suspiciously.

"I charge fifty quid for interviews."

"Nice try but I'm not a journalist."

"Gotta try, haven't you? Worked on the other three." He nodded his head towards two middle-aged-but-still-trying-to-look-trendy men and a hard-faced woman dressed for a night on the town, each sitting on their own and watching her intently. Callie thought she recognised the woman from the local television news. It seemed as though everyone had had the same idea as her.

She turned back to the bar as the barman leant forward.

"We get all sorts from the hospital in here, lab techs, nurses, porters. They all smoke like chimneys and boy, can they drink. And ready to jump anything with a pulse, too. Must be something about working with sick people, right?"

"And last week?" Callie persisted.

"Yeah, there was a group of four nurses in with the one that got killed. They were here about this time and they left about an hour or so later, said it was 'cos they had to be at work early but that's never stopped them before."

"So, why do you think they left?"

He shrugged again.

"Dunno. Maybe there wasn't anyone interesting in, it was quiet that night, or maybe they were being pestered by a bloke they didn't like, a groper or something, but they didn't say nothing to me or the bouncer I asked." He caught Callie's look of distaste. "Hey, it happens, all right?"

He wandered off to serve an overweight wannabe lothario who looked as though he had already had too much to drink and Callie took the opportunity to study the club. There seemed to be a lot of marks on the deep puce walls where notices had been put up and either taken down or moved elsewhere. The few notices that remained were so badly scuffed and, in some instances, graffiti covered, that it was hard to read what they said anyway. Ideally, she wanted to find herself a secluded corner where she would be able to sit out of sight and watch people come and go while, hopefully, remaining unmolested herself. One look inside the club had told her that she wouldn't be finding her soulmate and life partner in here but she would certainly find a wide variety of bacteria. All she was hoping for throughout the rest of the evening was to see if she could spot any likely regulars who might have been in last week and who might have seen what made the nurses leave early. She was already getting a picture of the sort of person who went to the club, although that impression might improve when a few more people arrived; it certainly couldn't get any worse. She was pretty sure that whoever killed Caro had followed her back to the hospital. Something had happened to spook the girl into leaving prematurely and it seemed too much of a coincidence that she should encounter a serious groper here and then run into a serial killer elsewhere, all in one night. But what did Callie know? Maybe there were millions of perverts out there, just waiting to pounce.

She spotted a table in a corner so dark she had to get quite close to be sure that no one was already sitting there and she surreptitiously gave the faux-leather banquette a quick wipe down with a tissue before sliding herself as far into the corner as possible. Taking a sip of her drink she settled back. She mustn't rush it, it was going to be a long night and she didn't want to have to make too many trips to the bar or the loo as both were the other side of the room and she would have to cross the currently empty dance floor in full, intensely scrutinising view of the other occupants of the club, to reach them.

The barman had been right when he said the place didn't get busy until everywhere else had closed. Callie glanced at her watch for the tenth time and was despondent to see that it was only just gone midnight. The club was still half empty; other than the journalists who clearly thought she was one of them, there were just a few sad singles peering dejectedly round, waiting for someone interesting to come in. Callie had tried talking to the couple of them who had ventured over and who looked as if they might be regulars but neither had been in last week. Both had been delighted to talk to her, and disappointed once she made it clear that she wasn't interested in them personally, but neither had been overly persistent or had tried to grope her. Clearly used to rejection by now, they had settled resignedly back on their stools and left her alone. Her fingers tapped against her glass and her head thumped in time to the music that was turned up way too high considering that there was no crush of bodies to soak it up. She was so tired she could barely keep her eyes open. How much longer could she stand it?

At last the door burst open and a mixed group of thirty-somethings crashed into the room, excited to be in such a notorious club, laughing loudly and acting as if they owned the place. They were soon followed by a younger group of boys on a grab-a-granny night, a couple of women in their forties who might just do for them and a strangely mixed group intent on carrying on partying, or at least pouring as much alcohol down their throats as was humanly possible, no matter what.

The dance floor was soon full, and the noise level increased by an alarming number of decibels as the DJ pumped up the volume. If Callie's head had been hurting before, it now felt like it was going to explode. There was no way she was going to be able to talk to anyone over the music and she was about to write the evening off to experience and leave when one of the young lads came and plonked himself down beside her. Callie realised a bit late the downside of sitting in the corner on a banquette, namely that there was no way out if anyone sat next to you, not without climbing over them, anyway.

The lad looked as if he was barely out of school, with his spiky gelled hair and no-need-to-shave-yet look, and something about the way he kept glancing over at his mates at the bar told Callie that he had probably been dared to chat her up. She was not amused. She was not a granny.

"So, what's your name then, love?" he bellowed.

"Emily," Callie replied. She had no intention of saying anything to this boy that might help him trace her later; a toyboy with a crush was the last thing she needed. "What's yours?"

"Paul," he replied and then looked round for inspiration as to what to say next. "Do you come here often?" was the best he could come up with, despite thinking hard.

"No, do you?" Callie was trying not to sound bored, just not very effectively.

"No. First time," he shouted and slid his arm along the back of the seat so that it was poised to drape over her shoulder. After a bit of long-distance encouragement from his friends he reached across and slipped his other hand onto her knee.

Callie picked it up and popped it back on his own leg.

"Excuse me." Her tone was distinctly icy. "I need the loo." There was an awkward shuffle as he had to get out of the way to let her out and she hurried across the packed dance floor, wanting to hold her hands up in the air in order not to touch anyone or anything too intimate, but restraining herself. Once she was safely in the ladies' room, she stood patiently in the queue and eavesdropped on the conversations of those in front of her.

She quickly realised that she should have been in the toilets the whole evening. Not only was it quieter and certainly the best place to chat or listen in on people who were chatting, despite being a little cramped, it had the distinct advantage of being ladies only.

"She was always a bit of a slapper, that one. Surprised she pulled a doctor, though, even if she met him at work," an overweight and very under-dressed woman was saying to a skinny friend with a face like a plucked chicken.

"Yeah," her friend agreed. "You ever had a doctor?" she continued as Callie tried not to look as though she was listening to them. She was pretty sure they must be talking about the victim.

"Nah, his type don't come in here, I'd've thought, but I did have an X-ray bloke once. Nice bum, shame about the rest."

They laughed and moved forward as two women came out of the stalls, but continued their conversation from adjoining cubicles.

"I wouldn't want to shag a doctor, mind, it's like you don't know where their hands have been all day, do you?"

"Do ya think seeing people's bodies all day would put you off sex?"

"Nah, my Terry looks at them all day on the internet and he's still up for it."

"You lucky cow."

"Lucky? Have you seen my Terry?"

They came out still laughing.

"Did you know Caro?" Callie asked them, standing back to let the woman behind her go into the cubicle ahead of her. The fat one looked at her suspiciously for a moment.

"What's it to you?"

"I knew Caro from work," Callie half-lied. "I just want to find out what happened to her. Did you see her last week?"

"Yeah, but she and her mates left early."

"Lucky for us." Her friend chipped in. "They always nick the good blokes, nurses do."

"Why did they leave, do you know?"

"Couple of them were really pissed." The skinny one was tweaking her rigid hair in the tiny mirror, whilst the fat one tried to see past to slap on more lipstick. Callie couldn't help but notice that neither had bothered to wash their hands.

"But they'd only just arrived."

"You must know what nurses are like if you work with them. Drinks are too expensive here, so they neck some supermarket vodka before coming out, only, like I say, a couple of them had overdone it. Even so, I think they might have stayed but that Caro had a go at some fat bloke who asked her to dance."

"Thought she was too good for him. Stuck up cow." The skinny one sniffed with disapproval, as if no one was too good for someone they met at the Adelaide.

"So, she flounced out and her mates all followed."

"This bloke she had a go at, do you know him?"

They both shook their heads.

"Might've seen him here before but not to speak to."

"He knew her though, or claimed to, but she denied all knowledge, said she couldn't be expected to remember losers like him."

"And he left soon after they did, I remember," the skinny one added.

"Do you think it was him then? That killed her? Not the doctor?" The two women were clearly excited by the thought that they might have actually seen the killer.

"I don't know," Callie told them, "but it's possible, isn't it?"

Chapter 31

When Callie came out of the ladies, she had to restrain herself from punching the air in elation. At last! She had a lead. She would go to the hospital first thing tomorrow morning and find Claire Crehan. She needed to ask her if she knew who it was Caro had seen here at the club and, if Claire did, then she had to get her to tell Miller, if she hadn't already done so. It was quite possible that Miller knew all about the fat man and had discounted him as a suspect, or maybe he was just too obsessed by the thought that Jonathon was the killer to bother looking at anyone else. Callie suspected the latter. Either way, she needed to make sure he had found out who the man was and that he had checked him out thoroughly but equally, she didn't want to go to him herself and admit that she'd been out snooping again. She suspected he wouldn't be pleased. That's why she had to get Claire to do it.

As she made her way towards the door, Callie's face dropped and the elation evaporated as she recognised Miller himself standing between her and the exit. She stopped dead in her tracks, trying to think what on earth she could do. He was the last person she wanted to see right now but she couldn't help giving him a second look all the same. He was casually dressed in black jeans, black T-shirt, and black jacket; a bottle of Mexican lager, untouched, in his hand. There were no two ways about it, he looked good, and he was attracting a certain amount of interest amongst the ladies although he was acting as if he was completely unaware of their attention.

Why on earth did he have to be here? Now? He was almost certainly undercover, doing much the same as she had been, and if he saw her, he was going to be very angry with her for getting in the way of his investigation again. Why, oh why, had she come? It had seemed like such a good idea at the time. And, in fact, it had been, she told herself, firmly. She had got some good information, hadn't she? All the same, she had to get out before he noticed her. She looked around for an escape route but there didn't seem to be one; the only way out involved passing right next to him to get to the main door. Callie turned to go back into the ladies' room, wondering how long she could feasibly stay in there. Maybe there was a way out from the back? A fire escape, perhaps? Surely there ought to be an emergency exit of some sort? As she hurried back towards the toilets, she felt someone grab her shoulder. She turned and found herself frowning straight into Miller's eyes. Miller's furious eyes.

"What the hell do you think you're doing?" he asked, shouting above the music.

"Going to the loo," she shouted back, as calmly as she could, given the noise.

"I think not. Outside. Now." And he pulled her firmly but gently towards the exit.

"I need my coat," she said, breaking free from his grasp and stopping at the cloakroom, seething. He had absolutely no right to treat her like this, as if she were one of his employees or a suspect. She was shaking with anger as she handed over her cloakroom ticket and waited for the girl to find her coat. When she located it at last, Callie grabbed it from her and was still pulling it on as she stormed out of the club.

Miller stood directly in front of her, forcing her to stop and look at him.

"So?" he asked belligerently.

"So what?" If he thought she was going to make it easy for him he was sadly mistaken.

"So, what are you doing here?" Callie had finally managed to get her coat on and started to walk round Miller.

"I came out for a drink."

"Rubbish! You've been snooping again, like when you and your friend went to the karaoke evening." He was keeping pace with her, arguing as they walked briskly back towards the Old Town.

"There's no law against it."

"You're messing with things you know nothing about and interfering in my investigation."

"Really? Like your investigation is getting anywhere."

"And yours is?"

"Actually, yes." She couldn't keep the smugness from her voice and he knew she had something.

"What do you mean?" She had his interest now, no doubt about it.

"I just found out from one of women in there that Caro Sharpe had a confrontation with a man at the club on the night she died. A man who seemed to know her. And also that he left shortly after she and her friends did. Or did you already know that?"

Miller stopped walking and Callie turned and regarded him triumphantly. She had him there and she knew it: he hadn't known about the incident.

"No. I didn't know that, but I will look into it. You have my word on it."

"You'd better do that, Detective Inspector Miller, because I will be checking up on you, you have my word on that." She turned on her heel and stalked off, pleased with herself and with the fact that she had set him so completely and comprehensively back on his heels.

She wondered what he would do now. Would he follow her? Try and question her some more and get her descriptions of the women she spoke to? Or would he go back in and try and find them for himself? She didn't pause for one moment to find out, walking quickly away from him through the underpass and along the sea front without so much as a backwards glance. She couldn't hear his footsteps behind her so she assumed he had gone back into the club.

She slowed down a little as she walked past the long-closed souvenir shops and cafés, letting her coat flap open despite the cool night air. After the heat and close atmosphere of the club it was nice to be outside, warmed by the healthy glow of self-righteousness.

The Old Town was quiet; most people were safely tucked up in bed at this time of night but it wasn't until she hurried along George Street and the last of the drunken, late night revellers had disappeared that she began to feel a little uneasy. She felt a tingling at the back of her head, as if someone was watching her. She turned quickly but could see no one. Maybe it was Miller after all, making sure she went straight home and didn't visit any more nightclubs. She hurried on. The feeling of being followed persisted. She hoped it was Miller. It was gone two in the morning, she was alone and she had been deliberately trying to look for a man who was a serial killer of lone women. Right now, that didn't seem like it had been quite such a smart idea.

Callie turned right at the end of George Street, back to the sea front, thinking that she might be able to get a taxi from the rank there but it was empty. She looked up and down the main street and the promenade but there was no one in sight and no taxis around either. The deserted mini fairground was dark and the carousels and roller coasters looked vaguely sinister without their bright lights and loud music disturbing the peace.

Callie hurried along the front, towards the tall, dark shapes of the net sheds, silhouetted against the night sky. She wanted to get home as quickly as possible and there seemed little point sticking to the main roads when they were as quiet as the backstreets so she took the narrow stairway straight up the East Cliff. She would go the shortest possible route, through the twittens, to get to her home. To safety.

As she hurried up the steps she paused to catch her breath and then froze, hardly daring to breath. What was that? She was sure that she had heard something. She waited a moment, listening hard, but there was nothing now.

"Go away, I am quite capable of taking care of myself," she said clearly, half of her hoping that it was Miller seeing her safely home and that he would ignore her request to go away, the other half indignant that he would treat her as some sort of weak and vapid woman in need of seeing safely home. Who was she kidding? Right now, she would be delighted to see him, even if she wouldn't necessarily show it.

She quickly ran up the next flight of steps and reached the road at the top. She looked along the street to the left and then back down the steps. There was no one visible but she could swear that she could hear footsteps some way behind her. She raced along the road and took the next shortcut up towards her own lane and the safety of home, positive now that she could hear someone behind her. She was taking the steps two at a time, running along the roughly paved horizontal sections, hoping fervently that she knew the path well enough that she wouldn't trip on a forgotten step or miss a turning in the dark. She could hear that the footsteps were gaining on her, despite her almost headlong flight. Panicking, she ran on and, startled by a cat that jumped out of nowhere, caught her foot on a plant pot partially blocking the way, going sprawling and banging her knee and jarring her wrist as she fell.

The cat had fled but the footsteps were louder, closer, accompanied by loud, wheezing breaths. The breaths of someone pretty unfit and unused to running uphill. Barely pausing, she sprang up and continued up the path at a run again. She was nearly there, nearly at the top where it opened out into her own lane, only a hundred yards from her front door and safety. She could still hear the heavy, laboured breathing behind her, but at a slightly greater distance; whoever was chasing her was finding it a struggle to keep up. She put in one last effort and broke out of the twitten and into the reassuring amber glow of a streetlight, gasping too loudly to hear if her follower was still close.

"You should go to the gym and get fit, Miller, then you'd be able to keep up." She shouted with the last of her breath and peered down the alley but could see no one in the shadows. She turned and was walking briskly towards her house, pulling her front door keys from her pocket at the same time.

"Are you all right?" Miller's voice shouted back at her from a distance.

She turned, relieved that her phantom, wheezing follower had been him after all but then dropped her keys in surprise. Miller was way down the far end of the lane, running towards her. She looked at where the twitten opened out under the streetlight, where moments ago she had heard footsteps getting closer, almost on her, and the heavy breathing, so loud she half wondered if it was her own. It hadn't been him behind her, couldn't have been him, not if he had come up the road.

He reached her, barely out of breath, clearly fit. A worried expression on his face as he registered her muddy knees and how she held her injured arm against her body.

"Someone was following me. Through there," she said, looking at the narrow gap between the two houses. She was shaking, exhausted by her run up the steep hill and her heart was pounding, as much from the adrenaline released by her fear as from the exertion.

He went down the first couple of steps.

"Is there anyone there?" he called but there was no reply and Callie couldn't hear anything other than the slight echo as his voice bounced off the canyon-like walls of the alley.

"There's no one there now," he told her, unnecessarily. "And it certainly wasn't me. I didn't think you'd be stupid enough to take the alleys, so I came up the main road."

Callie was far too frightened to take offence. Now that he said it, it did seem a bit stupid, more than a bit, in fact, and it wasn't even the first time she'd done something like that, either. Miller bent down and picked up her keys, took her firmly by her good elbow and walked her towards the front door of her house.

"There. Home safe." He had opened the door and was holding out her keys, looking at her with concern.

Probably wondering if she was going to come over all faint again, she thought.

Callie almost snatched the keys from him and stuck them straight in her pocket, trying to disguise the fact that her hands were shaking so badly that she was worried she might drop them again.

"Thank you," she said meekly, and went into the hallway before turning back. "Would you like a cup of coffee or something?" she asked, expecting him to refuse, to say he had to go back to the Adelaide, or home, or any other excuse he could come up with on the spur of the moment.

"Yes, that would be good. Thank you." She was too surprised to retract the invite and stepped back, allowing him to follow her into the communal hallway.

Callie wondered how on earth she got herself into these situations as she led the way up the two flights of stairs to her flat, and dug out her keys again to let him in. Why had he accepted? He clearly loathed her. She was nothing more than an irritant to him. So why subject himself to any more of her company than was strictly necessary?

It wasn't until they were both inside the flat that she remembered that she might have a slight problem with providing coffee. She switched on all the lights and closed the curtains, unable to resist a look in case there was anyone watching her or the flat but she couldn't see anyone. Only once the place was snug and secure did she go into the kitchen, anxious to keep busy, do anything to avoid dwelling on being followed home like that, stalked and spied on, beginning to see a pattern emerge. She filled the kettle, switched it on and then took a quick peek in the fridge. What a relief, there was a carton of milk. She gave it a shake and her heart sank. Yes, there was something in it but the contents didn't give a nice reassuring slosh as she shook it, there was a definite delay in the movement, a heaviness about it. She tried pouring a little into the sink and a bit of watery fluid came out before a lump clogged the spout. She wrinkled her nose in disgust at the rancid milk and turned to explain the situation to Miller, only to find him standing at the breakfast bar, watching her with an amused smile on his face. That was the downside of an open plan kitchen.

"I take it black," he said.

"Just as well," she replied. She took two mugs from a cupboard and hesitated. "You don't take sugar, do you?"

"I can live without." She wished that she was more organised, more prepared for unplanned entertaining, or entertaining of any sort for that matter. The sad fact was that she hardly ever had anyone back at her flat except Kate and whenever she came round she always arrived with everything she thought she might want because she knew just how bad her friend was at shopping.

She put the cups on a tray and was about to carry it through to the living area when he came up behind her.

"Let me." He took the tray from her. "Your hands are shaking so much you are bound to spill it."

She swallowed the retort that came automatically to her lips because he was right, she was still feeling a bit shaky, so she followed him meekly through to the living room and settled herself on the sofa, slipping off her shoes and curling her legs up under her, as he carefully placed the tray on the coffee table.

"Have you got anything stronger? Brandy? Whisky?" he asked her.

She pointed to the cupboard where she kept her mother's gin, when she remembered to buy any. There was about an inch left in a quarter bottle of brandy left over from last Christmas and he brought it out.

"That's it, I'm afraid. I'm not really a spirit drinker."

"Well, you are now." And he poured a healthy slug into her coffee before passing it back to her. She took it gingerly and cradled it in her hands.

"Are you warm enough?" He seemed concerned rather than irritated with her, confusing her once again. She wished that she could make this man out.

"I'm fine, well, better than I was, thanks," she reassured him. "It's just a bit of a shock to think that I was followed by someone. Other than you, that is."

He sat on the sofa, keeping a respectable distance between them, and sipped his coffee.

"I didn't see anyone follow you from the club, so we've no reason to think it's the killer."

"Oh great, it's just some other stray perv, that makes me feel much better."

He smiled.

"Now I know you're going to be all right."

She gave him a quizzical look.

"The smart alec comments are back," he explained.

She smiled back and closed her eyes, feeling the brandy begin to smooth down the rough edges of the night.

"Have you ever been to that sort of club before?" she asked him.

"No, not my kind of place at all," he told her, "besides, I'm married."

"There's an air of desperation around it, isn't there? All those sad lonely people, looking for someone, anyone more or less, to take home. Anything rather than spend another night alone. What they don't seem to realise, though, is that sometimes you're better off on your own."

"Not everyone's as bad as Jonathon Kane."

"Granted, it's just that right now it feels like I pick all the ones that are. They are all either bastards or married, or both." The brandy seemed to have gone straight to her head and she felt slightly woozy.

He stood up and went to the window, pulling the curtain aside and looked out.

"Can't see anyone there, but I'll take a walk round before I go."

Callie walked him to the door of her flat. He stopped as he was going out.

"Promise me you won't do that again. Put yourself in danger like that?"

Callie nodded.

"I promise."

"And lock the door after me."

"You can be sure of that."

He smiled and was gone. True to her word, Callie closed the door, locked it, dead-locked it and put the chain on.

Chapter 32

Despite the triple-locked door, Cassie spent the night tossing and turning and felt tired and washed out the next morning. As she read the Sunday papers, avoiding all the articles about the Hastings murders, her mind kept going back over the previous evening and in particular how it had ended. Was she sure she had been followed? Could it have been the murderer? What might have happened if Miller hadn't been there? How could she have been so stupid as to walk home alone? In the end she gave up on the papers. A brisk walk along the promenade, well wrapped up against the wind and rain, finally dispelled the circular questioning and self-recrimination and she was able to spend the evening catching up on paying her bills and answering emails and letters.

Next morning, after a better night's sleep, Callie was confident that she would be able to give at least half her attention to her patients. The first patient on her morning list was Mrs Lockwood, which was puzzling. Had something happened? Callie wondered if she had time to call the hospital, prepare herself for bad news, then decided against it. Whatever the reason for the visit, knowing in advance wouldn't make it any easier.

There was a knock at the door.

"Come in." Callie called out and Mrs Lockwood opened the door, as beautifully turned out as ever. Every bleached hair in place, every manicured nail expertly polished.

"How can I help you, Mrs Lockwood? How's Timothy?"

"Much better the hospital says, although he still seems very weak to me. Apparently his liver is beginning to work again and they think he will make a full recovery."

Mrs Lockwood didn't seem as thrilled about this news as Callie thought she should be.

"He's a very lucky boy. And you're lucky, too."

"I realise that. It was a close call and I appreciate all that you have done for my son. I really can't thank you enough." For a moment her lower lip seemed to quiver, but it was only momentary and then she was all business again, pulling a sheaf of papers from her bag.

"I've been talking to my lawyer and he thinks we need to go back to court to alter the terms of the custody agreement."

Callie took the papers that Mrs Lockwood was holding out to her and started looking at them, unsure of what the woman was expecting her to do.

"Whilst Timothy's father undoubtedly behaved stupidly, I'm not sure how that alters the situation." She flipped to the back page, which seemed to be a breakdown of expenses, including the cost of a live-in nurse, housekeeper and nanny, private home tuition, a staggeringly high premium for private health care and the cost of regular stays in health spas in exotic locations around the world.

"It means I need more money. After all, this is all his fault and it's going to be hard to care for Timothy at home – his insurance alone is going to go rocketing up."

"But you said the hospital think he will make a full recovery."

Mrs Lockwood was having none of that.

"That's easy for them to say. I nearly lost my son, thanks to Philip. The emotional toll, the strain of it all, has been considerable." Even Mrs Lockwood must have realised that this sounded a little selfish; either that or she caught sight of Callie's expression. "I've lost my confidence as a mother," she hurried on, in a more caring tone of voice. "Timothy might relapse. Who can say what these drugs have done to him? I can't let him go to school, it could be too much of a strain on him and the worry would certainly be too much for me." She pointed to the paperwork. "What my lawyer wants is a statement from you about how I need help to care for Tim as a result of Philip's actions, as per the list here" – she pointed to the balance sheet – "and if you could put in a bit about the mental strain on me that would be good as well."

"I am happy to write about the strain on you and Timothy but I can't justify your need for all these expenses, Mrs Lockwood. I have patients with far worse problems coping with much less help and support." Callie pushed the papers back to Mrs Lockwood, who looked surprised.

"Yes, but they don't have rich husbands who damn near killed their child, do they?"

She did have a point, Callie had to concede, but she still didn't feel she could justify claiming such an obscene amount of money, even if Philip Lockwood had behaved like a total plonker.

"Look, I will write a letter, of course I will, but what you and your lawyer claim, that's down to you. I really don't want to know."

It was a compromise that seemed acceptable to Mrs Lockwood.

"Thank you, Dr Hughes. That's all I ask," she stood up, "now I need to get back to the hospital and be with Timothy."

And she left Callie wondering if Mr Lockwood was going to be allowed to visit his son or if he had given up and already left the country.

* * *

Miller sat in the patient's chair in Callie's consulting room and placed a couple of files on her desk.

"I was on my way to the mortuary and thought I'd drop in and check you were okay, in light of what happened Saturday night."

"Did you check to see if it could have been Jonathon following me?" Callie was trying to be brisk and business-like. "Only it occurred to me that it could have been him doing that as well as watching the flat and leaving the silent phone messages."

"Watching the flat? Silent calls?"

"I've been getting a few recently. Didn't I mention it?" Callie tried to sound as if those sorts of things were minor incidents, little irritants that happened all the time, instead of the major anxiety-inducing occurrences that they had been.

"No." Miller seemed put out that she hadn't told him about them. "But I will certainly check up on him. As a matter of urgency."

"Thank you." She looked expectantly at him, waiting for him to take the hint and leave. He seemed reluctant but finally stood up.

"Well, seeing as you have everything under control, Dr Hughes, I'd best get back to work."

And he left.

It wasn't until later, much later, that she returned to her consulting room after doing her afternoon visits and realised that Miller had left the two files on her desk.

The files contained the second post-mortem report on Jade Trent and the first on Caro Sharpe, which Miller had been intending to drop off to Ian Dunbar for translation into simple English, and Callie couldn't resist the chance to be nosy.

She sat down, opened the first file and started to read.

Chapter 33

Linda looked up from the computer screen behind the reception desk as Callie came hurrying out of her consulting room clutching the two files.

"That scrummy policeman is on his way over, said he left a couple of files on your desk."

"Tell him to meet me at the mortuary. There's been a mistake. I've got to speak to Ian about these." Callie hurried out and drove as fast as she dared to the mortuary. She had tried calling Ian Dunbar but there had been no answer. This was not unusual or worrying. He could be conducting a post-mortem with Dave assisting or he could be cutting samples whilst Dave had been called away to collect a body from a ward. She just hoped that Ian wouldn't be too busy to take a look at the files and confirm the discrepancy that she thought she had found between the two post-mortems. She remembered him saying – or was it Dave? – about the swabs being negative when they were talking about the first autopsy, she was sure.

She was relieved to see that the hospital car park was no longer a crime scene and managed to find a parking space not too far from the mortuary. Snatching up the two files and her handbag, she locked her car and almost ran to the mortuary entrance.

The lift seemed to take an age and, as she hurried out of the lift into the mortuary proper, she slowed as she was struck once again by the stillness and silence of the place. She couldn't hear so much as the clatter of metal instruments on trays or the murmur of voices. It seemed almost indecent to hurry into a place as calm and quiet as this.

She walked at a more measured pace along the corridor, peeking through the porthole window into the first post-mortem room, which was empty, and then the second, which was also empty, save for a shrouded body on a trolley.

'Someone must be around,' Callie thought, knowing that Ian would never allow a body to be removed from the fridge unless he was about to start cutting. She stuck her head around the office door but there was no one there either.

The silence was beginning to feel oppressive and unsettling rather than calm.

'Don't be so silly,' she told herself, refusing to let it get to her.

"Ian?" she called out. "Dave? Is there anyone here?" Her voice seemed to echo along the corridor but there was no reply, no sound or sign of movement from anywhere. She walked back along the corridor, opening doors into changing rooms and store cupboards, but still saw no one.

Where could they be? Callie went into the second post-mortem room and walked past the body on the trolley, brushing lightly against it as she did so, to look into the adjoining storeroom. No one in there either. She was beginning to feel seriously spooked and she turned to leave.

That was when she saw it. The foot, or rather the boot. The sheet covering the body on the trolley had shifted slightly when she'd brushed against it, revealing the right foot, still in a boot. The fact that the body was still clothed was not unusual; bodies were often wheeled in fully dressed to have their clothing removed in the post-mortem room in order to preserve evidence, particularly in criminal cases. But bodies for autopsy rarely wore white rubber boots, unless they belonged to someone who worked in the mortuary.

Callie edged slowly forward, reluctant to take a closer look but unable to stop herself from doing so.

She reached the trolley and put out her hand to pull the sheet back from the head, then hesitated.

'Don't be so ridiculous,' she told herself, and swiftly whipped back the sheet, before gasping in horror and stepping back.

Ian Dunbar was lying on the trolley, dressed in his green scrubs, eyes bulging, purple tongue protruding from his mouth, with the yellow rubber tubing of a Foley's catheter cutting tightly into his neck. He was dead, very dead.

"I knew you'd come."

Callie jumped and let out a small involuntary cry. She hadn't heard Dave Ball come into the room.

"You startled me," she said, hurriedly, almost guiltily, replacing the sheet, hoping that he hadn't seen her look under it.

"I knew you'd work it out and come to me." He was standing squarely blocking the doorway, filling it like he filled his surgical scrubs to bursting point.

"What do you mean?" She looked around, knowing already that there was no other way out, but wildly hoping that there might be one she had forgotten. But no, unfortunately not. There were only the two doors, one was the way out, currently blocked by Dave, and the other was the door into the storeroom.

"He caught me." Dave nodded towards Ian Dunbar's shrouded body. "With Caro. In flagrante, as they say. Very careless of me, but that's why he had to die."

"You didn't have to do that, you know, kill him. I mean, okay, yes, you wouldn't be able to work in a mortuary again once it was known that you liked to, you know, have sex with them, the, uh, the dead, ah, bodies." She found it hard to even talk about it, something so awful, so alien to everything she held dear, that she couldn't even imagine what attraction there was to it.

"Necrophilia. I love that word. Necrophilia." He savoured the sound of it and took a pace towards her. "It wasn't until I worked down here and saw the bodies, so cool and still, that I realised what I was, realised my true nature, as they say. They were so tempting."

"I understand." She couldn't, but she needed to keep him talking while she thought of a way out of here.

"The first one, she was only thirty, died from breast cancer, very sad, a little on the scrawny side but that's to be expected in the circumstances."

Callie couldn't stop a shudder.

"Trouble was, once I'd discovered what I wanted, what I liked, nothing else would do. I tried so many times because the standard of the bodies round here, well, most of them are horrid old bags, to be frank, not many are in good shape, only scrawny and sick-looking or the morbidly obese who've stroked out. And all so old. Not exactly a turn on, know what I mean?" He moved a step or two closer and it took all Callie's strength of will not to recoil in horror, to step quickly away, anything to keep her distance from him.

"Not really." She was surprised at how steady her voice sounded, under the circumstances. She put her handbag down on the shrouded body.

"So, I kept trying with the living but, well, I just couldn't seem to get it up anymore and then that Jade bird, the tart, she had the nerve to laugh at me and I lost it. Strangled her with her own tights. And there she was. Dead. The ultimate turn on. Didn't have sex with her there, though, I know all about trace evidence, believe me,

I even took her fake nails with me to make sure there was nothing left at the scene. I knew there was no hurry, you see, she was going to be with me, here, for weeks. I had loads of time."

"But you made a mistake, didn't you, Dave?"

Callie began to very slowly sidle round the trolley as she listened to him talk, trying to put it between them.

"Yes. I didn't know they did a second PM for the defence. Stupid mistake, really, but we don't get a lot of criminal cases here. And once that happened, I knew it was just a matter of time before someone put two and two together."

"What about Denise, the till girl? She wasn't exactly your finest hour, was she?"

Callie was at the head of the trolley now, her hands lightly resting on the side rail.

"Callie, Callie, you are so right." Dave moved forward again, smiling and shaking his head in admiration at her cleverness. "She was such a loner no one found her body until she was well past her use-by date. And she wasn't exactly a looker when she was fresh. You can be assured I let her rest in peace. Putrefaction isn't a turn on, I've found."

Callie inched a little further round, moving her hands down to the trolley head, hidden from Dave's view by Dr Dunbar's body. She had known from the moment she saw the second post-mortem report on Jade Trent, where it stated that the vagina contained dead sperm, enough dead sperm for a swab to be sent for DNA testing, that someone must have had sex with her corpse. The first autopsy had found no sperm at all, the swabs were negative. There was only the trace of lubricant from a condom, or condoms more likely, given Jade's occupation. The question Callie couldn't answer was who had done it, and it hadn't even occurred to her that it was happening on a regular basis, or to other corpses as well as Jade. Well, she knew now and the thought of him, Dave, someone she knew and had worked with, shared a joke with at times, desecrating the dead, was horrific. Not to mention the fact that he was killing them in the first place in order to have access to the bodies for sex.

"That's when I got the idea that I didn't need to stick to the fat ugly dollops that I usually ended up with. No, you see, that's the beauty of this job. I could have anyone. Any girl in the whole, wide world I wanted. I could have Caro, even though she thought she was too good for me. She learned, she did, not to reject me. And of course, my ultimate choice, the one person in the world I really wanted, Callie. You."

Dave was moving forward again as he spoke and Callie had been ready to push the trolley into him, but this final revelation gave her pause for thought, just a moment's hesitation, and he started round the trolley towards her. He was at the wrong angle now, she wouldn't be able to push the trolley into him, she had missed her chance.

"All those nights I watched, I even saw that prick Kane stay with you."

"You scratched his car."

"I was tempted to do more than that, but I didn't want you to know I was watching you. I called you on the telephone, I liked to hear your voice on the machine, and the thought that you were there, listening to me breathe."

Callie began to work her way round the trolley again, slowly, a step at a time.

"Once you started going to those places, the bars and clubs, I knew you'd worked it out so I made my plans. Got ready. Ready to take you away with me."

"What on earth makes you think I'd go away with you?"

"You have no choice, Callie, believe me, no choice at all."

Dave moved forward again and Callie moved to the side and tensed, ready to push the trolley into him. The room was suddenly filled with the sound of arpeggios played on the piano. For one second it seemed, eerily, to be coming from Dr Dunbar's body, but then both Callie and Dave realised at the same moment that it was coming from her bag, that it was her mobile phone ring tone. Callie lunged for her bag but Dave got there first and threw it across the room. The contents of her bag scattered across the room and the ring tone stopped as the mobile phone hit the wall and clattered onto the floor.

Dave lunged for Callie but, in the time that he had taken throwing the bag across the room, she had moved round and taken a firm hold of the trolley rails and shoved it as hard as she could into him, not waiting to see the effect, to see if she had stopped him or not, before turning and running in the only direction left open to her, into the storeroom.

She slammed the door shut behind her and tried to drag a metal shelving unit across the door to block it. She had no idea how long it would be before someone would come looking for Dr Dunbar or herself but she prayed fervently that Linda had passed on her message to Miller to meet her at the mortuary and that he was on his way.

The door handle turned and rattled as Dave tried to push it open. Callie leaned hard against the door and pulled again, harder this time, at the shelving unit, complete with the stocks of sterile packs, couch rolls, and specimen pots that were on it. She had it half across the door when Dave threw himself at it from the other side, sending Callie and the unit flying across the room, the contents of the shelves skittering across the floor. Callie landed awkwardly, her head hitting another metal shelf and her wrist cracking, as she hit the heel of her hand against the floor. A wave of nausea and pain washed over her. Her eyes were closed but she could feel the wet and warm feel of blood trickling down the side of her face. She shook her head slightly to clear it and decided very quickly that that had been a mistake. The floor tipped away from her and she could feel herself sliding into unconsciousness. She took a deep breath and tried to open her eyes again.

"You can't get away. There's no way out." Dave was filling the doorway, looking at her with a small smile playing on his lips and a slight sheen of sweat across his brow. There was no doubt he was going to enjoy this. Callie recoiled, clutching her broken right arm to her chest, crouching, huddled against the far wall, and looked around desperately but he was right. There was nowhere to go and no way out past him. She reached out with her left hand, her fingers searching for something that she could use as a weapon, anything at all. As Dave moved forward again, her hand closed around a small plastic container, a cytology pot.

A couple of feet from her, Dave bent down and picked up a sterile catheter pack that had fallen from the shelves and opened it, pulling out the rubber catheter tubing and snapping it in his hands. There was little doubt in Callie's mind about his intent. She was to become the latest victim, strangled with a urinary catheter wielded by a necrophiliac mortuary attendant. What a way to go.

"You won't get away with this," she said desperately as she tried to work off the lid of the specimen pot one handed, but it was closed tight and she couldn't shift it. She had to stall him. Give herself time to open the pot. "Miller knows I was coming down here, that I had found a discrepancy in the reports. He will be on his way here by now." She certainly hoped he was.

"He'll be too late. We'll be long gone by the time he gets here. I've got everything ready." Dave was getting closer, and Callie tried to shuffle to the right but her way was blocked by the drug cupboard. That was no use to her because it was not only locked but had to be fixed to the wall by law, so she would never be able to open it or move it. She tried the lid of the cytology pot again and this time it moved, just a fraction, but it was a start. It gave her hope. She had to keep him talking, just a little longer, while her fingers worked on it some more.

"Where are you taking me?" she asked.

"Somewhere no one will ever find us," he said blissfully as he reached down to her, bending over her with the rubber tubing in his hands, leaning closer, so close that she could smell his rancid breath and the stale sweat that was beginning to stain his scrubs.

At last the lid came free and Callie jerked her left hand forward, throwing the contents of the specimen pot, the formalin used to fix the cells sampled, into Dave's eyes.

There was a moment of shocked hesitation and then he screamed and lurched back, dropping the rubber tubing and scratching at his eyes, trying to claw away the liquid that was instantly killing and fixing the cells of his corneae, blinding him.

Callie took her chance to jump up and hurtle across the room and out of the door, straight into the arms of DCI Miller. She clutched hold of him, sobbing into his chest, relieved to feel his arms come round and hold her tight, only vaguely aware of Jeffries and a hospital security guard moving rapidly past them into the storeroom, to where Dave was still blundering about, screaming.

"In there." She heard Miller tell two uniformed policemen who arrived as back up, but still she didn't lift her head, keeping it deeply buried in his chest, and he didn't stop holding her, tightly, and uttering soothing phrases.

"It's over, you're okay now. It's all right."

At last, she felt strong enough to lift her head, and look round as Jeffries brought Dave, in handcuffs, out of the storeroom. His eyes were squeezed shut and he was whimpering.

"I can't see, that bitch blinded me, I can't see anything."

Callie pushed herself away from Miller and took a deep breath.

"You'd better take him to casualty. I chucked formalin in his eyes and it will have to be washed out if there's any hope of saving his sight," Callie told them.

"Right," Jeffries said as he pushed Dave forward, then turned and spoke to Callie. "And should we take him the short way or the long way?"

"The short way, sergeant, if you please," she said firmly but, as she looked at Dr Dunbar, lying on the trolley, dead through no fault of his own, Callie wasn't absolutely sure that she meant it.

Chapter 34

Callie was shown out into the casualty waiting area by one of the staff nurses, who was looking a bit concerned that this patient didn't seem to be listening to her advice. Doctors: they always made the worst patients. Callie was surprised and relieved to see Miller waiting for her and the nurse was happy to hand her over to him.

"There's no way you're fit to drive," he explained in defence of his presence and Callie had to agree: it was nothing to do with the fact that her arm was in plaster or that she had six sutures holding her scalp laceration together, it was just that she felt pretty weak and wobbly.

"It's all that local anaesthetic," she agreed, "leaves you a bit shaky."

"Not to mention the rest." Miller clearly wasn't taken in by her excuses. He took her arm and began to lead her out to the car park. Callie stopped and looked around.

"Linda was waiting for me, to take me home."

"I sent her away," Miller told her. "I hope you don't mind. I promised her I'd take charge of you."

Callie didn't mind at all, there was no doubt that it felt reassuringly good to have his strong arm to lean on.

As they walked across the car park, Callie could see Jeffries over by the mortuary, standing next to a large lorry, a low loader, onto which a white van was being lifted.

"What's that? Is it Dave's or something?" she asked.

"Um, yes." Miller seemed suddenly and uncharacteristically embarrassed. "My car's just over here." He tried to hurry her away but she, obstinate as ever, and alerted by his anxiety to move her on out of the way, stopped to give the van a closer look as it swayed awkwardly in the air, ready to be lowered onto the trailer.

"It's a refrigerated van," she finally exclaimed in horror. "He was going to kill me and keep my body in a refrigerated van so that he could, could carry on, with me for—" Like the van, Callie was beginning to sway slightly. Her hand came up to her throat with the sheer horror of what Dave had planned for her. Miller grabbed her good arm to steady her but quickly realised that that was not going to be enough, so he swept her up and carried her back to one of the benches just outside the main entrance doors.

"Put your head between your knees," he ordered.

"Don't start that again," she said, staying as upright as possible. "Anyway, I'd probably be sick." So, she just closed her eyes for a moment, leaning slightly against Miller. She heard someone close by clear their throat and she opened her eyes to see Jeffries. She moved slightly away from Miller and tried not to blush, a hopeless task.

"Sorry about that, guv," Jeffries said.

"My fault," Miller contended, "my timing was impeccable as always." He tossed his keys to his sergeant. "Fetch the car over here, will you, Bob? I don't think she'll make it that far." And Jeffries scurried away to bring the car closer.

Callie straightened her shoulders and composed herself.

"I'm okay, honestly, you don't have to drive me back, I could get a taxi."

"No." He was firm. "I'm taking you home and I'm not taking no for an answer."

For once, Callie didn't argue.

As he drove her back up the East Hill, he told her that Jonathon had denied all knowledge of the vandalism to her car, following her or making the phone calls. He had, in fact, suggested it was wishful thinking on her part, trying to make out she was more important to him than she was, which Miller admitted had made him quite angry. A check of phone records and duty logs seemed to support his story, however. He was also no longer a serious suspect for the murders as another woman had come forward and reluctantly given him an alibi for Jade's murder. It had set Miller thinking that perhaps the incidents meant that Callie might be being targeted by the killer because she knew him. So, once he got the message that she had gone haring up to the mortuary because of problems with the post-mortem reports, he'd put two and two together and realised that it could be someone from the mortuary.

"The stupid thing is, I never suspected Dave was the killer, I just realised that he was having, you know—"

"Sex with the corpses?" He smiled, still amused at her inability to talk about sex.

"That's right."

"We were ahead of you there, then, we had already worked out that it had to be someone from the hospital because the professor had been pretty sure the murder weapon in Caro's case had been surgical tubing of some sort, and I did listen to your opinion that it wasn't that prat Kane. So, it was no great leap to realise that it might be someone from the mortuary."

"He was going to use a catheter on me too, can you believe it?" She felt her lip tremble slightly at the thought, the realisation of just how close she had come to being the next victim, and they continued the rest of the journey in silence, each alone with their thoughts and fears. It seemed no time at all before they arrived outside Callie's home.

Miller switched the engine off and came around to the passenger side to open the door and help her out.

"My keys!" Callie suddenly realised that she didn't have her handbag with her.

"Your bag is still part of the crime scene, I'm afraid, but I did rescue these for you." Miller held out her keys and Callie took them. She opened the door and went reluctantly into the hallway and then turned. Miller was still standing in the street, looking in.

"You must have lots to do," she said, making his excuses for him.

"Are you going to be okay?" he asked gently.

She nodded.

"You should call a friend or family member, ask them to come round and be with you."

"I'm fine," she said firmly. "They'll be round as soon as they hear, to be honest, I could do with a little time to myself."

He gave her a long, hard look but then nodded and turned quickly, going back to his car. She watched silently as he drove away – a little too fast, wheels skidding slightly on the loose gravel – before closing the door, and making her way up the stairs to her own front door, finally allowing the tears to come.

THE END

If you enjoyed this book, please let others know by leaving a quick review on Amazon. Also, if you spot anything untoward in the paperback, get in touch. We strive for the best quality and appreciate reader feedback.

editor@thebookfolks.com

www.thebookfolks.com

BODY HEAT – Book 2

A series of deadly arson attacks piques the curiosity of Hastings police doctor Callie Hughes. Faced with police incompetence, once again she tries to find the killer herself, but her meddling won't win her any favours and in fact puts her in a compromising position.

GUILTY PARTY – Book 3

A lawyer in a twist at his home. Another dead in a private pool. Someone has targeted powerful individuals in the coastal town of Hastings. Dr Callie Hughes uses her medical expertise to find the guilty party.

VITAL SIGNS – Book 4

When bodies of migrants begin to wash up on the Sussex coast, police doctor Callie Hughes has the unenviable task of inspecting them. But one body stands out to her as different. Convinced that finding the victim's identity will help crack the people smuggling ring, she decides to start her own investigation.

DEADLY REMEDIES – Book 5

When two elderly individuals pass away, it is not an unusual occurrence for seaside town doctor and medical examiner Callie Hughes. But she notices that both of the deceased had a suitcase packed, and her suspicions are aroused. Who is the killer that is prematurely taking them to their final destination?

MURDER LUST – Book 6

After noticing strange marks on the body of a woman found dead in a holiday let, police doctor Callie Hughes probes further. The police take her concerns about a serial killer seriously, but achieve little when another body if found. Callie is possibly the only obstacle to the murderer getting away with the crime, and that makes her a potential target.

OTHER TITLES OF INTEREST

IMPURITY by Ray Clark

Someone is out for revenge. A grotto worker is murdered in the lead up to Christmas. He won't be the first. Can DI Gardener stop the killer, or is he saving his biggest gift till last?

Available on Kindle, in paperback, and audio.

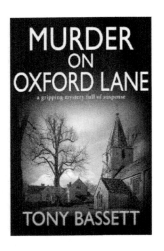

MURDER ON OXFORD LANE by Tony Bassett

A budding chorister doesn't return home from practice but his wife doesn't appear concerned. DS Sunita Roy becomes convinced he has been murdered but she has her own problems in the form of an ex-boyfriend who won't take no for an answer. Will she keep her eye on the ball when all expect her to fail?

Available on Kindle, in paperback, and audio.

Printed in Great Britain
by Amazon

17905664R00154